THE BAD
GUYS ARE
WINNING

To the commuting flight crew

THE BAD GUYS ARE WINNING

A Max Power Flying Adventure

NOTE GLOSSARY

Captain Trig Johnston

AUTHOR'S NOTE

I am fond of saying that this book could have been finished years ago had I duct taped a crayon to a certain portion of my anatomy and scribbled my thoughts on a Red Man tablet. But *the* Chief Pilot, whose face we see in the thunderstorms that march over the horizon to bring necessary conflict to our journeys, has a way of orchestrating things so that it all works out in the end.

Bad Guys was written in the crew bunk of 747's over the Pacific, aboard the Nuclear Submarine *Phoenix* deep beneath the seas off Pearl Harbor, in the delightful town of Morro Bay, on Guam, and in Tacoma. The locations are real, the characters composites. The Submarine *Dogfish* SS 379 is of course mythical, but her sister ship the *Bowfin* is not. Major portions of this work were written aboard that famous boat. For a real treat, Captain Hofwolt invites you to come to Pearl Harbor to visit the USS *Bowfin* Submarine Museum and Park (www.bowfin.org). Then pick up an autographed copy of this book in their gift shop, go aboard, find yourself a niche, and *experience the adventure aboard the submarine!* If you haven't been to Hawaii, it's time you went and you damn well know it.

With apologies to my many friends in the FAA and our government who may suffer undeservedly and a **"take that"** to the few who spit on the rights of others and wipe their behinds on the Constitution of the United States of America.

My thanks:

- To my airline friends and colleagues and especially Captain's Lehman, Thomas, Whitesell, Bellamy, Kullman, and Smith for keeping my memories fresh.
- To the Phoenix Parks & Recreation 702 Society, that opened the doors to Commander DJ Murphy and the superb crew of the USS *Tucson* who are at this writing in harm's way guarding our freedoms.
- To Clive Cussler for a leg up in a new endeavor.
- To my copy-editorette–the one who got away much to her good fortune–who refuses to be identified with such a delightfully politically incorrect story with deliberate run-on sentences, and grammatically incorrect airline jargon.
- To my son, Logan, who inspired me to continue on the many occasions when I wanted to set fire to the manuscript.
- And to my late friend, the real Master Chief Manny Burruell, combat veteran of thirteen war patrols in the diesel submarines and eternal member in good standing of the greatest generation that ever lived.

5% of the profits of this book will be donated to the USS Bowfin in memory of M/C Manny Burruell

PROLOGUE

On August 7, 1945, the day after Hiroshima at the close of WW II, the newly commissioned Balao class Submarine *Dogfish* SS 379 was dispatched to an equally new submarine base at Morro Bay, California.

Soon after the Japanese surrendered aboard the battleship *Missouri* in Tokyo Bay, the base was no longer required and was closed. Crews and base personnel were reassigned except for nineteen-year old Electrician's Mate Manuel Burruel, who was assigned to guard the boat until relieved.

The winter storms of 1955 destroyed the base pier, rolling the *Dogfish* 30° to starboard. Winds and erosion slowly covered most of the boat and what few buildings remained with sand from Morro Bay's live sand dunes.

After ten years of guarding the boat, Manny Burruel rightly concluded that the Navy had forgotten all about him and the Submarine *Dogfish*.

"Oh, you work for the airlines?
Then you get to fly for free!"
—Unknown

CHAPTER 1

The Bad Guys are Winning

Flight Deck
Mariah Air Transport flight 266
N 56°35'.04 E 176° 25'.22
Tokyo—Los Angeles

"Here we are, Max, teriyaki chicken." Frannie tried to slip one by me. She'd slung her first drink when they were still called stewardesses, and she knew all of the tricks. A short, strawberry blonde with dimples, she taught aerobics and still had the body of a twenty-five year old with a golden, Arizona tan. I looked for lines in that tan at every opportunity with negative results. If the rigors of a hard life in the air were visible at all, they were limited to the crow's feet at the corners of her baby browns. The frequent oceanic crossings that bridge nineteen time zones each and a few red-eyes out of Japan for Guam didn't seem to bother Fran Olson. Me? I always feel like I've been run over by a garbage truck.

"Hold it a second, Frannie, this is a coach meal! Where's my captain's gold-foil dinner?" I turned in my nine-way adjustable, sheep-skin lined captain's chair to raise an eyebrow at her as I lifted the silver foil off the steaming steerage entrée of mystery meat.

Frannie bent over to examine the meal tray, giving me an opportunity to look for more tan lines. I could tell she was a little miffed, not because I was ogling her cleavage—I frequently see a lot more of her around the hotel pools—but because I called her Frannie. She insists I call her Fran. It's a sensuous name that fits her like her Mariah Air Transport uniform. Like a cougar wears its pelt, clinging to her curves and accentuating her mysterious valleys. She knew it all right. She'd planned it that way. Her flashing baby browns, Arizona tan, and spontaneous nature were the trademarks of a spunky little creature that loved to curl up and purr. Or fight. We'd done both several airplanes ago. Those days, with tension in the airline high enough to prevent the proverbial needle from penetrating a tick's rectum even with the aid of a sledgehammer, we mostly fought.

She'd surrendered her innocence long ago, but put up a good front. She wore her sweet-sixteen smile but had a knack of transforming drunks, obnoxious big shots, and movie stars—as well as a pilot or two—into cowering mice with just a lash of her tongue, the envy of any serpent. Under that sheath of tanned, curvaceous flesh was one tough broad.

"Frannie, dear, what the hell is this?" I held up a strand of golden hair for all to see. "About two-feet long and strawberry blonde wouldn't you say, TJ?"

"Dammit, Max, don't call me Frannie!" She boffed me on the head with a serving mitt. "It sounds like something right out of Hee-Haw!" she said, referring to the old '70s TV series.

"Well, I dunno, it does look like one of yours. Straight as a—" She cut me off.

"Oh, Max," she whined, "I don't want to hear about the preacher again! Dammit, Max, you're . . . you're just a . . . a, oh shit!" she said and turned to storm out of the cockpit.

TJ, the first officer, was bent over in stitches. At six feet four inches, the F-18 squadron commander with a slender runner's build was nearly opposite my weight lifter's frame. But I've got all my hair and it's still brown. Well, most of it is. A relatively new-hire pilot, the second officer just chuckled politely to himself. It seemed, well, a bit out of step from the rest of us. A pilot's position during his first year with an airline is notoriously precarious, where he can be fired for anything, little things like not wearing his uniform hat that management loves to call a cap, another little dig in Mariah's continuing war between management and pilots. Or he could be fired for insignificant things such as the way he combs his hair which in his case was not much of a problem, or even his laughter. I just chalked it up to new-hire nerves.

I thought the hair in my food might be a souvenir from some scrofulous blood donor doing community service in the flight kitchen. A prize in one of our truly horrible endless servings of Chicken Ala King or whatever it was.

Frannie slammed the cockpit door, returning with the entrée labeled "Pilot." "Here's your damned gold-foil—"

In *Alice and Wonderland* fashion, time slowed to a crawl. Frannie was cut-off by a muffled explosion. Instantly the orderly cockpit was transformed into a bedlam of charts, flashlights, pencils, dry-roasted peanuts—or pilot pellets as the fight attendants call them—silverware, manuals, and coffee cups, while little round globules of coffee floated in the weightless environment around us. Silverware and a coffee cup scattered behind the rudder pedals in a black hole known to attract Cross pens, money clips, and car keys that are never to be seen again.

The autopilot disconnect alarm was screaming. Its associated warning lights were flashing on the instrument panel before me as I wrestled the control yoke in an attempt to regain control of the flying behemoth. As individual specks of dust rose from the flight deck, suspended in space, passing slowly through my field of vision I couldn't help but holler, "*W h a t t h e f u c k w a s t h a t!*" I don't think anyone heard me over the fire warning bell, the autopilot alarm, screaming passengers, and the sawing, grinding sound of one of those mammoth engines that was eating itself to death. My voice seemed exaggeratedly slow and distant to me. I hollered out the command, "Engine Fire Checklist!"

Out of my peripheral vision I saw that TJ, the first officer, was already reaching for the checklist, but the instrument panel where it is stored was shaking so violently, he was having trouble grasping it. I had to stand on the left rudder to keep the 747 flying straight. Just when I thought I had a handle on the situation, it got worse. Even with the left rudder to the floor, the airplane yawed violently to the right, alternately threatening to roll over on her back to the left accompanied by a surge of engine power, sound, and blinking annunciator lights. One of the throttles, it looked like No. 3, but I couldn't be sure as the cockpit shuddered violently, was moving on its own from the *firewall* position, or Max Power—which strangely enough is my name—to flight idle. Its amber, REV OP annunciator light alternately flashing on and off was an indication that one of those nasty things that can't happen—was. Engines don't reverse course by themselves, but one of the engines on the starboard side was doing just that. The distant thought that I might be losing control of the airplane produced a massive jolt of adrenaline. As I was gingerly feeding in some left aileron to counter the yaw to the right, and back pressure on the elevator to climb, I mentally coaxed the 747 as if it were a recalcitrant mule. Suddenly I heard a heavy thud against the flight deck. I glanced over my right shoulder and didn't like what I saw. The climb back to altitude had reintroduced normal positive G-forces, landing Fran face down amidst the second officer's crew meal and assorted cockpit debris. Blood was pulsing from a wound caused by a stainless steel fork with the Mariah Air Transport logo protruding from her throat.

"Don!" I hollered to the second officer, Don Adoni, while I pointed aft towards Fran. He'd already seen her.

"I'm on it," he cried, the flight interphone pressed to his right ear summoning help from the cabin as he battled his intricate panel with his left hand, seemingly in slow motion.

I've seen this before. A time shift where seconds last for hours and a minute is an eternity. There was an issue heavy on my mind, the dreaded merger with North Air America, Francisco Franco's cancerous airline. It would mean disaster for my career, but I pushed it aside like the leavings of so many flies.

Even with my senses on full alert from multiple jolts of

adrenaline, I could only make out the major sections of flight and engine instruments. The smaller brake pressure gauges, flap indicators, toggle switches, gear and flap handles, and the values on the engine instruments were lost in a crashing blur. Popping circuit breakers sounded like automatic weapon fire as the emergencies compounded one upon the other in the deadly snowball syndrome that can bring down even the biggest, most advanced airliner in the sky.

"Captain, I've lost the cabin!" Adoni, an Air Force veteran C-141 pilot, was short, nearly bald, dumpy, and a scratch golfer. In my periphery over my right shoulder, his arms were a blur in an effort to regain cabin pressure. "It's going through ten thousand!" He shouted over the pandemonium of a flight deck gone mad. The frigging engine fire bell was loud enough to give anyone a heart attack, even without the fire. It could be silenced if only the panel would stand still long enough to push the appropriate button. At 14,000 feet cabin altitude, the cabin pressure alarm would sound, adding to the cacophony.

I made the command, "Oh-two masks and interphone on, crew check in—go ahead and drop the masks, Don!" We each donned our oxygen masks. I hoped the passengers would reach for theirs. "Captain on," I said noting an adrenaline-induced tremble in my voice.

"First officer on." TJ was alert, but calm.

"Second officer on!" Adoni's voice was more excited than I would have cared for, nearly shouting into the oxygen mask's microphone, and therefore difficult to understand.

I wasn't surprised to hear TJ make the call "fire in number three!" But I was surprised to hear Adoni sing out that we had a fire in the forward cargo compartment.

Adoni continued to sing out abnormals that might be expected with a failing engine, "Number three generator off the line! Number three *and four* hydraulic pressure and quantity zero!"

The forces at work on the rudders should confirm what we had. Dead foot, dead engine: basic multiengine flying. But this was like peddling a kiddy-car, massive pressure on the left rudder, then from the right. What the hell was going on? I was aghast at the thought that either the No. 3 inboard or No. 4, the outboard engine, was in reverse thrust. Combined with the dancing thrust lever, the tripped generator, and loss of hydraulic system three pretty well assured me that it was the No. 3 engine. But I knew that if I shut down the wrong engine with the other in reverse, I'd send the 747 into a long, flat spin from which there would be no recovery. There would be plenty of time on the way down to think about things, possibly making a transmission to aid the NTSB accident investigators. The passengers might even get in a call home to say goodbye to their loved ones on the Mariah Sky Phone before we impacted the Pacific some seven-plus miles beneath our feet.

Company policy and our training required us to follow the checklists we live by. They outline specific emergency procedures for every conceivable type of problem except, of course, this one. We are directed to follow a detailed list of troubleshooting items. There are four ways to shut down an engine—by the fuel control lever used for normal engine start and shut down, the overhead fire handle, the fuel shut-off valve on the second officer's panel, or a flock of ducks. We were fresh out of ducks.

We are trained that when an engine is to be shut down during an emergency, it *shall* be done with the fire handle that also isolates the engine from all pneumatic, hydraulic, and fuel sources, trips its generator off the line, as well as arming the fire extinguishing system. But that night there was no time. The airplane was bucking so violently, I couldn't grasp the overhead fire handles to save my life. All 358 of our lives, and that was precisely the case.

"Shutting down number three!" I hollered more for the benefit of the cockpit voice recorder in case we didn't make it. I flashed on the flaming wreckage of TWA 800 floating on the surface of Long Island Sound while submersibles searched the depths for the flight data and voice recorders. In my strange slow-motion state, other flight numbers came to me. American 191 at Chicago, Alaska 261 off Port Hueneme, our own 774 that disappeared without a trace over the South China Sea, and PSA 182 as it plunged into San

Diego city streets—the first officer transmitting, "I love you, Ma," while the 727 was in a vertical dive, seconds from impact. It took every ounce of my strength, more mental than physical, but I flatly refused to add Mariah 266 to the list.

To avoid being dashed against my side window, I was holding onto the yoke with my left hand. With one of the throttles acting like a meat cleaver, I held onto the pedestal between the two pilot positions with my right hand. This is where the fuel control levers are located. Grasping the first lever, I counted over to No. 3, again confirming to myself that I had my hand on No. 3. *But was it No. 3?* I recalled TJ calling a fire in No. 3, Adoni crying No. 3 *and 4* pressure and quantity zero. It looked like the No. 3 throttle that was moving on its own, but with the flight deck shaking as bad as it was . . .

I punched the safety release button that prevents unintentional movement of the fuel control lever with my thumb and hollered, "Number three!"

Far away and through the commotion I heard "Roger, concur number three!" TJ's movements were still in slow motion in my peripheral vision.

"Very well!" I thought to myself. It was one of *those* moments in life. First day of school, raising your right hand swearing to defend the constitution, slipping a band of gold on your bride's ring finger. This was bigger than an accumulation of a lifetime of those experiences. I took what could be my last deep breath and slammed the fuel control lever down into the idle, cutoff position. Instantly the bucking, yawing bull ride was over. The roar of flight resumed as the cockpit returned to flight level silence, and time— like a slap in the face—returned to normal.

*   *   *

A glance at the second officer's INS unit showed Anchorage, our nearest point of dry land, to be 843 miles distant. "TJ, pull that number three fire handle, then declare an emergency. Get us a clearance direct Anchorage, and request a discretionary descent to one zero thousand!"

"Yes, sir! Standing by with the Engine Failure Checklist!" His expression was grim. She was badly out of trim, and fighting me, trying to roll over on her back.

After feeding in substantial left rudder trim, plenty of left aileron, and reducing power on the No. 1 outboard engine, she seemed to fly all right, although she was shaking and shuddering badly. The S/O had his hands full, but I couldn't take my hands off the controls to punch in direct ANC on my INS and TJ was busy on the radio. So, I loaded the second officer up with another chore, "Adoni, give me a heading for direct Anchorage!" I began a slow left turn with a shallow bank in the general direction of Alaska. Under emergency conditions the regs cut us some slack, allowing us to lawfully worry about ATC clearance later. TJ was transmitting the "Mayday" to Honolulu while below us in first class some of the passengers had given up already. They'd surrendered their dignity and were screaming for their lives as if that would do any good. They sound a bit like screamers on a roller coaster, but somehow there was a difference in their voices. They're a little more urgent, more believable. Because those screams were for real.

"When I was in the Air Force—"

"Not now, Don!" I heard that at least fifty times a day.

"Heading is three four zero for Anchorage, sir!" I nodded to Adoni and thanked God for my three-man crew. Fact is nothing ever happens by itself in the cockpit. One little devil stabs you in the ass with his pitchfork, and his buddy is sure to stick one in your ear at the same time. I've never seen it fail. I'll always remember that flight, when the emergencies compounded one upon the other, then another, and another as the night of the Grim Reaper who slithered into the jump seat behind me, patiently waiting for the moment when I would be overcome.

"Captain, cabin pressure is passing eleven thousand feet and I can't stop it!" The flight attendant chime sounded. TJ knew that I had my hands full of airplane, so he answered the call, spoke a few words into the handset and then returned it to its cradle.

His expression was grim. "Smoke in the forward cabin, boss."

I turned to the right for a quick look at the flight engineer's panel, but instead I saw Fran out cold on the deck, a growing pool of blood under her neck. "Alright, gentlemen, stand by for emergency descent!" I reached overhead for the flight attendant call button and rang it four times, signaling the cabin crew that we needed immediate help in the cockpit, in this case for Fran.

Cockpit crews speak with each other over the interphone through microphones in their oxygen masks. We receive through our hearing-aid style, molded ear piece that we use for ATC communications, on board announcements, etc. It also magnifies the sound of our breathing. "How you coming with the clearance, TJ?"

"Standby, I'm working Honolulu right now." TJ was holding up a *wait one* finger, because he too was juggling flaming swords. "OK . . ." By depressing the first of the two positions on the yoke-mounted, rocker-type switch he returned to Honolulu AIRINC, who was relaying our ATC clearance through the cacophony of wheezing static and the transmission of other flights thousands of miles distant. "OK, go ahead Honolulu for Mariah 266." I turned to glance at the cabin pressure indicator. It was still climbing and nearing 14,000 feet where the oxygen masks in the cabin would drop automatically had we not already done so manually. I flipped up a toggle switch labeled HF-1, our antiquated but long distance radio, to monitor our clearance. It is essential that at least two pilots, and preferably all three, copy any ATC clearances, especially when things on the flight deck are hot.

Through the whining, frizzy static that is HF radio I heard a far off electronic voice coming from Hawaii where I desperately wished I was. "All other traffic standby-standby, emergency in progress, break-break, Mariah two six six, Mariah two six six, cleared present position direct Anchorage. Unable your descent at this time, maintain flight level three seven zero, crossing traffic is a United seven forty seven at your ten o'clock, one five miles, northwest bound at flight level three four zero. We're working on lower for you." The operator signed off with the AIRINC signature "Honolulu." Then as an afterthought "Good luck, gentlemen." The frequency, normally a jumble of multiple transmissions overriding each other had become silent, as flight crews scattered over the Pacific, both north and south, listened in on our emergency. They knew it could be them at any moment, and we knew they were all pulling for us.

TJ and I made a quick visual sweep in the darkness where the United flight was supposed to be. "Got him!" TJ pointed to a position just to the left of our nose. I searched the black of night for a moment longer until I too spied their strobe lights

"Eleven o'clock?" My target was just to the left of our nose.

"That's him!" said TJ just as the United flight showed a landing light to aid in the identification. TJ punched the VHF 1 button on his COM panel, "Gotcha. Thanks, United."

A reassuring "Good Luck, Mariah" followed in our ear pieces on the oceanic air-to-air frequency. That night, all pilots sharing the sky over the Pacific were brothers. Only after the emergency was over would the rivalry and bickering between pilot groups resume.

"Cabin leaving one four thousand!" cried Adoni. Predictably the cabin-pressure alarm sounded, the effect not unlike someone torching off the siren from a fire engine in your shower. It could be heard by the passengers in the upper deck, and possibly even below us in first class.

How could the passengers be holding up? The screams from the cabin told the story all too well. How I wished to reassure them. To put on my uniform coat with the four gold stripes on my sleeves, wings of gold upon my chest, and my hat festooned with company emblem and gold braid to visit the cabin To hold the hand of some terrified grandmother, and calmly explain our situation. To stand in the aisle, shaking hands and explaining all the while that, yes, we are going to make it through the night, that we will all see the sun rise in the morning, that they will see their loved ones again and soon. To explain patiently to our passengers who have entrusted their lives to us that not only will we as a crew not let them down, but neither will this magnificent airplane, the very best ever built. Yes, we do have challenges to face and things to think about such as lowering the gear in an emergency descent with the No. 4 hydraulic system out. We'll get the gear down for badly needed drag during the dive, but won't be able to bring it back up again for the cruise portion of the trip to Anchorage. But we will make it. We will. I would ask each of them to pull together, to pray, and to be confident. But this I cannot do because I must fly the frigging airplane.

"TJ, advise Honolulu we have the United in sight and are beginning emergency descent to one zero thousand now!"

As he transmitted, I sensed an increase in the noise level, and felt an almost imperceptible change in the pressure on my ears. The cockpit door had opened and I heard a gasp. Turning my head quickly to investigate, as if I needed any distractions, I saw two flight attendants working on Frannie with a first aid kit. It was getting crowded with three extra people in the comparatively small cockpit adding to the feeling that things were jamming up in snowball fashion which pilots are trained to recognize as a fatal trend. I engaged the autopilot to reduce my work load that would enable me to better prioritize my actions, each and every one of which I knew would be studied, analyzed, and second-guessed for years to come.

Back on the interphone the hissing, sucking sound of pressurized breathing under stress dominated. "Adoni, get on the PA and advise the passengers we'll be making a *controlled* emergency descent. Tell them the truth, and that is that the situation is under control, we're headed for Anchorage, and will be on the ground in . . ." I glanced at Adoni's inertial navigation unit. " . . . make it . . ."

TJ chimed in, "one plus two five!" I quickly calculate my own

ETA, not because I don't trust my first officer, but because that's the way we do things. I check on you, you double check me, and the flight engineer—thank God again and again for a three-man crew—checks out both of us. Mistakes are easy to make, especially when the heat is on. We could afford no mistakes that night. No, not even one.

"Concur, one hour and twenty-five minutes." Things were happening fast, but that was the scenario we train for in the simulator. Having assessed the situation, and with a firm grip on the control yoke, I punched off the autopilot since this maneuver would be beyond its capabilities. There was the familiar sigh from the air conditioning packs as I grabbed a handful of throttles and retarded them smoothly to idle. Pulling the speed-brake lever fully aft that normally would hydraulically extend four large panels on top of each wing into the airstream produced a mild, barely noticeable buffeting. With No. 4 hydraulic system out, we had only two spoiler panels in operation on each wing, but even the reduced number of panels would help to keep our airspeed down during the descent. As we slowed, my eyes were glued to the mach/airspeed indicator. I dare not add to our problems by ripping off the gear doors with too much airspeed. While transferring my grip on the throttles to the yoke I turned briefly to TJ and Adoni. "You know once that gear's down, it isn't going to come up again." It wasn't a question. They responded with two grave expressions that said they understood. "OK, then." The verbal and visual thumb-down commands were totally out of place at altitude. "Gear down!"

"Roger, gear down," said TJ lowering the big landing gear lever, "and standing by on that Engine Fire/Failure Checklist." TJ is an excellent first officer because he was a captain at his airline until it was swallowed by Mariah Air Transport. As the eighteen wheels extended into the airstream we were pressured against our seat belts and shoulder straps, adding to the noise level and increasing the vibration even more. The three altimeters before me began to unwind slowly at first, then faster as I shoved the nose over into a steep 20° dive. The passengers had to be scared to death. Regardless of Adoni's words to the contrary, most will imagine this to be their final descent.

"Honolulu—Honolulu, Mariah two six six!" TJ was transmitting HF radio, "stepping on" other flights' transmissions with the required report, hoping Honolulu would hear us. He transmitted in the blind, "Mariah two six six has United in sight, leaving flight level three seven zero for one zero thousand."

"TJ, stay with me on this emergency descent at all times, but see if you can raise dispatch. Advise them what's going on. We have one injury that we know of, possibly more. I suspect when that engine let go, she punched a few holes in the fuselage, maybe started a fire in the forward cargo or it could be an indication problem, but I don't think so. It's 'FR' for now."

TJ seemed puzzled, "FR?"

"For Real," I said. His expression said he should have caught that one.

Firmly established in the low-speed descent, a quick assessment of our situation satisfied me that we were well *ahead* of the emergency. All three crew members were at their positions, up to speed, and ready for anything. It was past time to talk to the passengers, but I couldn't get to them just yet. I only hoped Adoni's announcement got the point across that we were under control. I learned later that the second officer had punched the wrong button on his communications jack box, thereby selecting the wrong frequency, and had transmitted his PA announcement over the company VHF frequency, unusable from our position over the ocean. The passengers heard nothing from the cockpit and were convinced the hour of their death had arrived.

"Leaving three zero zero." TJ's voice was calm, all business, betraying no emotion. But as he tapped my shoulder and pointed to a gelatinous glob that was Fran's blood slowly flowing down the flight deck, I saw terror under control in his eyes. There was nothing either of us could do for her other than to *fly the airplane!*

"I'm off," said TJ switching back to the company frequency.

I nodded that I understood, then thought better of it and

announced, "Roger that," for the benefit of the CVR—cockpit voice recorder. I sensed the cockpit door opening again, then slamming quickly closed.

"Captain, I have the cabin damage report." It was Pat Gergen, whom I'd flown with for many years. She has proved herself under emergency conditions more than once. I trusted her. She was breathing from a walk around bottle of oxygen, and was forced to lift the mask temporarily away from her face in order to speak. Since standing in a steep dive is difficult, I directed her into the aft jump seat where she could strap herself in and use one of the observers' O^2 masks that would allow her to communicate on the interphone.

"Fran has a bad cut on the back of her head, but she is conscious and responsive. Her pupils, though, are unequal and slow to respond. We think she has a concussion. She's lost a lot of blood from the wound in her throat." While listening to her report, I had to concentrate on *flying the airplane*, the absolute key to our survival in this emergency. My eyes were glued to the flight instruments before me. The ship's four altimeters, three on the forward panel and one on the second officer's panel, were unwinding rapidly. Twin rate-of-climb indicators were pegged at a 6,000-feet-per-minute rate of descent that would get us down to 10,000 feet and breathable air quickly. Passengers rarely experience such an emergency descent. In the cabin, it seems as if the airplane is going straight down. The effect can be terrifying.

"There are six jagged holes in the cabin wall near door three-right," Patty said confirming my suspicions. "Two passengers were hit by flying metal from the engines . . ."

TJ cut in on the interphone to transmit, "Leaving two five zero looking for one zero thousand." Then was off and back on the radio with our dispatcher in Los Angeles.

"We think we can see fuel spraying from under the wing . . ." said Pat.

"Back with ya," said TJ, "dispatch advised. Said they'd call back."

"Swell. Adoni, any sign of venting fuel?" My mouth was full of cotton. I felt as if I would choke if I tried to swallow.

"Uh . . . no, not so far—I'll keep an eye on it!" He expertly marked the value of each fuel gauge with the flight engineer's ubiquitous grease pencil. In that way, any uneven fuel burn would be easy to spot even though the airplane and consequently his panel were shaking badly in the descent.

I continued to listen to Patty's damage report on the interphone, but then the HF Cell Call started paging us. It's a warbling tone designed to get your attention quickly to notify the crew there is an inbound radio transmission. It did. TJ reached to the center overhead panel and silenced the tones, then answered the call. "Make sure to tell them we think we're losing fuel." TJ was nodding that he understood while transmitting.

I turned my attention back to the flight attendant and her damage report. "Go ahead, Patty." Her sensuous, slightly husky voice was heavy with emotion. Her hands were shaking slightly. There was no question that we were all scared. We just didn't have the time to indulge in it. That would come later.

"The passengers are terrified. Several have fainted. One passenger has gone into labor. Maybe you could say something to them?" she asked. As captain, it is part of my job. I can delegate it, but I know the people want to hear the captain's voice telling them everything's going to be all right. Even if it isn't.

"Alright, Patty, I'll say something when we level at ten thousand."

"Captain, there's—"

TJ cut Pat off, his brows knitted in consternation. "You aren't going to believe this, but dispatch wants us to go to Los Angeles!"

"*Los Angeles?* That's ridiculous!" He nodded in agreement. "Did you tell them we're operating on three engines with the gear hanging out?"

"Yes, sir, I did. Also told them we have injuries and may be losing fuel, but they're adamant that they want us to proceed direct L. A."

"They're crazy!" I said.

"Previously established." It could have come from anyone in the cockpit.

Patty risked a scolding by cutting in on the interphone without permission. "Captain, that isn't the worst of it . . ."

TJ called, "Leaving two zero zero for one zero thousand." We got a taste of what impact would be like when a thick, stratus layer of cloud rose, slowly at first, then faster and faster to meet us. We thundered into it, then in the next instant exploded through the base of the cloud as we plummeted towards the ocean like an 800,000-pound bank vault.

Then Adoni cut in, "Definitely losing fuel from the right main tank, sir—standby for a rate!"

"Open the cross feeds, and feed number two and four from the right main until it's dry!" With the center tank fuel gone, we needed to use the right main's fuel first, or risk going for a swim. No.1 would burn from its respective main tank to avoid flaming out all three engines when the tank feeding engines No. 2 and 4 ran dry.

"Yessir!" Adoni had only six months with the company, but was doing a fine job under considerable pressure. Fuel management on the 747 is one of its more challenging tasks.

"Captain . . ." I knew Pat had important information because she called me Captain, instead of Max, but I couldn't get to her just then.

"Stand by one, Patty . . ."

TJ continued with the standard emergency descent calls, "Leaving one five thousand, five to go!"

I was formulating my announcement for the passengers when I sensed Patty had moved into the forward jump seat. I felt a hand on my shoulder, her breath on the back of my neck. I caught a whiff of her perfume.

"Max, I . . ."

"What?" I was mildly irritated for I was concentrating on leveling the airplane and did not appreciate distractions. We got one break, having descended past 14,000 feet, the cabin pressure alarm ceased its squawking, easing the tension somewhat.

"Th—those jagged holes in the cabin wall?" She was having trouble with this—it sounded as if she might cry. That's all I'd need.

"Two to go, out of twelve for one zero thousand!" said TJ.

"We've *caught the cabin*!" Adoni's announcement was accompanied by significant pressure in our ears, so with a little back-pressure on the controls, I shallowed out our descent. Our passengers had suffered enough discomfort without my adding to it. I double-checked the seat belt sign as we entered an undercast with its predictable mild turbulence. 747s normally cruise above altitudes where icing is a distinct possibility. I used my flashlight to inspect the rain repellent nozzle on the other side of the two-inch thick, heated windshield for traces of ice. We were getting some.

As TJ was busy on the radio, I called out to Don, "Heat us up, please." After a moment's hesitation, he understood and activated the engine anti-ice on the overhead panel. I chided myself for not using the correct terminology. The days of casual cockpit commands are over, but old habits are hard to break. "Wings, too." Remembering the old days, I thought to myself that this was a great night to *not* be out night freighting in a small airplane. Rime ice was accumulating rapidly, though with our hot-bleed air for the engines, wings, and antennas, it would pose no operational problem for us. I continued to level the airplane, rolling in nose-up trim with the yoke-mounted toggle switch, "OK, Patty, go ahead." But before she could continue, TJ made another call, pointing to the altitude alerter.

"One to go, out of eleven for ten." A thousand feet to go.

I repeated the call, and continued to shallow out the descent while slowly retracting the speed brakes. Patty continued, "Well, those holes . . . there were hot pieces of metal from the engine that made those holes. They looked like tracers when they came through the cabin wall!" I allowed the airspeed to bleed off until we were below the max gear retract limitation speed, then interrupted Patty with the command for TJ to raise the gear.

"It ain't coming up, Boss!" he said. Instantly I felt like a complete fool, but I forced myself to get over it quickly. Even airline captains make mistakes—that's why there are three of us up there.

Patty continued, "Some of them lodged in the closet by door two-right and started a small fire. We used the CO_2 extinguishers, but . . ."

With the speed brakes retracted our ride smoothed out considerably as we reached 10,000 feet. The passengers would like that. I fed in some power to engines No. 1 and No. 4, leaving No. 2 at idle to avoid unbalanced, asymmetrical thrust. The airplane now established in cruise configuration, I turned my attention back to Patty. I had a bad feeling about what she was trying to tell me. If they weren't able to put out the fires, we were in a lot more trouble that I realized.

"Did you try the Halon extinguishers?"

"Uh, no, no, it's not that. We put the fires out OK, but one of those pieces of hot metal that started the fire went right through the passenger in 32G. Max . . . he's dead!"

Stunned. Slowly I accepted the fact that I was responsible for the death of a passenger who had entrusted his life to me, and that this was the initial moment of a haunting that would follow me for the rest of my life. Glancing at my reflection in the windshield under the stark white lights, the standard lighting configuration for an over ocean flight during darkness, I saw the reflection of a killer. Fighter-pilot haircut, graying with age from past emergencies, half-frame reading glasses, blue-water tan, muscles toned, good shape. Crisp white shirt with four gold stripes, black tie. I didn't like what I saw. I announced, "Rigging for red," turned off the harsh fluorescent lighting in favor of the soft, red overheads, and back-lit instrument panels. My image was one of red and black, the impression of Lucifer himself.

TJ rescued me from introspection with the Anchorage weather. "You aren't going to like this." We knew Anchorage had been

forecast to be near minimums in snow showers and fog, but from
TJ's tone, it was going to be worse. "Anchorage is on its ass in snow
and fog, the RVRs are eight hundred, six hundred, and six hundred.
All of Alaska is down. Vancouver's closed. Seattle is *WOXOF*.
Dispatch says no one's been in there all day. I guess that's why
they want us to go to Los Angeles."

Adoni cut in, "Sir, I don't have enough fuel to make Los
Angeles." *We*, Adoni, we. Even if you're alone in a single seat
airplane, you and the machine are a team.

TJ answered another call from the flight attendants, then
announced as he replaced the handset, "Smoke continuing in the
cabin, looks like a real fire in the cargo compartment." As my
senses slowly returned to normal I became aware of a sonorous
rumbling. Ice forming on some jagged hunk of aluminum hanging
out in the slip stream was creating a gentle rolling vibration that
was traveling through our feet, right to left, as we bored on through
the ink, just two miles above the icy North Pacific.

"Your flight is wide open!"
—Reservations agent

CHAPTER 2

Johnston

Aboard N9TL,
Los Angeles—Morro Bay

TJ and I flew our last trip of the month on the afternoon of our disastrous meeting with Buck Don Breeding, Mariah's excuse for a Chief Pilot. Director of Flight Operations and one time Sheriff of Leesville, Louisiana, Buck's real name was Eugene Donald. He picked his own nickname to offset his actual persona, that of a skinny, shifty-eyed, poorly-bred mistake. He chose a pencil-thin mustache thinking it made him look dashing, but in reality all focus was on his shoes that were rumored to be elevator models.

Six days later after chewing on Buckie's bullshit over several oceans, hemispheres, and continents, TJ was flying two weary aviators home in his classic float plane, a 1946 DeHavilland Beaver. Departing from Marina del Rey, we followed the shoreline towards Ventura staying right on the deck to get our speed fix. Even so, the mood in the airplane was somber. TJ held a 280° heading, generally following the coast for direct Morro Bay while I pretended to watch the grid-locked world slide by on US 1. But it was Breeding's mousy face I was seeing as I mulled that meeting over again and again in my mind. That Breeding had regressed into an earthling did not surprise me. You stay out of the cockpit long enough and that will happen. Buck was at one time a pretty good stick, buddies with the pilots, all the time retaining information to be used against them. He was a real bastard, but I was shocked that even he would manipulate the transcript of our CVR tape. ALPA had warned about such things for years, but we no longer had ALPA as a result of the first buyout of Mariah and the corporate maneuverings of the surviving carrier. They had quietly decertified three years earlier, a move initiated by our beloved, incompetent Buck who preferred a cubicle to the cockpit, or better yet an office with windows since he had failed a first officer's check ride early in his career. Apparently he'd assessed his abilities, deciding his way out was to brown-nose his way into the very political training department, there administering check rides that he himself could not handle. Check rides between the pilots in the clique were given to each other in a manner that positively assured a sterling performance and the paperwork to go with it. With that in mind, I wasn't just pissed at having been given a month off without pay, I was stunned! It was *unbelievable* to me that we had been disciplined for following the Federal Aviation Regulations! The normally reserved TJ was visibly hostile. We both remembered the utter feeling of exhaustion after we'd set the parking brake on 266 while still on the runway at Anchorage. The passengers cheering for their deliverance could be heard over the sirens from the fire equipment, but Mariah wasn't happy. Their position was that we recklessly endangered the lives of the passengers, crew, and of course the airplane by making a zero zero landing in Anchorage. Their second-guessing would have had us flying an additional five hours to Los Angeles. When I pointed out that we simply did not have the fuel to reach Los Angeles or even San Francisco with the gear hanging out, Mariah denied it claiming that the remaining fuel on board would have been sufficient. The old governmental line, straight from Goebbles and the ministry of propaganda—repeat the lie until it is accepted and finally believed.

Breeding brought in the VP of maintenance, Christopher Cheney, the same man who had told me we would have lost the wing had I not shut the engine down when I did. Now he wasn't so sure. They couldn't locate the source of a fuel leak. Indeed, they couldn't find any evidence of one. Adoni's memory had failed him. All very convenient. Anyone not familiar with the facts reading the report could only conclude that Mariah's logic was perfect and that my decisions were arrived at through horribly poor judgment.

The media was all over it. "Pilots disciplined for heroic performance" and things of that nature. Several of the passengers told their stories on talk radio. One was writing a book about the experience where his life hung suspended in space for over two hours. Discovery produced an hour-long documentary clearly telling the story of our ordeal, featuring interviews from passengers and crew. Mariah didn't seem to care, acting as if they were immune to public opinion. Any negative feelings generated could easily be swept away with a round of fare wars that Mariah was always eager to start. And if things really got hot, free Mai-Tais with a little umbrella on the Hawaii flights always seemed to do the trick. Since the ruling came from the top, there was nowhere else to go for appeal.

Over gyoza and beer in Tokyo, I made the sardonic suggestion that we sell the airplane to the Japanese on our next trip. A moment of polite laughter died quickly. As far as bad ideas go, it was pretty good. It would certainly solve our retirement problems. But it was a ridiculous notion, and I'd all but dismissed the idea as nuts when I spotted an ad in *Trade-A-Plane* offering "top dollar for transport category aircraft whether running or not" with a Miami phone number. I called the number after clearing customs at LAX. Yes, they were always looking for equipment. No, documentation would not be a problem. No, while it is always desirable to have the airplane's maintenance history, in this case it wouldn't be absolutely necessary as these airplanes were to be "scrapped" the man said. Doing the arithmetic in my head was easy. If the aluminum in the airplanes they were buying was scrapped, someone was paying a pretty high price for it, somewhere around $21 per pound when the going rate was around 35¢. They could be dopers, gunrunners, or even slavers but whatever they were, they weren't in the aluminum siding business.

When TJ started a gentle descent passing San Luis Obispo my sleepy day dream evaporated into a view of picturesque Morro Bay that grew larger until, on short final approach, sailboat masts on either side of us were a kaleidoscopic blur of speed. Poking his head out, a seal freaked at the sight of the flying monster bearing down on him, ducking just as TJ was about to kiss the water with his Beaver.

Crews returning from international flights have a saying: "Welcome to America, where nothing works." Don't believe me? Does "For assistance in English, press one" mean anything to you? When I gave TJ a polite golf clap for his landing, the Beaver's voice activated interphone clipped the first and last part of his reply. All I heard was an electronic "psstt-sshole-psst."

As the Beaver slowed to taxi speed, she settled further and further into the water until I was convinced we were going to sink. At idle power, her shock mounted instrument panel jiggled to the "pocketa-pocketa" song of the radial engine. It's a combination of her throaty, belching exhaust, the sound of a whirling propeller amidst a background of thousands of moving engine parts, all in perfect harmony. That nostalgic melody is known to bring mist to the eyes of pilots, line boys, passengers, and lovers who park by the grass runways that still dot what's left of America the Beautiful.

TJ and I were worn out from our week of flying. Imagine going to work normally at 9:00 AM on Monday and returning home around 6:00 in the evening, beginning an eighteen-hour shift at midnight on Tuesday, another one on Thursday. Take ten hours off, then report for work at 2 PM that same afternoon to work through the night finishing your trip to arrive back at your base at 5 PM on Monday that is really Sunday, thanks to the International Date Line. Then factor in trying to sleep in the machine-shop environment of a daytime hotel with its droning Hoover uprights and screeching maids. It's easy to locate the crew rooms, just look for the ice machine or an elevator. You'll find us close by. It's pitch dark at high noon. If you can imagine your system turned inside out by the infamous jet lag, suffering insult through frisking several times each day to keep up the government's illusion of security, then you might have a fair idea of a flight crew's thirty-hour work week. That's thirty hours the airplane is *moving* for the purpose of flight. Time preparing flight plans and the airplane, tedious hours spent in revising our "Jepp" manuals, or just sitting around the airport waiting for the arrival of our inbound airplane can easily exceed our paid thirty hours.

I felt as if I'd been run over by a freight train after flying a series of trips and our meeting with "Captain" Buck. A beer would slide down very well. After securing the Beaver and making her fast to the dock, I looked over at TJ and said in my mixed Japanese-Mexican dialect, "Anato-wa frio cervesa?"

TJ, a fresh drop of engine oil on his white uniform shirt and looking a bit haggard, shook his head no. "Keiko des, amigo," for no thanks. "I just wanna go home to Mama," he said referring to his wife, Terrie. I didn't envy him since his ten-year old daughter had reached puberty while we were in Tokyo.

"Yeah. Me too," I said, "but the tide's not out yet."

When he stared straight ahead for a couple of beats, I knew I had him. Studying the double half-hitch I used to secure the nose of the right float to the seaplane dock, he inclined his head a few degrees to the right, working his mustache quizzically as if attempting to formulate a question he didn't quite comprehend. But he wasn't about to admit he didn't understand why I couldn't go home until the tide was out. So when he finally did get a question out, he caught me off guard.

"Didja mean it?"

"Mean what?" I asked innocently.

"Selling the airplane to the Japanese on our next layover."

"Jeeze! TJ," I said in a mock serious tone. "What the hell kind of man do you think I am?"

He stammered a bit, "Well, I, uh, you . . . uh, well hell, Max!" he said straightening to his full height, and staring me directly in the eye to drive his point home. "That's exactly the kind of guy you are, and you damn well know it!!"

"Oh, be still!"

"Just don't do anything stupid!" TJ was looking at me like a high school vice-principal, smacking his hand with the assault paddle.

"Never." He wasn't convinced. "Really, it's OK"

"Max . . . ?" TJ was staring me down.

I said nothing for a few moments. "To hell with you then," I said not willing to divulge any information. "I'm headed for Rose's and a frosty one." TJ gave a half-hearted wave and turned to start the short walk down the Embarcadero to his floating home, the 110-feet tugboat, *High Dozo*. The name was a left over from her previous owners after she was seized hauling a barge allegedly, *but not for certain*, stuffed with bales of "happy herb." I flashed my best imitation of a John Wayne salute, "Later, amigo."

Rose's Cantina, home to the seaplane dock, is a nautically flavored saloon decorated with hanging fishnets, Japanese glass floats, and old paintings of ships at sea. Still in my summer uniform of white shirt, black Mariah tie, and gold epaulettes, I made straight for the men's room. My hat stays at the airport here it belongs with my flight bag. The routine is to place my aged aluminum suitcase on the trash can, dial in the dual combinations 727 on the left and 747 on the right, and pop open my bag to extract my disguise, in this case a black cashmere pull over sweater vest. "Poof!" I was a civilian. Snapping the latches home, I headed for my favorite window seat in the saloon.

"Hey, Captain, you look like hell!"

"Angie, you look good enough to eat, as always." I couldn't tell if Angie was nineteen or thirty-five. In either case she was beyond blushing. "How 'bout a Sapporo for a night freighter low on fuel?"

"Promises, promises," she said as she fished out a frosted mug from the freezer and a Sapporo from a small wooden sailing dinghy that had been converted to an ice chest. Leaving me to contemplate my lecherous thoughts, she jiggled off in pursuit of my usual bowl of chowder and steamed, sourdough bread.

The word "home" means something different to all of us. As

the view from my living room is somewhat compromised, the view from Rose's Cantina that looks out over the bay, my front yard, is the vision of "home" to me. Boats lashed to mooring rings all facing the same direction in the current and flying colorful windsocks from their masts. The few stinkpots—diesel powered trawlers—mixed in among the sailboats were decorated with potted plants and a bicycle or two identifying them as live-aboards. The *Pilar'* and the *Joanna K*, where Angie lived with her dirt-bag boy friend, were tied up north of the seaplane dock. And then there was Dirty Dave's quarters, the *Katy 'Chell*, an old wooden hulk up on blocks next to the street in Jonah's marine salvage yard that would never make way again. The seiners and other fishing boats were further north except the *Sara J* that lived in front of the Fish Peddler restaurant next door. Across the bay, the dunes have all but covered the remains of the old submarine base with only a few pilings and boulders still visible. Massive Morro Rock to the north of the harbor still serves as a beacon for mariners as it has for centuries. A whistler cried its mournful tune from the breakwater. In all my worldly travels I'd never seen a more beautiful little town. Well, maybe Scottsdale before the developers got into the Mayorette's pants and ruined it.

I was trying not to listen to Angie's TV soap opera. She returned, treating me to a delightful view of her gravity defying charms as she set the bowl of steaming chowder before me.

"Where'd ya go this time?" she asked.

"Land of Rising Sun." Same question, same answer as always.

"Where's that?" *Ah, so Angie was nineteen!*

"Well Angie, It's ah . . ." I was moving over to the window for a look-see when sweet Angie took off for another order. The pilings were dry to the water line, but my mark was still an inch under water. My el cheapo grande watch and the tide tables Rose's displays on the wall next to the pay phone told me the tide was as far out as it was going to go that day. Barring a global catastrophe, it would be coming back in shortly. After savoring my chowder, I left Angie a fiver in appreciation of her playful display of flesh, grabbed my bag, and left.

The gulls were laughing at me as I wound around under the restaurant amidst the odorous pilings encrusted with crackling barnacles, mussels, urchins, and an assortment of salt water critters as I made for the big boat I call *The Dog*. My roommate calls it *Rosa*.

I caught myself daydreaming on how incredibly easy airplanes are to steal. TJ's $100,000+ supercharged DeHavilland Beaver, like the airliners, has no key. It could be had by untying a simple line and flying it away—if one knew how.

Our slippery walkway that winds through the maze of pilings eventually leads to several large fish nets that appear to be hung out to dry. I parted the fish scented nets, stepping onto a deck that went "clink" rather than the usual "clunk." It took two hands to turn the wheel and a fair amount of force to raise the partially submerged hatch. As seawater poured into my front door, boat smell combined with garlic, cumin, freshly made corn tortillas, and cigarette smoke came out. I knew what was in store for me.

"Hijo de puta, *Pendejo!*" echoed from far below.

I secured a line to my bag, and sent it below. Manning the ladder, I grasped a lanyard to close the hatch behind me and began a rapid descent along with a thousand pounds of seawater. After securing the hatch, I swapped ladders and slid down into the control room of the Submarine *Dogfish*, face to face with my roommate, seventy-three-year-old Many Burruell. Wearing *Dogfish* sweats, a ball cap, flip-flops, and a T-shirt with a pack of Camels rolled in his sleve, his silver belt buckle was engraved with a submarine and the inscription "Pride Runs Deep."

"Ju in such a hurry ju can wait for low tide?"

"It's out!"

"What?"

"I said it's out! . . . Say, ah, that isn't cigarette smoke there, is it, Chief?"

"Como?" Manny's Spanish is conveniently selective. He broke the moment by staring at my feet as he would at a child who had peed his pants. I tried to ignore the icy seawater that had gone down my back, warmed to body temperature in my shoes, and was making little puddles on the old green and white linoleum decking. "An dat's Master Chief!"

"Sorry, amigo. Tide's about as low as it's gonna get today." Manny used to be taller than I, but age has bent his frame until my six feet towers over him. His rock solid handshake came complete with a quarter spoonful of heavy-duty marine grease.

"Das what I said, dammit! Eeef ju don' know ju have to wait for low tide by now." Then his tone of voice changed to that of a small child caught red handed in the cookie jar, "I—I don' smell no smoke."

"Where's that Miracle ear, amigo?"

"Como? Ayee, Chiwawa! She's in San Diego weeth her mother! Now, ju gonna mop up thees sheet or am I?"

Ignoring him, I made for the wardroom, in the forward battery compartment known as "officers' country" with Manny in tow. The practiced leg-body-leg maneuver through the watertight hatch was a little slow today.

"Jeez, I'm stiff." It had been a long day that began on the other side of the world.

"Jur' steef?" Steadying himself with his left hand on the braided grab bar over the hatch, he bent over slowly to put his left leg through. He had to use his right hand to help lift the weak leg and had a terrible time bending his neck. In the war, he'd made it through these same hatches at a dead run. He was mumbling in rapid-fire Mexicanese, then he said, "I'm getting too old for dis sheet."

In the wardroom where officers take their meals and shoot the shit, I poured Manny's fifty-weight coffee into our sturdy US Navy mugs that were hot in more ways than one. As usual, it tasted as if it were made from bilge water.

"You figure you're gonna need any parts soon?" I asked. My airline paycheck keeps the submarine in parts while Manny and his pals supply the know-how and labor.

"Hijo de puta, Pendejo, ju don' please to mumble at me! Now, what'd ju say?"

"I asked if you are going to need any parts soon, you crotchety old fart!"

Whether he knew it or not, he was lip reading, staring at my lips as I spoke. "What?" I repeated myself mildly irritated at the old sailor for ditching the hearing aid I bought to avoid exchanges just like the one we were having.

"We need thee leetheum greeze an' the 16-751A tubes for the LF transmitter, an' . . . hey! I ain't old, goddammit!" He turned to look at me as if I was crazy. "An I steel need thee bearing for—wait a minute—ju going somewhere, Pendejo?"

As the tidewaters of the Pacific covered the bridge and slowly climbed our periscope shears, a really depressing picture of a massive concrete structure along the Missouri River entered my mind. "Uh, yeah. Kansas, maybe."

CHAPTER 3

Johnston

Flight Deck, Mariah Flight 267
Boeing 747-2B, Ship 9881
Los Angeles—Tokyo

"**Mariah two six seven, Mariah two six seven, Los Angeles center, *over?*"**

Rats! Distracted over the situation at Mariah, I'd missed a call. It happens. I roger'd the call and was given clearance direct to our next way point and a frequency change to the next ATC sector. After confirming the flight plan coordinates for HEMLO, our "coast-out" way point off the southern tip of Oregon beyond which lies only open ocean until reaching the coast of Japan, we each punched in the command for direct. The behemoth's 2° turn seaward would be unnoticed by even the most savvy passenger, yet that turn would shorten our flight by some 26 miles. Satisfied that the three INS units were in agreement, that the headings and distances were reasonable, I made the call.

"Los Angeles center, Mariah two six seven climbing to two four oh, direct HEMLO."

The reply was instantaneous. "Mariah two six seven, Los Angeles, roger, maintain flight level three six zero, resume normal navigation and contact oceanic on eight nine five four, primary two nine five two secondary, squawk two four zero zero. And Mariah

Visit GOLF WORLD on the Web—
http://www.golfdigest.com

BUSINESS REPLY MAIL

FIRST-CLASS MAIL   PERMIT NO. 128   HARLAN IA

POSTAGE WILL BE PAID BY ADDRESSEE

GolfWorld®

P O BOX 3262
HARLAN IA 51593-2442

HAPPY HOLIDAYS!

HOLIDAY SAVINGS:
1 YEAR (46 ISSUES) OF GOLF WORLD FOR ONLY $31.77.

☐ **YES!**
SEND MY GIFT SUBSCRIPTION TO:

Name: _____

Address: _____

City/State/Zip: _____

E-mail: _____

Free gift cards and envelopes will be
forwarded to you.

List additional gifts on a separate sheet of paper.

GIFT IS FROM:

Name: _____

Address: _____

City/State/Zip: _____

E-mail: _____

☐ Enter or ☐ extend my own subscription
for $53.97.
☐ Payment enclosed.
☐ Bill me later.

GOLF WORLD

Golf World®

For Canada, U.S. $56.46 per gift (includes 7% GST). GOLF WORLD
is published weekly, January 11 - November 8, plus 3 more times
through December. Please allow 3-6 weeks for delivery of first issue.

L031JS4

two six seven, maintain mach point eight four. Have a nice trip, gentlemen."

Since it was my leg to navigate, I set the oceanic altitude in the Flight Management System and roger'd the call. Mach .84 is our normal cruising speed, so there was no adjustment required there. I dialed in the primary HF frequency on the overhead No. 1 HF radio, and the secondary in No. 2 and tuned the antennas. Until we reached Japanese airspace and a radar environment, we'd make hourly position reports with land-based stations either in Honolulu or Okinawa with the WW II era radios.

Flight 267 was a full boat, as we call them when every seat is full. We were right on flight plan, making good 480 knots over the ground, climbing out of two four oh at a leisurely 1,300 feet per minute. Not bad for three-quarters of a million pounds. On our great circle route, Narita-san airport and Tokyo were a mere twelve hours away.

The slip stream and the sound made by four huge engines at climb power and a conversation between the first and second officers made for a noisy cockpit in my right ear with the hectic ATC frequency in my left. I was performing the critical coast-out INS accuracy check when two hundred twenty pounds worth of light loafers barged into the cockpit with Frannie Olson, my personal irritant, right on his heels. It was Blake, our *galley queen* for sure and exactly the last person I wished to see.

We almost always have one or two of "them" on board. They make great waiters and seem to gravitate to the airlines. He crouched down conspiratorially between the two pilots' seats while Frannie snuggled unseen into the jump seat behind me and began massaging my shoulders. She always wears this intoxicating perfume, Caroline something or other, so I knew right away it was her. Blake, with his intricately styled unnaturally blonde hair, moved closer into my personal space and I didn't like it. I turned to him as if to ask what he wanted. He was grinning, but it failed to tip me off as to what was coming.

"So, Captain, we hear you're going to steal one of the airplanes?" he swished. My head jerked back and my body jumped.

"WHAT!"

Fran gave a little lady laugh as she restrained me. "Sit," she said, as she dug what remained of her nails into my neck.

"Blake, where the in *the* hell did you hear that!"

TJ grinned an I-told-you-so. Turning to his right, he pretended he was looking outside, but gave up and broke into a belly laugh, chest heaving with sobs of laughter. He reached over Blake to pound me on the shoulder, unable to speak, tears of laughter streaming down his cheeks. Flip, our second officer for that trip, was right on the verge of it, but so far he didn't get the joke. He was sitting there with a prepared smile on his face, following what he could hear, "Yeah? Yeah?" He was trying to laugh, but it just wasn't working for him.

"Oh, Captain," swished Blake, "you know the airline rumor mill is the fastest in all the world!" Flaming gay voices are like chalk on a blackboard to me and TJ knew it, sending him off into guffawdom again.

"Kevin," he said lifting his eyes heavenward, "he's my flying partner. We met in Belize? And well . . ."

"I don't want to hear it!" I said.

Flip engaged a lever with his heel to swivel his chair forward, leaning in to hear the conversation, still chuckling, turning his head to favor his left ear in order to hear every word in the noisy cockpit and really trying to get into it. Yes, we laugh in the cockpit, as often as possible, but only above 10,000 feet out of the sterile cockpit environment. Find a pilot who doesn't laugh, especially at himself, and you'd better get off his airplane.

I let the crew yuk it up at my expense as I know from experience there will be no stopping it until the laughter dies its own natural death. Even then, sometimes incidents of jest are immortalized by a single word, such as "Alpo."

One of our captains was conned into investing in a couple of racing dogs that were to provide him triple write-off against his staggering tax liability. $350,000 and two imaginary dogs later, the scam was revealed by our beloved Internal Revenue Service as phony. Maybe it was because the captain was such a good target, an ideal victim, or perhaps it mirrored society's sick humor. Whatever the cause, he became known as Captain Woof and could count on finding several cans of dog food in his mailbox or in his flight bag before every trip. I did not care to be immortalized in a similar fashion. Neither was I going to drop the idea because of a couple of airhead flight attendants. But the plan was exposed. There were at least two credible witnesses, TJ and Flip. If one of Mariah's airplanes turned up missing, there was no way they wouldn't remember the conversation. I turned sideways in my seat thereby terminating my neck massage. If I could mainstream the subject, maybe it wouldn't be quite so obvious who was behind it.

I said, "With Franco running the show, we're faced with a situation previously unknown in the history of aviation. Do you realize what I'm saying? This is new!"

"Max, it has been established that every thought, every sound we come up with has been thought of before. Everything's been done!"

"Well, darlin', this one hasn't." Fran stiffened at my using the word "darling." Subconsciously, I suppose, she pulled her blouse closer together, this from a woman whom I'd seen wearing thong bikinis in Japan where such things are simply not done, which is why we fly boat loads of Japanese to Hawaii where such things are done.

Then the swish kicked in, "Captain, it's been proven mathematically that—"

"Max, she's right," said TJ. Flip was nodding in agreement.

"No, now wait a second. I'm not suggesting that there is anything new with their evil intentions. Only their methods are new. Not only are we in danger from what they intend to do and in fact are doing at Air America right now, but they are endangering the seniority system." I drew a collective groan on that one. Everyone hates the seniority system. Some feel it provides protection for the weak and that one weak captain is much more than enough.

"Gee, that would be terrible, wouldn't it?" asked Flip.

"Now, just a minute. It's true that we all hate the system, but think of the consequences of getting rid of it!"

"Yeah, I'm for that! Get me off of this damned panel and into the left seat!"

"Exactly my point. And you'd do whatever you had to do to accomplish that, wouldn't you, Flip?"

"You're damned right I would!"

"OK, now imagine a guy like Buck pulling the strings. He knows he can get men, such as you, qualified in the left seat quickly. He understands what that means. He knows that reaching the left seat is the achievement of the ultimate, lifetime goal to any pilot. It is also true that your reaction times are much faster, that your night vision is much clearer than that of Captain Woof. But so are your contemporaries'. Therefore, competition is introduced and in this one instance, I say it is bad!"

Frannie freaked, "What are you talking about? This isn't like you, Max! Competition is good! You'd be practically guaranteed to have the sharpest crew available for every flight!"

"Would you, now? Frannie dear, your naivete is showing. Picture Buck pulling the strings on such an operation. Do you honestly think he'd pick captains based on merit? Or would his criteria for selection include a generous greasing of palm under the table? And the grease would come from other directions as well. The feds would grease for each minority he would place in the cockpit. Crews are being hired right now for their skin color or whether they stand or sit to pee rather than their ability to fly. With the increasing automation in the cockpit, Buck feels the captain is along for the ride anyway. He'd hire a computer expert, teach a little about flying, and send her out the door.

Fran dug her fingers deeper into my neck as Blake swished, "Well, Captain, we won't tell a soul about any of this . . . but we *do* want to work the trip!"

"A T'submareene ees a beeg hole een the agua where ju put jur
dinero ... an jur life."
—Master Chief Manny Burruell

CHAPTER 4

Johnston

Captain's cabin
Submarine *Dogfish*

I was having one of the two standard airline pilot nightmares—feeling as if I'm walking through honey, I am across town struggling through an endless succession of impossible obstructions that keep me from the airport at departure time while an airplane full of people is waiting for me—when I awoke with a start, thinking I'd heard a distant scream. I was still fogged with sleep, trying to tell the time from the large, repeater depth gauge on the bulkhead at my feet. It looked like 7:35 PM, but was actually reading zero feet. When I first took up residence aboard the submarine, I thought for sure she was haunted. But this boat had never been in combat, so the only ghost aboard turned out to be my roommate and his nightmares that continue to haunt him.

I rolled over the restraining bar designed to keep the captain in his bunk in heavy seas vaguely thinking I'd slept in, still under the influence of the dream. Parting the heavy, green curtain I stepped out into the darkened companionway, did a left 90°, took five steps aft, pivoted on my right foot for a hard-left turn into the boat's small office where we keep our reel-to-reel tape recorder of WW II music. As in hotels, I can make my way around the boat with my eyes closed. The trick is to remember where you are.

We keep the music down so low you hardly notice it, but it does add a lot to the atmosphere aboard the *Dogfish*. In the small pantry that adjoins the officers' wardroom, I poured Manny's swill from the stainless coffeepot down the drain as Dinah Shore sang *Candy*. It is customary aboard submarines to have fresh, hot coffee available twenty-four hours a day. Manny has kept up the tradition since 1945, but his taste in coffee is a bit different from mine.

I finished making a fresh pot of Seattle's Best, placed the pot on the warmer, and slid two cups through the serving window that separates pantry from the wardroom when I heard the old sailor. He was grunting his way through the water tight door separating the forward torpedo room from the forward battery compartment. Dressed in sweat pants, T-shirt, and his SS 379 *Dogfish* ball cap, he slid his arthritic frame slowly into a seat at the table, smoothing the antique, hunter-green, double-dolphin tablecloth into place.

"Guess I woke ju," he said sheepishly.

"Didn't hear a thing," I lied to the soft muted trumpet of a big band.

His eyes moistened and his voice grew thick. The music obviously brought forth vivid memories to him just as a little Jan & Dean brings back my memories of cruising Broadway in a white '63 rag-top 'Vette. He tried to say something, then gave up. Wincing at the coffee, he stared into space for maybe a minute, worked his jaw muscles, then said, "Uh . . . eet vas the *Wahoo* again . . . 'so damned *real!*"

I sipped my Seattle's Best as I listened to Manny's story. Over the years I have heard many of his tales, first-hand accounts of what it was like to crew on a WW II fleet boat. Stories of courage and bravery under fire, unmatched in the history of mankind from a frail old man I have adopted, and am proud to call my friend.

"I vas on thee breakwater at Midway—" He looked at me to make sure I knew it was Midway Island he was referring to. I grunted affirmatively. "When t'chee left on her seventh patrol. I vas a plank owner, ju know, I helped to beeld thee boat." He was viewing the past by staring at the wardroom tablecloth. Antique music, *Anapola*, fit the mood. Leisurely moments passed.

"Jes," he nodded slowly. Then he looked up at me with a sudden energy, a questioning expression that meant no matter how eloquently he told the story, and how much I wanted to experience it, I could never really know, never be there to experience the adventures and terrors of our country's finest hour.

"I served five patrols on da *Wahoo*, three with *O'Kane*," he said, referring to Admiral Richard O'Kane, famous sub skipper and author, "and two with Mush Morton. I didn't like O'Kane, but Mush? He and I were *friends*," he said breaking into a brief, reflective smile. "One day, hee pulled me aside and said, 'Manny, ju got five patrols on dis boat. Dat's enough. Any more, and eet ees jus' bad luck for ju!'" He came back to the present for a moment, raising his eyes to meet mine. "I didn't want to do eet . . . I didn't want to leave, . . . but, I deed what hee tol' me to do."

His head drooped again for a moment, then raised slightly. The Glen Miller selection seemed to catch his attention. He looked up and seemed to stare right through me as if I weren't there, at locker No. 8, one of the featureless stainless steel cabinets that line the far bulkhead. When you live aboard a real WW II United States Submarine where the calendars read October 1945 and the music is of the era it is easy to get into the mood, so Manny drifted off again, returning to 1943. He was really there, seeing it all over again, live.

"I can see heem so clearly. Right now! He ees beckoning to me from thee bridge. Hees face—it has thees empty—how do you say—vacant look. Hee is looking right at me," he said somberly, "and hee . . . hee has no goddamned eyes!" His face was contorted with agony, tears unashamedly streaming down his grizzled face. "*Wahoo* never came back," he sniffed, mopping tears with his handkerchief. "Shee vas lost weeth all hands—all of my friends. I can see them so clearly trying to shore up thee boat and stop thee leaking. Thee batteries, you know, they give off thee chlorine gas when they come in contact with salt water." I nodded that I

understood. "I can see them," his voice catching, "breathing eet."
He broke into sobs, laying his head down on the table.

I guess it was the atmosphere aboard the antique submarine,
the music, the 1945 calendar, or the fact that I was sitting across
the table from a man who had really been there—a real, honest-
to-God hero. Somehow I made the jump. In a kind of *Twilight
Zone* fashion I was *there*, for just an instant, experiencing the terror
of being trapped 400 feet below the Sea of Japan surrounded by
billions of tons of water. Water tight doors closed, some
compartments flooded, I could feel the icy tendrils of claustrophobia
gently at first on my shoulders as the mortally wounded sub lay at
an angle on the bottom with up and down not quite where they
should be. Suffocating from lack of oxygen in the dark with only a
mixture of spent foul air and chlorine gas to breathe, preparing to
drown, icy salt water licking at my ankles knowing there was no
escape, no way out.

"Thee lights are out and everybody is coughing freezing and
scared t'chitless 'cause they know what ees going to happen to
them, but they are brave men and I t'chud have been there to help
them! They can't stop the leaks! Maybe eef I . . . maybe one more
man. That might have made thee difference." He peered into his
heavy Navy coffee mug as if it were a portal into the past. "I see
thee boat as she ees filling slowly weeth salt water that ees as cold,
no, colder than ice. I can . . . even in the darkness I can see them
drowning, all of my friends. Eet e . . . horrible!" Manny closed his
eyes with his high cheekbones resting in his palms, eyes covered,
shaking his head slowly.

I cuffed him on the shoulder. "Más café, amigo?"

"Ju should have made some fretch. Thees tc'heet ees getting
pretty old."

"Yeah, well."

"Now!" He said quickly wiping away his tears with the back of
his hands that seemed to break the spell. "Vat 'chu up to, *Pendejo?*"
We were back in the present time. But the crew of the *Wahoo* was,
and still is on patrol at the bottom of the Tsushima Straits, off the

west coast of the Japanese Island of Honshu. "I can tell when sometheeng ees up. Qué es?" The pressure was off Manny and onto me. I looked innocently back at him, but the wise old man knew something was up. It was time.

"We . . ." How the hell was I going to explain this? "You know I told you about this guy Franco. They call him a "corporate raider." He's a pirate all right. Wall Street, hell even Rush Limbaugh loves him! He's selling the airline off piece by piece and pretty soon there will be no airline, and everyone including me will be out on the street selling shoes. No pension, no severance pay 'cause Franco's spent it all!"

One of my perverted theories is that the only possible alternative to flying the big silver bird is to sell shoes. It makes revising manuals easier.

"He's liquidating our pensions right now, at this very moment, and there is nothing we can do about it! Pilots, the mechanic's union, and the flight attendants have a suit filed against him in federal court, but this guy pulled the same thing at Atlantic Airways and a couple of other airlines that aren't flying anymore *and got away with it!* I called the attorney representing the pilots to get a progress report and all I can get are recordings that are essentially press releases. 'Push one for this, and two for that, but I can't get through to talk with anyone human. The whole world's going to shit that way, Manny. If you'd ever get out of Morro Bay, you'd see that for yourself.

"I like eet here." It was good to see him beaming, to see that old face in a broad grin. He viewed the world from a different perspective and seemed to enjoy my ranting.

"You buy yourself an electric tooth brush and you can just bet the tooth paste will last longer than it will! Just *try* to make a phone call from a pay phone!" I didn't want to get started on this, but he asked. "They smell like latrines, take your money, and all you get is a dial tone or a recording of an address where you can write to the Jerkwater Telephone Company to get your thirty-five cents back two months later!" Manny shook his head and chuckled, stirring an additional spoonful of sugar into his coffee. He was enjoying this.

"Hell, you go to the grocery store on a busy day, and out of sixteen check stands, they might have two open. Buy anything anymore and the emphasis is on the warranty instead of the product you're buying because it is understood that you're about to buy another piece of junk! You're gonna get greased and the only thing you can do is bend over! Remember what the airport was like when we went to Japan?"

Manny looked up for a moment, gazing at the repeater depth gauge on the wardroom bulkhead. "Kinda busy, but eet vas OK once we got on thee airplane."

"That's just what I'm talking about. At least there the crews have some control over how your flight's going to go. You get a crew that's rested and in a good mood, you have a great flight. You draw one that's been run into the ground—so to speak—for a week while the boss is raiding their pensions and you might not have such a good time."

I squeezed out of my seat to get fresh coffee for both of us. The sound of a propeller from a small boat could easily be heard through the hull and was blending with early Frank Sinatra as it churned up Morro Bay's harbor, setting me again to wonder what a Japanese destroyer at flank speed would sound like. Because our periscope shears were camouflaged with fishing nets, the *Dogfish* continued to do what she does really well: Hide.

"Passengers miss their flights because they're still standing in line at the ticket counter when the plane pushes back!" I was getting steamed. "People standing in line have heart attacks from the stress! Really! Out of twenty-four counter positions the airline might staff four, just like the grocery stores. The line snakes around a maze and goes clear the hell outside! They've got one of their little bean counters watching that line. When he sees passengers starting to leave to go to another airline, they bring out another ticket agent but not before! Same thing when you call to make a reservation. The computer that plays Johnny Mathis in your ear also tells them just how long the average passenger is going to wait before he gets fed up with the elevator music and hangs up. That way they can staff twenty rez agents instead of the fifty they should have. Sure, they lose a few so they overbook the flights to compensate, knowing damn well that even if everyone does show up, all they have to do is give out a free ticket to Hawaii that costs them nothing. Then the bean counters bitch because the Hawaiian flights are full of people flying for free. The result in the airport is chaos! The corporate mentality has taken the *fun* out of flying! And now they're going to screw me out of my retirement knowing there isn't a damn thing I can do about it because they've got the judge in their pocket! I gotta *do something!* Manny, I can't just let them screw me blind and do nothing about it!"

I relayed my information that ended with a no-questions-asked Colombian "scrap" buyer. Accomplices were available. There was TJ and probably a lot of other pilots enraged over the loss of their pensions, and the two flight attendants I was stuck with who threatened to blow the story wide open unless they could go along for a stake in the proceeds. The old guy's reaction shocked me a bit, but as he was coming from a time before doublespeak and political correctness, when black was black, white was white, and not corporate gray. It didn't surprise me.

"Caca de toro!" hollered the old sailor as he pounded his fist hard on the wardroom table spilling coffee from both cups. He stood up, seemingly invigorated and strong, placing his gnarled hands flat on the table and frying my conscience with his intense gaze. "Bull'tchit! I know ju, Max Power! Ju ain' no thief! I've seen ju! Dat time wee had lunch in the aeropuerto and dat woman gave you a twenty instead of a five you had coming in change? Dey vas charging five times what dey should have for comer del gato but ju gave her el dinero back anyway!" When the old sailor gets excited he reverts to his native Sonoran Spanish. And he was right, the $8 tuna sandwich did resemble cat food.

"Calm down, Manny," I said, but I could see that wasn't going to happen.

"Not 'cause she was nice to ju eether, 'cause she vas a real *puta*! But that leettle voice inside jur head said to give thee money back or hee wouldn't let ju forget it. Ju're an honest man, Pendejo. Ju go fly someone else's avion."

We'd had that discussion before.

"Manny, I've got eight years left 'til the mandatory age sixty retirement. If I put every dime I make as a new hire pilot for another airline into food, I'd starve to death. They won't hire me anyway because I'm too old. I don't know how, but they get around the EEOC. Besides that, I'm divorced!"

"Ju told me dis guy Franco would hire ju at hees other airline!"

"Dammit, Manny, I just can't do it! A man's integrity's at stake here. I'd be giving into his plans. If that bastard gets away with it *again*, it's going to roll back pilots wages forty years! That all adds up to no parts for your purloined submarine!" I thought if I used a word other than stealing, we might get by this rough spot for once.

"I told ju before, goddamn it, I didn't *esteal* it! Thee chief of thee boat ordered me to guard thees focking boat 'til I am relieved. So, that ees what I'm doing! I'm guarding thees goddamned boat, because I have not been relieved!"

"For fifty-two years! Don't bullshit me, Manny. Navy ever finds out you're *guarding* their submarine, they'll relieve you alright—just before they march your ass onto the gallows so they don't have to clean up after you! Somehow you and the boat were misfiled, lost in the confusion after the war, that's all. That's why you keep getting survivor benefits made out to your wife who's been dead for twenty-three years!"

Manny's eyes filled again at the mention of his beloved Rosa. "Navy's been good to me. I take care of thees boat like it vas my own." With good reason: It *was* his own.

"Eeef thee Navy got hold of thee *Dogfish*, they would make bote de cervesa, out of her!" he shrieked. He was probably right there. I had visions of rows upon rows of B-17s, P-51s, and other groovy airplanes being melted into ingots. Manny's Rosa would melt down into a lot of beer cans. "Any way ju vant to tweest thee words around, eet still comes out thee same way, Max Power. Ju're an honest man, and ju ain' gonna e'steal no goddamned airliner."

"I'll take the chicken."
—*Captain's prerogative*

CHAPTER 5

Johnston

Flight Deck, Ship 782
Mariah Cargo Facility, LAX

"Gear lever and lights?"

"Down, three green."

"Do I really say 'fire warning'?" asked Blake.

"Yes, dammit, say 'fire warning' and read the checklist like we discussed!"

"OK, fire warning?" he swished.

"Checked!" No one would ever believe this. That's the one reason I felt it would work, just like D.B. Cooper. One time only.

"Circuit Breakers?"

"Checked."

There was an annoying pause, a break in the reading of the checklist. I turned part way in my seat to look over my right shoulder for the cause of the delay, "Blake!"

"What?" he lisped as he marveled over the second officer's panel.

"Read the next item, dammit. It's yaw dampers!"

"Alright, yaw dampers! You don't have to be so rude! If you know what it is, why do I have to read it?"

"Gimme that!" I said snatching the plasticized checklist. I ran over the rest of the items, with a little extra caution, by myself. He shrugged off my irritation by catching up on the soaps with Fran, whom I would have to chase downstairs again.

Due to the sadistic bastards that make up airline schedules, it isn't unusual to see a flight crew reporting for duty at three o'clock in the morning. I'd instructed Blake to wear black slacks, black shoes, and a uniform white shirt with my F/O stripes so that I could pass him off as our second officer—*providing he kept his mouth shut*. A flamer, if he said anything, and any of the airline people heard him, the jig would be up. To make matters worse, he flatly refused to cut his wavy blonde hair. I finished the checklist with the airplane configured for engine start when Fran, who had conspired with Blake to force their way onto the trip, appeared at my shoulder as she had on so many flights.

"Coffee?" She was wearing that damned, door-opening perfume.

"Sure. Y'know, you look pretty good in those coveralls." The Mariah coveralls came with a fuel truck we'd liberated in the deserted main hangar. Good looking as she is, she underscores my basic philosophy: Boats, even submarine boats, airplanes, motorcycles, and other toys—or a woman. But you can't have it both ways and expect to live a peaceful life. "Blake can work the galley, Fran. You just go watch that frigging fuel truck like I asked!" I said. "Please?"

"Well, I just thought you, I mean I . . ."

"It's OK, Fran . . . just go watch the truck, *p l e a s e*?"

I almost got my feelings hurt. Here I was in the commission of a capital crime that could send me to the Big Resort on the Missouri, and I was having to play nursemaid to Fran and Blake's sensitive personalities. This flight was over crewed and undermanned. If it got much worse, it would be like a real flight! Fran's expression looked like a little kid who had been sent to bed for being bad.

"OK, Max, but I . . ."

Admiring hers, I said, "No buts!" pointing aft towards the air stair. She turned and left with her feelings hurt. I hoped to God she didn't intend to pout because pouting is one of the things I decided I would no longer participate in when my ex-bride, the D.L. for Dragon Lady, left me for being the pilot she had earlier pursued, then much to my delight. I sent the pouter packing, along with everything I owned as well as half of my now nonexistent pension wondering how in hell I'd ever spent so much as a single night with her. Franco's raiding of the pilots' pension fund would be an expensive last laugh on her.

We were short a fueler and a "momback"—that's what we call the guy with the flashlight wands who directs the airplanes in and out of the parking spots. The term was coined from a decidedly nonpolitically correct joke about the guy behind the garbage truck who has since been replaced by an OSHA mandated, back-up beeper that also serves as a pre-wakeup alarm in many neighborhoods. When one of the feds turned us in for use of the term, the red-faced airline insisted we call him a "marshaler," so we compromised by using our own word. It was another step backwards, like when we finally gave up pasting photos from the centerfolds in the checklists, behind panels, and so forth. Our airlines were being drained by sexual harassment suits from the lady pilots they hired who, since they couldn't fly worth a shit, decided on a sort of brief, modified legal career instead. We survived without the photos of God's little playthings, so I guess we could handle taxiing without a momback. It was a straight shot out of the ramp to the taxiway; we'd fake it without one.

After I parked the hydrant truck in position and got my hands dirty hooking up the hose to our single-point, fueling manifold, I asked Fran to monitor the pumping because Blake was afraid of the truck's noise. The only duty involved having to shut down the power takeoff by pushing a single lever after the truck shut off automatically. As there is always a chance that any machine won't do as it's told, I explained to her that in an emergency, she would push in the same PTO lever, and how to call the cockpit from the ground service interphone. The plan was then for me to dash outside, disconnect the truck and replace it in the hangar before the day shift became the wiser. As we would find out all too soon, something was about to go fatally wrong.

I can operate a 727 by myself in my sleep, provided all goes well. Pilots who have flown her agree she's the best flying airplane ever made. It's comfortable, flies beautifully, and appears to be doing 300 knots while sitting at the gate. The *72'* is self-contained, requiring no ground support equipment, provided everything is working, which in this case it wasn't.

The only 727 on the ramp and available for theft was 7816, the City of Leesville. Colombian client wants a "three-holer," it might as well be a model 2M with the big engines and fuel tanks. She was parked outside the hangar awaiting a "C" check, second only to the heavy check where the big airplanes are disassembled with each and every part on the airplane inspected and replaced if necessary.

A review of her logbooks revealed a number of reccurring write-ups that positively must be fixed before she flew again. Larceny being what it is, I decided that a little rescheduling was in order. She would fly at least one more time before wrench one was turned, and it wouldn't be Francisco Franco's wrench. If it flew in, it ought to fly out. We'd find out soon enough.

The most serious problem was with the APU, or auxiliary power unit, a small jet engine mounted transversely in the main landing gear wheel well. It had been written up as surging and having had multiple fire warnings, and it was placarded inoperative. Occasionally a sick APU will shoot a 12-feet tongue of flame on starting that has been known to scare passengers to the point of initiating a ground evacuation all by themselves. Those who bother to pay any attention to the pre-flight safety briefings have been instructed on the operation of the doors and over wing exits on each flight. They've been known to use them, the airplane shedding passengers off the wings as she waddles along the taxiway.

Our sick APU would have to provide 30 PSI of pneumatic pressure to start the engines, so the collared circuit breaker that prevented its use had just been reactivated.

"Receiving aircraft check is complete, *sir!*" I said it aloud to myself. It's an industry policy I insist my crews follow religiously. If for some reason I'm distracted, I want my crew to make sure I know the checklist has been run.

Loosening my tie further, I turned in my seat to face what could loosely be coined "the crew" for my standard preflight briefing that wasn't so standard. Fran was back again, and sat in the jump seat directly behind me wearing Caroline Herrera, her potent gardenia scented weapon for offensive maneuvers against the opposite sex. I took a refill, told her for the thousandth time that I didn't want cream or sugar, and told her I didn't particularly like the sound of the NOGOTs and INOPs myself.

I continued the briefing, "We will operate this flight as a standard maintenance ferry. With no passengers, we'd be legal to *ferry,*" I said with a glance towards Blake. "That is if we had the proper permits from the FAA and of course if the airline knew anything about it. This is a risky operation. It's not too late, you can bail out now." No one moved towards the exit. "OK then, Frannie, get your cute little butt down stairs and watch that fuel truck!"

ACARS is a small computer that relays the departure and arrival times of a flight automatically to the dispatchers. Another of its several functions allows a flight to obtain its ATC clearance in writing thereby eliminating the often-frenetic process of dealing with the clearance delivery frequency. I punched in the request, the crisp clear clicks of each digit sounding like rifle shots in the still of the night. After a few moments, the screen flip-flopped to the clearance display. Not what I wanted to see: "Clearance not on file."

"Shit!"

"What?"

"No clearance!" No clearance—no go. It's not an unusual response, but in this situation it was definitely not a good omen.

I thought that this must be what Simon and Garfunkle used to sing about. The silence in a cockpit absent of normal ambient noise from the APU, hydraulic pumps, and assorted electronics was deafening. Annoyingly, my head-stereo plunked the 45 on the turntable in my mind and began to play what I wasn't in the mood to hear. Like they say, there's a time and a place for everything—and this was not the time.

Reset-reset. "Hello darkness my old friend . . ."

I turned to Blake who sat at the S/O's table, "You have the news?"

I had to give that one to Blake. Not only did he not have it, he didn't know what it was. "I give up, what's the news?"

I was referring to the ATIS, what I call the Automatic Terminal Insurance Statement. It's a recording that broadcasts valuable information to pilots telling of the weather, altimeter setting, runways in use, and any NOTAMs—Notices to Airmen that tell of inoperative components—often droning on and on for what seems like an eternity at the end of which is your phonetic prize. With a mildly tainted attitude, one could conclude that the latter portion of it is the handiwork of the FAA's legal department engaged in a little CYA. Rather than fix an inoperative taxiway light, they merely tell you that it is burned out. The pilot is expected to memorize where—on an unfamiliar airport—the offending taxiway light or closed intersection might be, and thence avoid it. That way, if something does happen, it's the pilot's fault, not the airport's. The prize at the end of the transmission must be given to the controller in order to obtain an ATC clearance as well as clearly establish your guilt on tape should you wander onto a closed taxiway, etc. The prize was "Kilo." Indefinite ceiling, 300 obscured, higher broken and overcast layers, viz was a quarter mile in fog, altimeter three zero one one, runway two five right for departure. I set the altimeters to 30.11, cross-checked the airport elevation with that indicated on two electric and my captain's standby barometric altimeter, then coached Blake into setting the one on the second officer's panel.

"You mean I just twist this little knob here?" he said.

"That's it," I said patiently. The S/O's altimeter was out of tolerances, reading 300 feet when it should have been reading the LAX elevation of 18 feet, plus or minus 50. Not legal for departure. Oh well.

"Alright, let's quit screwing around and get the hell out of here," I said. It was nearly 0320. The mechanics working the 4-1 shift would be rolling in soon; the last thing we needed was company. I selected 124.55 in the No. 2 VHF, brought the mike to my lips, keyed it and said, "G'morning, Los Angeles, Mariah ferry two eight one two with Kilo, IFR to Ontario."

No answer.

It wasn't terribly unusual, especially given the hour where one controller works several frequencies, but it was unnerving given what we were up to. This was where they could get us. Thanks to information I'd passed along from my knowledge of dispatch I'd picked up over the years, Frannie, our computer nut, had figured out how to bring up the dispatcher's program on one of the flight attendant computer stations to file the all important flight plan. We were about to see how well she did.

One more time. "Los Angeles, good morning, Mariah maintenance ferry two eight one two, IFR Ontario with Kilo."

"Mariah two eight one eight, Los Angeles, standby one."

"Roger, Mariah two eight one **two**."

The plan was to hold off on starting the APU until we had obtained a proper ATC clearance to Mariah's major maintenance facility in Ontario, just 36 air miles east of Los Angeles. If for some reason they were wise to us, the plan was to abandon ship and haul ass out of there, hopefully leaving nothing but my pathetically disguised voice on the ATC recorder to identify us.

"Mariah two eight one eight, clearance." Ahhh. A short sigh of relief. "Mariah two eight one eight, we have nothing on you. Say your proposed departure time and destination and advise if you have information Kilo." Even Blake knew it was an "UH—OH!"

"Ah, ground it's Mariah two eight one two, two eight one two, and we're proposed off at three five, destination Ontario, with information Kilo." Blake, among other things, is a well-dressed person. As the screws began to tighten, and the pressure increased it became obvious to all that this was one of those heavy moments in life. Fastidious Blake unbuttoned his collar and loosened his tie. Mine already was.

"Mariah two eight one two, nothing in the computer for you, sir. Suggest you have company re-file. Information Kilo is current."

Bad news. It looked as if we were shot down before we even

got started. Decision time. I decided to try a maneuver best suited for light airplanes flying between two small towns in close proximity. It might work. "Uh, ground Mariah two eight one two with Kilo, uh, given the hour, any chance of a tower-to-tower clearance? No one in the office just now." It was a stupid lie I hoped the controller didn't catch. There is *always* someone in dispatch monitoring the red-eyes while everyone else is asleep. He had to know that. It all boiled down to what kind of mood our controller was in.

"Uh . . . Mariah two eight one eight, correction Mariah two eight one two, roger, I'll check—standby . . ." The silence in the cockpit was absolutely deafening.

At that moment a Mariah mechanic in greasy coveralls and a modified pompadour, smoldering stogie clenched in his teeth, stomped into the cockpit. In thick New York City, Queens, I'd guess, he said, "Hey, Cap wha'da fug?"

"Oh, ah, G'morning. What's up?" I studied his eyes. He didn't know.

"Cap, uh, lemme ask youse a question? Where'd yure freeking fuelah go?" *Why do they always ask you if they can ask you a question?*

Real good question, "Ah . . ." Since he had a name embroidered on his coveralls I knew he'd been around a while. "Ah, Vinny . . . he was there a few moments ago."

"Well, he ain't der now!"

"Aw, shit!"

"Youse got dat right! Listen, ah, Cap, I, uh, disconnected da truck, but youse guys just pumped bettah'n two hundred freeking gallons of Frankie's jet fuel tru de overflows, and it's all ovah my god damned ramp!"

"You're shitting me!"

"I positively ain't shittin' youse! An, Cap," he said chewing on his stogie, "I'd advise youse guys not ta smoke anything, cause your ass is sittin' in da middle of a pretty freeking good size puddle a kerosene!"

"Pull back to make the houses look smaller."
—Unknown

CHAPTER 6

Johnston

Cockpit—City of Leesville, (Before)

Vinny had unknowingly compromised the plan. He advised us not to use the radios as if we didn't know, and rushed off to call the Airport Fire Department to wash down our fuel spill. He was about to spill the beans too.

It was now or never. Everything hung on that one moment. We would either pull one off on old Franco or we'd be right back at Mariah Airlines waiting for our pink slips. Or maybe in jail. I knew my conscience would bother me, so I had made the GO/ NO-GO decision earlier. This wasn't really stealing, I told myself. It was a recapture of assets during wartime, and we were definitely at corporate war, that called for modern, updated thinking similar to the style favored by our Commander and Chief with the big, red nose in the White House. It was time to start the APU, fire up the engines, and get the hell out of Dodge!

"Blake, you know about the fifteen minutes of fame?" He turned to look at me over his shoulder with jaundiced cow eyes. "Here comes your big moment. To your right . . ." Using my pointer, I directed him to the APU control panel located amidst a thousand circuit breakers. "Put your finger on, but do not move, that silver toggle switch right—no—the other one." He was having the usual difficulty in finding the switch for the first time.

"This one?" he swished.

"Yes! That one! You're going to start the APU now, Blake. You've heard it whine a thousand times, but this time you're going to make it happen."

I reached for the PA handset, and punched the blue, overhead-button indicator light to make sure Fran heard me. "Frannie!" I said, "OK on the door!" It was time to raise the aft stairs and reach for the sky! I waited until I saw the AFT STAIRS annunciator light on the S/O panel change from green to amber, meaning Frannie was bringing up the stairs.

"OK, now, Blake, move that switch up to the START position and hold it until I tell you to stop."

"Like this?"

CHAPTER 7

Johnston

Cockpit—City of Leesville—(After)

I was surprised to feel the heat so fast. Responding to the orange ball of flame that enveloped the entire airplane, I instinctively reached for my oxygen mask. With a "Whomp" our world had turned to a dull orange and at once it seemed stuffy in the cockpit. Murphy was our ground crew that morning because the APU ignited the spilled jet fuel, enclosing us in a huge, mushroom cloud of fire and oily black smoke. The TAT probe was pegged on +46C. There was no way to measure the temperature, but I knew it was pretty warm when the windshield wipers began to burn. If they were on fire, the tires would be too, along with hydraulic lines and door seals. Fire was everywhere. We had mere seconds to live.

As I watched the APU spool up I became aware of *that* sensation, the now familiar one where terror turns mili-seconds to hours and minutes into a ghastly eternity. For the second time in three months I felt Lucifer slither into the jump seat behind me—felt his hot, rancid breath on the back of my neck and his cotton in my mouth. Dammit, it was happening again.

I knew the tower controller had punched the *crash* button and that as I fought for my first breath I realized that he was calling us from far away in another dimension. We were burning to death.

"Mariah two eight one two, observing an explosion and large

fire in your vicinity, advise if you require assistance! Mariah two eight one two! Mariah two eight one two, Los Angeles ground, over!" For him, the moment was nearly as bad as it was for me . . . working a flight normally one moment, not getting an answer the next, and knowing in the pit of his stomach why.

There was just no time to respond. Blake was scared shitless and so was I.

We are trapped! We are on fire! We must get out! My voice sounded low and far away—there was no time for this, no time to do anything but to *run, to flee!* But we had to methodically start an engine and get moving! That was our only means of escape. "Blake, move the APU air switch up . . . yes, that's—good! Now . . ." As I was talking him through the configuring of the APU for engine start, with liberal use of my pointer, it began to surge. The RPM was unsteady and she was farting out compressor stalls. The little jet was suffocating from lack of oxygen just as we were about to do. And Blake had forgotten to go on oxygen. One sniff of the toxic smoke and it would be all over for him. His lungs would involuntarily shut down. I raised my oxygen mask to holler at him, "Blake, oh two and interphone!" In my periphery I saw him fumble only once with the quick-don oxygen mask. In a moment he was sucking down Mariah's oxygen—probably not his favorite, but it would have to do.

I reached overhead, pushed and turned the rotary switch that would open the start valve for No. 1 engine. It was very hot and getting hotter rapidly. Without the cool oxygen from our masks, we'd already have been unconscious. I felt perspiration running down my forehead forming little rivers that ran around my oxygen mask and onto my chest. The fire had been burning for perhaps two seconds. Little tendrils of smoke began to issue forth from the ceiling and side walls of the fuselage. It seemed to take hours before the engine started to rotate.

"CAPTAIN, GET US OUT OF HERE!" Blake's electronic voice was coming to me from the end of a long tunnel. I was pleased to hear that he was under control, but aware that he was also on the verge of surrendering to panic. We had been engulfed in fire for nearly six, long, agonizing seconds.

"Stay with me!" Far away I heard the controller issuing directions to the crash crew amidst frantic transmissions to us.

"Fire one, fire six, the explosion was in the vicinity of Mariah's maintenance facility off the two five left parallel, cleared to cross all runways and taxiways break-break, Mariah two eight one two, Los Angeles ground, over!"

The engine had reached 8%, and would accelerate no more. But we needed 20% for start, or at the very least 17%. Stupidly, I reached overhead to force the start switch to the stop as if that would result in more speed. Orange flames mixed with an oily black smoke were licking at the cockpit windows and had set the captain's wiper blade on fire. The little APU, strangling in the heat and rarified air inside our mushroom cloud of flame and smoke, surged and backfired with vigor.

Run! Escape! Get out of here!

But I couldn't. I knew that the only way out, that our sole means of escape was for me to stay in the seat and get an engine started or die trying! I had to fight the instinct to unstrap that Boeing from my ass and run like hell!

More compressor stalls; the APU was in her death throes and wasn't able to give one more cc of desperately needed pneumatic power. The No. 1 engine started to decelerate. We were roasting alive. I knew that if I didn't do something right then, at that very moment, we would die. But if I attempted to start the engine at such a low RPM, it most likely would blow itself to pieces, sealing our fate. I recalled conversations on the line about hot weather engine starts . . . You're supposed to have 20% N1 to start, but you've just *gotta* have at least 17% unless you can't get that from a weak APU in which case you *might* get by with 15% . . . or *maybe* at the very, very least 11% if you're out in B.F. Egypt away from maintenance. We were fresh out of options, the fire was everywhere *and it wanted to come inside!* As I mentally crossed my fingers, I raised the engine start lever at 7% to introduce fuel and ignition.

For an eternity nothing happened. Then with a loud "POOF" that shook the airplane she lit off! The EGT was buried in the red, but she slowly spooled towards idle power.

You know that sound. The increasing whine that only comes from the starting of a jet engine. It's rescued me from some lousy situations, marked the passing of major life events, and the painful loss of a lover. But never had that sound, that crescendo of jet engine whine, ever sounded so damned good to me! I felt my chest swell with excitement and promise. Even before the start switch had cut out automatically, I reached overhead to select GRD on the start panel for the No. 2 engine, repeating the process. The instant No. 1 engine reached idle, I released the parking brake and shoved the throttle smoothly forward.

"Whomp-Whomp!" Compressor stalls. Like the now dead little APU, No. 1 wasn't getting the oxygen needed to maintain combustion. But we had to get out, *right now!* Not another moment, not another second could we delay. "Whomp-Whomp-Whomp!" Slowly at first, then rapidly the engine spooled up; her high-pressure bleed valves closed—kicking us in the ass by a smartly accelerating Boeing 727.

We exploded from the fireball to a beautiful sight. Trailing burning rubber and heavy black smoke that rolled off our airfoils, we burst into the clean, clear smog of another Southern California predawn. We might live to see the sunrise. I yanked open the sliding cockpit window, bathing the cockpit in the blessed, cool, Pacific air. Jerking my oxygen mask off in favor of some real air I was suddenly unable to hold back my imitation of a rebel yell, so I burned off a little tension with a "YEEHAW!" It scared poor Blake who was already petrified.

"Jesus Christ, Captain!" He had a death grip on the S/O's table with both hands.

We had been prisoners of fire for less than a minute and a half. Involuntarily, my head-stereo began to play:

"Get your motor running,

Head out on the highway,

Looking for adventure . . ." Steppenwolf. *Born to be Wild*. That time I let 'er play!

Having raised the No. 2 start lever, she was midway through the start sequence when I reached overhead to engage the No. 3 start switch. At our twelve o'clock, I observed the flashing red and blue lights of the crash trucks headed for us at high speed. I squeezed the top of the yoke-mounted rocker switch to transmit a warning, but my mind was working lightening quick. I pointed over my shoulder at the S/O's jackbox. "Blake, punch up number one VHF, push the PTT button and say 'coming through!'" I realized just in time that my undisguised voice had nearly been recorded for the entire free world and probably the commies too for the 6 o'clock news.

Blake's mind must have been awash in adrenaline too, because without hesitation he transmitted the requested words in a dialect that kept the federalies scratching for a while. Like a fairy on a CB radio he flamed, "Stand aside, boys, we're coming through!"

The chartreuse fire trucks moved aside to let us pass but the one on our left was squeezed by some Mariah ground equipment the ramp rats had parked too close to the taxiway. Frigging slow motion again. Shit! I tried at the last minute to turn into him, which would move our left wing tip away from the crash truck, but it wasn't enough. Like a gentle tug on my sleeve the wing tip sheared off their light bar and antennas in an explosion of sparks and jagged shards of plastic.

On any normal flight, the captain taxis the airplane slowly enough to ensure passenger comfort and avoid bouncing the flight attendants off the cabin walls, thereby providing sufficient time to complete the many tasks necessary to configure a jet airliner for flight. But that morning, I was taxiing the machine fast towards runway 25L, operating on *Twilight Zone* time, unable to divide my attention from the world outside to the forward instrument panel.

That really was no way to run an airline. Even Mariah.

I introduced fuel to the No. 3 engine at what I estimated

would be 20% N1 by counting champinzees in my spare time. Yes, I said champinzees. She was getting pneumatic power from the No. 1 engine bleed air and though I couldn't hear her whine, I knew she would wind up quickly. I moved my hand over a few inches to wrestle the flap lever through the flaps-two safety gate, and selected 15°, the standard takeoff flap setting. While herding the jet much too fast down the taxiway, I was cognizant of abnormal indications as the 727 wing "disassembled itself" into the takeoff configuration. The amber light I saw out of the corner of my eye was a disagreement indication that told me we weren't getting the flap setting that I selected, not surprising since I'd used the wing tip as a cleaver. Even though the fog was thick, sighting down the left wing I could see that the No.1 slat on the left wing was damaged and wasn't going to extend. I dreamt of the luxury of doing a "180," returning to the ramp, and calling for maintenance to the sweet sound of groaning passengers. But it wasn't going to happen.

With a touch of my left thumb, I rolled the STAB TRIM to the forward edge of the green band on the trim indicator. At our light weight of 170,000 or so pounds, that would be in the ballpark, it would be easy to retrim as necessary on the takeoff roll. I felt as if I was handling the situation as well as one might expect under these circumstances when time, with the customary, stinging slap-in-the-face, returned to normal.

But wait! Things were happening too fast! My hands were too full, the snowball was piling up on me! I wasn't ready for time to speed up, but, dammit, it had anyway! Apparently the Chief Pilot in the Sky thought I could handle things from there on. I shuddered at the thought of what the Biggest Boss would have in store for me as a result of that flight. Had I known what else was coming, I would have stood on the brakes, parked the machine, shut down the engines, and cheerfully awaited arrest.

"Mariah two eight one two, Los Angeles ground, advise your status, over!" The controller was in the dark, but the fire boss brought him up to date.

"Ground, fire one!" Excitement caused him to shout into the

microphone, which resulted in a scratchy, over-modulated, garbled mess . . . sort of like you hear when the guy asks if you want fries with your order. "That Mariah Tri-jet is northbound on taxiway Bravo, and he's on fire! Tell him to stop so we can squirt him!" I continued the fast taxi as they talked back and forth trying to unravel the mystery.

Memory is never good enough for a checklist, but that morning, it was all I had time for. As the blue taxiway lights appeared one at a time out of the fog, I ran through the checklist mentally. Then as the taxiway lights gave way to the amber runway lights for two five left, meaning time was running out, I double-checked myself with an old non-sked technique. *Are the doors closed? Is there fuel in the tanks? Are the flaps extended? Is the trim set? Are the engines running?* A CIGAR check for the jet. That basic check was passed along to me by a grizzly old C-46 pilot, a final check for the checklist when taking the active runway. It may sound odd to ask if the engines are running, but in a 727 they can't be heard in the cockpit aside from a weak whine that could be from one engine or three. So I nearly had a heart attack when I realized engine three was *not* operating and that the aft stairs were *not* in the up and locked position!

I glanced at the N2 RPM indicator for engine No. 3. It seemed to be hung at 3%. Something was inhibiting its rotation. The obvious answer was that something from the explosion had been sucked into the inlet. Just then an electrical shock ascended from my ass to my head. The preflight! Damn, we'd somehow missed it! The No. 3 engine had to be plugged with a catering cover!

CHAPTER 8

Johnston

City of Leesville—Taxi for takeoff

Runway. Runway is the length and breadth of an aviator's life. Runway is safety. Runway is our departure point from this earth, but most of all, runway is home. The mere sight of a runway appearing ghostlike through the ink of a stormy night has been known to mist the eyes of even the most hardened warrior. Cockpits fill with a choir of angels singing *Glory Hallelujah* at the mere sight of her approach lights reaching up to the aviator out of the black of night. For runway is deliverance. Runway is life itself. In our flight bags we carry the statistics for every useable runway in the world and we call them affectionately by their first and last names. One zero left, two eight right; zero two, two zero; one six, three four. Like the natural in-and-out, up-and-down rhythms of life, one of which I am especially fond of. Runway is our constant objective and we can never have enough of it. But the only runway available to us in the wee hours of that fateful morning was two five left. The airport was fogged in. Our runway was closed. And we . . . were fucked.

"Ground, fire one! Tell that 727 that his wheels are on fire!"

"What about Fran? Captain, for God's sake, you can't leave Fran behind!"

"Aircraft on the high speed taxiway, runway two five left is closed! Men and equipment on the runway, I say again, the runway is closed!"

I remembered hearing a faint scream. Not unusual as Frannie screams at lots of things. She sure as hell would scream at *our* fire, so it had to be her. Fran was either on board or she wasn't. There was no time to think of her now; that would come later. If she were alive, she'd have to take care of herself.

She was heavy on my mind while I dealt with the runway. Closed or not, I would have used it, but with heavy equipment on it, not only was it out of the question, it was certain death. The airplane was still on fire. I'd moved Blake to the F/O position, so I had a homo for a copilot, no second officer at all, and one crew member missing. One engine was not going to start and I wasn't too sure about keeping the other two running. I was being chased by the fire department and those who make the rules would point out that, oh, by the way, I was in the midst of committing a capital crime.

I was cornered, and when cornered I fight. With a sneer in my voice I growled out my own name "Max Power!" Blake turned to look at me as if I was crazy, but apparently the look on my face told him to keep his mouth shut. With the nose-wheel tiller hard over to port, I spooled up, then shoved the throttles to the firewall! What was left of the jet's nose-wheel tires screamed in protest of the aeronautical "Brodie" to the left. I wondered about collapsing the right main gear, but Boeing builds 'em strong! A maze of soft blue taxiway lights slued around until they formed a border on either side of us leading off into the infinity of darkness and fog. I could only see three of the blue taxiway lights on each side, and those began to accelerate out of the foggy darkness.

Runway—sometimes we make our own.

The clunking of the flaming nose-wheel tire sounded at first like rapid pistol fire, then a BAR, and finally a machine gun. Large pieces of burning rubber were being shed against the belly making a hell of a racket. Blake turned to say something to me, but I shut him up. "Just watch out for traffic!" At our weight the airspeed came quickly in spite of having an engine out. "One hundred knots!" I made the verbal call myself. At 110 knots Blake screamed again; I could see him pointing ahead and pounding on the glare shield. The million plus gigabyte computer resting on my shoulders sensed ground equipment on the taxiway. If he could see it, we would hit it, unless . . . "Flaps twenty-five!" This time, when it really counted, I was able to maneuver the flap lever through the gate to the next higher setting without difficulty. I hauled back on the controls and prayed to God for help. She was too slow and crippled to fly, but the Tri-jet, arguably the best airplane ever built, lifted her nose towards the heavens and clawed for the sky! I felt the smooth, welcome release, the transition from ground to flight. A quarter instant later, headlights passed beneath the nose and then we creamed whatever used to be attached to them with the right main gear. There was a loud "BANG" and a momentary shudder, but we were still in one piece, still in the air and flying!

It's funny, sort of, the things your senses will pick up at times of great crisis. I caught the aroma of Blake's high-dollar cologne, blended with fresh human urine. "Gear up, Blake!" I glanced over at him. His eyes were as big as Frisbees. Knowing his survival depended on it, he raised the gear handle quickly. As with the indications when reconfiguring the wings, abnormal indications of gear retraction leapt out at me. The red light over the gear handle meant that the right main wasn't gong to tuck into the wheel well. There was no time to mess with it. The jet was flying in "ground effect," and we were rapidly running out of ground. In order to clear the sand dunes at the west end of the airport, it was necessary to lower the nose a half degree at a time to gain enough airspeed to climb. But we were already on the deck and didn't have a half degree to spare! Airspeed came to us agonizingly slow, in spite of the two screaming Dash 17Rs whose EGTs were both buried in the red. The stick shaker quit. Using the FD 110 flight director's speed command for a guide, I risked raising the nose a degree. The IVSI showed a 200-feet-per-minute rate of climb. It might just be enough.

When the soft-blue glow of the taxiway lights turned black, the radar altimeter dropped to zero, then instantly to a hundred feet. We'd cleared the dunes! Almost. I tried to dismiss the mild bump but I knew damn well we'd hit the sand dune. Accelerating, I called to Blake to raise the flaps to 15°. Out of breath from fright, he still responded with what I wanted to hear, "Flaps fifteen."

Just then the APU fire warning sounded. Damn! I'd missed that one! "Blake, heave it out of that seat and shut the APU down!" It should have shut down by itself when it sensed a fire, but I wanted to make sure. While Blake was wrestling himself out of the seat, not an easy chore under ideal conditions, his wet butt was nearly in my face. I reached around him and raised the flaps to five, then two. Since I'd mashed the fire equipment with the left wing, I was not surprised to see an amber LED indication that should have changed to green. Without looking I knew that the outboard slat on the left wing was going to remain partially extended.

I'd never put a scratch on an airplane before, but that morning I'd personally transformed a pretty neat airplane into a pile of junk. But, like her ancestors returning all shot up from a raid, she flew. I gave the machine her lead, throttles still to the wall, the two engines screaming like a millennium falcon at light speed. Both EGTs were in the red, so I backed off on the throttles an RCH. Through 200, 210, 250, 300 and then the "clack-clack-clack" of the over-speed warning. We were doing 400 knots, literally at sea level, the Tri-jet shuddering more and more with the increased airflow over the damaged slat and landing gear. Yarding back on the yoke until my cheeks sagged, the IVSI pegged at 6,000 feet per minute. In an instant we exploded through the top of the fog into the predawn like the projectile we were, rocketing to 5,000 feet in seconds. I'd seen the footage of Tex Johnston rolling a 707 over Elliot Bay in Seattle back in the early '60s and, like most pilots, always wanted to try it. Standing on the left rudder, I fed in full left aileron and pushed hard on the yoke. The airspeed had petered out to near stall speed, deadly in a "T-tail" jet, but as soon as the nose was pointed toward the ocean floor, it began to roll up rapidly again towards the barber pole. I brought the throttles to flight idle, but dismissed the use of speed brakes in the dive since investigators would be pouring over the radar tapes with a fine-tooth comb. I wanted this to appear like a real crash. That way, they'd be looking for me as an oil slick on the water rather than chasing us down with the Air Force.

With the nose in a steep dive, the overspeed clacking again, we screamed through 1000 feet, semi-inverted and midway through a roll-and-a-half to the left. Blake had his eyes shut and his jaw clenched holding onto the glare shield with both hands, but at least he was quiet and didn't barf. The urge to recover was strong, but I couldn't pull out yet. Two seconds later at 500 feet, I pulled hard on the yoke while activating the primary trim with my left thumb and feeding in significant right aileron with the yoke to roll out on a southerly heading. Hot damn, it worked! We must have pulled six Gs in the dive because I saw my vision going to black. The 727 is stressed for three.

The radar altimeter was reading the Pacific Ocean, and was rapidly approaching zero. I hoped like hell it was calibrated correctly. As I advanced the power I heard the thunder of the engines bouncing off the water. We were very, very close, indeed.

I turned off the transponder that would eliminate our encoded return on the controllers' radar. As far as they knew, we were down. I took up a heading of 122°, southeast for Mexican airspace, climbed all the way to 100 feet and engaged the autopilot. Only then did I realize my shirt was soaked in perspiration. Blake turned to me from the right seat, seemingly in shock, and said quietly, "Holy Shit."

"Wanna do it again?" I asked. He flinched.

"No, I do not want to do that again! You're a disturbed man, Captain! Now, what about Frannie?"

A problem I couldn't solve. There wasn't a damn thing I could do. She was either OK or she wasn't. "I don't know. You can take a look in the stairwell. Maybe she boogied when the fuel torched off, or . . . ." *Yeah, or what? Death by fire?* I flashed momentarily on a picture of Frannie wearing kerosene soaked coveralls inside that mushroom cloud of fire. "Better just go change your clothes. And take that seat cushion with you, please."

With the immediate crisis over, I had time to think about Fran as I tuned the radar. Where indeed is Fran? Or is it *was* Fran? This was something I had not bargained for. As airmen, we are by nature indestructible. We must believe that. We back up that belief with skill and all of the knowledge we can acquire. But one of my crew was missing and probably dead. I felt like shit.

CHAPTER 9

Johnston

3 Miles Offshore
Near Carlsbad, California

I have a personal stereo that was implanted in my cranium prior to my birth. "They" say you can only hear one instrument at a time, but those of us that are head-stereo equipped know that's b.s. At will, I am able to call up any tune, any melody, or even a symphony. Sometimes it can provide great comfort but at times like that one when it wouldn't shut off, it could become a pain in the ass.

The heading was one seven five for Mexican airspace. Frannie was . . . well, where was Frannie? I'd sent Blake aft to investigate, hoping she was somewhere in the cabin, but knowing in my mind she wasn't. I kept punching the reset button on my mental jukebox, but all it did was to start the tune over again. Jimmy Buffett in a melancholy mood, "I made enough money to buy Miami, but I pissed it away so fast." Yeah. Something like that. Except instead of money, I knew it was little Frannie.

I felt Blake running back up the aisle, "Captain, she's gone! I can't find her anywhere!" The nightmare I had been dreading since the kero lit off came true. Sweet, dear, little Frannie had been roasted alive in the conflagration. My heart sank to the deck.

"Did you look in the stairwell?" Under different circumstances I would have cracked up, for I had incurred the wrath of a 220 pound sissy with his dander up.

"Of course I looked in the stairwell! There's nothing there, and the stairs are hanging down about a foot! She's just not here. W—what do you think happened to her?" I saw his eyes brimming at the realization, and behind him the AFT STAIRS light blinking rhythmically away with each bounce in the airstream as if to remind me that I now carried the burden of two lives snuffed out by Max Power, the killer.

"She probably hot-footed it away from the plane when the fire started." I rolled in two units of nose up with the alternate trim to compensate for Blake's bulk. "Maybe she's alright," I lied.

Blake didn't believe it either, and retreated to the first class section. At our low speed, the cockpit was whisper quiet, and I had no difficulty hearing him sobbing like a baby while I fought back that tight feeling in the back of my throat and the suggestion of tears forming in my own eyes. No kid ever wanted to grow up faster than I. Had I known that things of this nature would await me, I'd still be playing in the cat box with my bucket and shovel. I had to shake it off, at least for now.

In a few minutes he was back wearing a fresh pair of jeans, installing a fresh seat cushion for the F/O's chair that he'd cannibalized from the aft jump seat. His color was ashen. "Captain, I'm so embarrassed."

"Forget it. Any coffee left?" He gave a quick nod. In a moment he was back, eyes still moist with grief. Swish, maybe, but he was also a man, something I would never have believed before.

He sat on the edge of the S/O's chair holding the pewter coffeepot, and asked me a matter of fact question, "Captain, are we going to survive this?" That again. Even though his hands were trembling slightly he was able to aim the stream of coffee accurately into my cup and didn't spill a drop. "Cream or sugar?"

"Ah . . . no, thanks. Are we going to survive this? Well, let's see. Number three engine—along with its generator—is out, but we've got two good ones, so electrical power is no problem. Number three doesn't have a hydraulic pump as do the other two, so at least we're fortunate not to have lost any hydraulic power. We had an APU fire on takeoff, sustaining unknown damage, but we won't be needing that."

"Why was that?" he asked.

"This APU, unlike most others, is a ground-op-only unit. Its exhaust is over the wing, which in flight creates a strong suction— you like that, right?" He didn't. I think he was getting a little tired of my wit. "So it sucked the little darling into an over-speed condition which can cause a fire." I could see him painting the picture in his mind. Fire damage to tires which is probably what's keeping them from retracting fully; number one slat on the left wing damaged and partially extended. "Can you feel that vibration? Sorta like a landing light extended on a DC-9?"

He rolled his eyes up and to the right, "Oh, right, I do feel it." I craned my neck around to sight down the wing again for another look at where the left wing tip should be. It was gone, and the outboard slat was mangled, jagged fragments of aluminum were trailing in the slip stream.

"The right main gear was damaged when we creamed what ever that was on the taxiway, and it too is partially extended. Could be the tire, or maybe something structural. I'll have you take a look through the periscope in a bit to find out which."

"Periscope? Periscopes are on submarines!" Blake thought I was pulling his leg.

Yes, they are on submarines . . . two of them, as a matter of fact. "Yeah, and we have two of them also, one for each main gear." I wondered if one day they would load this damage assessment into some poor bastard's check ride. "The aft stairs are unlocked and trailing in the slip stream. We can't open the door and retract them now because the "Cooper switch" that's designed to keep the stairs from opening in flight also prevents it from closing.

"Cooper switch? You mean like D. B. Cooper, the first successful skyjacker?" I nodded again. "But we can still fly, right?" Blake didn't like the time I used up in making another answer while I did a slow scan of the instrument panels. He sat up a little straighter to hear the answer.

"Yeah, but we've got some damage and every little rivet—to say nothing of all the shit we have hanging out—will create more drag that requires more power and therefore fuel, to overcome it."

"Do you have to be so vulgar?"

"Fuck you, Blake," I said matter of factly. As I was assessing the situation, the lazy movement of a gauge on the second officer's panel caught my eye, followed rapidly by amber warning lights on the F/O's hydraulic panel and low lights back on the S/O's annunciator panel. "Aw, shit!"

"What! What now for Christ's sake!" he shrieked. What little of his tanning-salon color remained, drained away.

"We just lost the "B" system, that's our secondary hydraulic power and with that the brakes, inboard flight spoilers, the upper rudder, and aft stair control." I was almost expecting that one, probably from a hydraulic line weakened by the fire. "All of this damage is going to play havoc with our fuel consumption. All of the time and distance formulas for our fuel endurance are out the frigging window." There was nothing to do but keep on trucking. We sure as hell couldn't go back.

Like most airline pilots, if I can see the ground, I can easily navigate anywhere in the USA without a chart. Even though I'd flown many trips into Mazatlan and Puerto Vallarta, I had only flown into Guadalajara and Mexico City a couple of times. The rest of Mexico and all of South America were unfamiliar territory to me. Blake laid his head down on the second officer's table while I organized the charts I would need to find our mysterious Colombian airport. As this model 727 was equipped only for navigation within the established airways systems, carrying no INS or other sophisticated navigation equipment, I'd brought my own Columbia Navigator GPS I'd picked up in Morro Bay for $475. I'd carried the tiny hand held navigation device on several of the Tokyo trips comparing it to our onboard, ring-laser gyro, Inertial

Navigation Systems, costing several hundred thousand dollars each, and was astonished to find its accuracy as good or better. And the Columbia Navigator would interface with a Sky Pager or cell phone, or it could send its position to my home base computer aboard the *Dogfish* along with a short comment for Manny. The entire caper could depend on this little device. I made several cross-checks against onshore VORs, and was satisfied that it was accurate. I had drawn out our course on marine charts that would allow me to fix our position frequently. My larcenous mind had formulated a plan that called for a cruising speed of 205 knots, the approximate cruising speed of many, light, twin-engine airplanes. At an altitude of 100 feet a couple of miles offshore, I hoped to remain under the radar coverage while hiding in the fog. If somehow we were spotted, I hoped that whoever was watching us on radar would mistake us for a light airplane. There are many electronic eyes maintaining a watch on our border for smugglers attempting to bring their cargo north into our country. In my demented theory, the feds would be less interested in someone headed south, away from the USA. To further the ruse, I'd filed a flight plan using my old airplane's "N" number from Torrance to Ensanada. Out of habit, I used the No. 2 VHF to call in and activate the flight plan.

In a few minutes, Blake came to with the question I have been asked thousands of times. "Would you like some coffee, Captain?" Each time I reply the same way: "Yes, please, a cup of black for me."

I knew it was coming. "Cream or sugar?" I've fantasized that on the flight attendants' final exam after their rather intense training. The sky hop to be is to approach a make believe passenger who is in reality their instructor. He is to ask if the gentleman wishes a cup of coffee. Regardless of the response, he is to be asked if he wishes cream or sugar. If he asks, he passes the final exam. Frannie'd said it every time she brought me coffee for the last twenty-five years. Little Frannie. Damn.

My reverie was broken by the sensation of speed. While 200 knots is very slow for the jet, it can still be impressive, and in this case frightening. The fog bank that was our cover was breaking up, the remaining tendrils were scooting right on by the windows. We were rapidly nearing San Diego and the border, after which we would be comparatively safe. I could see that the fog was thicker to our right, a mile or so further from shore, so using the autopilot turn knob, I put the machine into a shallow 15° bank and made for the safety of the fog. It was time to implement the next stage of my ruse. I dialed in 118.1 on the No. 1 VHF, listened for a break in the action, and transmitted, "Lindbergh tower, Twin Comanche eight four forty-one alpha."

"Twin Comanche forty-one-alpha, Lindbergh tower, go ahead."

"Forty-one alpha is ten miles north, squawking one two zero zero, VFR for Ensanada."

"Forty-one alpha, roger, stand by, Continental niner three taxi into position and hold, United seven one eight left turn at Yankee, ground point seven, Southwest three one three Lindbergh tower, cleared to land runway two seven, Touchdown RVR two thousand six hundred, mid one thousand nine hundred, roll out is inoperative, wind calm altimeter two niner niner eight, American one eight five report REEBO."

Good. The controller was busy with a string of red-eyes arriving from the East Coast and a few early morning departures. The flights roger'd their clearances, an America West flight with the call sign Cactus 512 checked in at REEBO, the final approach fix for the localizer 27 approach to San Diego, while Southwest 93 stood by at the hold short line for runway 27.

"Forty-one alpha, San Diego is IFR, maintain VFR and remain clear of the TCA, altimeter two niner niner eight."

I imitated a private pilot. "Forty-one alpha, roger, I'll stay low and offshore."

"Forty-one alpha, say your altitude." It was working.

"I'm on top at two hundred feet." In order to disguise the 727's powerful radios, I'd directed air from the captain's eyeball vent over the microphone as I transmitted with the mike several inches from my lips, simulating the background noise of a light twin. The controller admonished me to stay at least three miles offshore, and again to maintain VFR.

"Forty-one alpha, roger." Things were calming down, getting into the routine of flight. The hours-and-hours-of-boredom part would be a welcome change from the moments, many moments, of stark terror.

"Here we are, Captain." I hadn't paid much attention to Blake leaving the cockpit. Proper etiquette requires he notify the captain when leaving, but I let it slide. Poor Blake was pretty much overloaded. When he returned in a few moments, I was expecting the usual cup of airborne swill and a bag of pilot pellets but much to my delight Blake presented me with a hot cinnamon roll from Cinnabon and a cappuccino.

"Starbucks?" He looked at me as if I was a two-year old, his eyes still red with grief.

"No, it's our Seattle's Best blend."

"Blake, you're a constant source of amazement to me." And that made the corners of his mouth rise slightly.

"I am? Why?" He sat back down in the flight engineers chair, apparently interested.

"Here, uh, use your right heel to push that lever there . . . yeah, now you can swivel the chair forward, it makes it easier to talk." The flight engineer's chair is a complicated device that everyone has trouble with at first, but he managed quickly.

"I, uh, well, I just don't understand. You know, uh." I was stumbling.

"You mean why I'm gay?" That was it and he read my expression. "I couldn't explain it to you. I just knew."

I thought it was a shame, although having him on the other side did cut down on my competition. Blake was a big man with a powerful physique, a weight lifter's build similar to my own. "But, jeeze, man, how the hell can you . . . ?" I caught sight of the three fuel gauges on his panel and Blake followed my gaze.

"What is it?" He almost walked into a one-liner from the movie *Airplane*, but I let it pass.

"Uh, shit. I don't like what I see there."

"Where, w—what's wrong *now!*" This time rather than complete alarm, he showed interest as well.

"The fuel gauges, take a look at them." This time unable to coax the chair into turning he finally gave up and turned towards the panel.

"So? They're full, isn't that what we want?" I was working out the problem in my mind, and it was a simple one.

"Well, yeah, we sure do, but that's pretend fuel you're looking at. We've been burning out of the center tank for nearly twenty minutes but its indicator hasn't moved." Blake was looking at the hydraulic quantity, so I pulled out my pointer. "Uh, push the test button there, uh, between the, ah, yeah good, that's it."

He placed his finger on, but did not push, the test button until I told him it was OK. Good Blake. When he did, nothing happened confirming my suspicions. Someone was really fighting us on this trip. "Damn!"

"What!" he started lisping again.

"Aw, shit! Shit! Shit! Shit! When you push test, the indicators and digital quantity are supposed to drive towards zero, then revert to the correct level when the test button is released. The damned fueling door out on the right wing must be open. Remember the mechanic?"

"Vinny? He was kind of cu—" I cut him off.

"Enough of that shit!" We had a short, tense moment that passed quickly. "Yeah, I guess that was his name. I recall him saying he'd disconnected the hydrant truck, but he must not have shut the door. If the refueling door panel is open, the fuel gauges in the cockpit won't work. It's designed to avoid taxiing away with the fuel truck still attached to the airplane or situations precisely like this one. Shit! Now we have no way of knowing how much fuel we have or where it is. Damn! With only one operating fuel flow meter on the No. 2 engine, No. 1 placarded INOP, we can't figure our fuel consumption accurately, so we don't know if we have enough fuel to make Columbia and we sure as hell can't stop for gas along the way." When I turned in my seat to look forward at the No. 2 fuel flow gauge, I instinctively hollered out, "Duck!" I should have said, "Gull!"

There was not even time to close my eyes, but there was time for me to pray to God that I hadn't missed the windshield heat during the confusion. Out of the corner of my eye, I could see the four green lights high on the F/O's overhead panel. They were all on, insuring our inch-thick glass would be resistant to bird strikes. Geese, seagulls, and especially starlings have been known to bring down bigger jets than this one. I thought we would have been safe in the fog, because birds are not supposed to be instrument rated and are thought by some to receive our weather radar signals as a warning. This squadron of gulls was IFR equipped and seemed to have used our radar as a homing device. The gull impacted my windshield with the force of a cannon ball. The machine took several other solid strikes, shaking the airplane badly with their impact. No. 2 burped out a compressor stall "Whomp!" *Oh please, please, don't take out an engine!* An old saying came to mind, "Place your faith in God and Pratt & Whitney." The No. 2 RPM indicators were unsteady for a moment, but the engine kept running!

While I did the calculations, Blake took one look at the gull guts and headed aft for a barf bag. Half the mass times velocity squared gave us a little over a two-ton impact with each bird. The flight leader's blood, feathers, and entrails were streaming aft, all over my windshield, completely obscuring my vision. Grotesquely, his mashed head and part of one foot were now glued to the windshield. The heat that keeps the glass pliable for just such an occasion was cooking his guts nicely. If it would ever come off at all, it would take a putty knife and the windshield would have to be overhauled before anyone would be able to see through it again.

From my position, we were blind.

CHAPTER 10

Johnston

Near Isla Angel de la Guarda
Gulf of California

We slid over Baja while the pretty people of the morning news were motoring out to the "crash site" in the predawn. As they were practicing their airplane crash voices and expressions on each other, I was grooving on the beauty of low level flight at dawn. Seagull blood and guts forced me into the right seat that thankfully had a dry cushion and a reasonably unobstructed forward view. I had to look through the smoke trails and parts of the gull that were smeared all over the windshield. As is always the case with a suicidal insect or marauding wiper blade, the gull guts obscuring my vision in the left seat were precisely at eye level as if they had been placed there by design.

Having successfully de-infiltrated the United States, I felt we were safe enough in Mexican airspace to risk a climb to a midlevel altitude for better fuel economy, but it was a hard decision to make. The fog evaporated just south of Ensenada giving way to a breathtaking view of the Pacific screaming by seemingly close enough to touch. The seas on the Gulf side of the Baja were calm, not a wind ripple in sight, reflecting the image of the jet like a mirror. It was simply spectacular. If we survived, we'd be on the ground in Colombia before the morning news.

The radio was dead quiet save for the occasional night freighter out logging a few more hours, risking his ass to deliver cancelled bank checks or medicines in hopes of that big day when the airline would call him for an interview.

As beautiful as the turquoise waters were gliding by at high speed, I found myself hungering for normalcy. When one pilot leaves the cockpit to, as the feds put it, "see to his physiological needs," the other two crew members are usually slightly, almost imperceptibly uncomfortable. Like flying with the cockpit door open—we don't like it. It makes us uneasy. With two crew positions open, it was a surreal atmosphere, almost the same feeling as when a pilot makes his first solo flight. There is no one in the right seat, but there should be, but there isn't, but there should be and on and on. Blake was in the cabin and I was flat-assed on my own.

Maintaining a position about a mile offshore that would imitate a southbound, light twin should we be spotted on radar or by satellite, reality set in. I would catch a light or two on shore and a glimpse of the blur that was salt water ocean. It seemed close enough to touch reminding me of night freighting, "scud running" along the Oregon coast with an airplane load of radioactive pharmaceuticals. Somehow I managed to survive those days in Twin Comanche forty-one alpha, though I have often wondered how. Now if I could only handle the same situation in this heavy "twin." And that got me to thinking again.

I'd made the "GO" decision in L. A. before arriving at the airport. But my conscience continued to bother me about the dastardly thing I was doing. My entire life had been invested in an airline career that I was not about to surrender to Francisco Franco. But had I disgraced the brotherhood of my profession, the one thing in life that was really, really important to me? Surely I would go down in history as the outcast rogue aviator—a Blackguard in the eyes of society or just a plain criminal. Or would I?

Just how far was I and indeed *are we* prepared to bend over? How much of our paychecks are we willing to contribute to the hip pocket of the Francos of Wall Street and what appears to be a thoroughly corrupt government that is selling us down the Yangtze

River? Certainly it wasn't my place to formulate national or corporate policy, but on the other hand it has to start somewhere, and placing any trust in the corporate world or government, that frequently seems to be one and the same, has proven itself to be a losing proposition. As long as we are willing to bend over, they will be happy to stick it to us.

Some say that on November 22, 1963, a coup took place in America with the assassination of President Kennedy. Since our government steadfastly refuses to tell us what actually did happen, and has been caught red-handed in several conspiracies to defraud its populace, as well as squandering our resources with great gusto, those forces have my attention.

I am fiercely American. But the America I grew up in is gone and it is time we admit it to ourselves. Something is fundamentally wrong with a government that teaches our children a re-written version of our history in favor of multi-culturalism, while totally disregarding the will of its people as it hides behind the sham that we are it.

We were it.

Who will you vote for in the next election, Senator Foghorn Leghorn or Governor Leghorn Foghorn, because that's the only choice you're going to get. What happens when the rules are changed in mid-play? When our government ignores its own Constitution and the basic principles upon which our country was founded, We The People are duty bound by that same Constitution to do something about it. The question has been what the hell can we do? How do you fight a sitting president who looks you right in the eye on national television, commits perjury before your very eyes, does the same thing while under oath before a grand jury *and gets away with it?*

We are told to change things at the ballot box, a concept our founding fathers soundly rejected in dealing with King George. The ballot box has been found to be rigged in Miami, Phoenix, and other cities, yet that damning information is kept secret by the very press we depend upon to expose it.

Our elected public servants have become Kings and Queens. I believe that roughly 80% of our income is confiscated through income taxes, sales taxes, property taxes, luxury taxes, taxes like the $500 each trucker must pay the feds annually simply for being a truck . . . and that's per truck. Federal taxes, state taxes, county taxes, city taxes, and let us not forget corporate taxes which the consumer pays in the end, so to speak, or the taxes we pay at the very end: death taxes. Taxes imposed without consulting the voter that sounds very much like taxation without representation. Then we have fees, which are merely charges for using the "services" of our government that we have already supported with our . . . taxes. We have interest on taxes owed and penalties on top of that should we encounter some resistance along the way in earning the fed's money for them. It's their money, not ours. And should we be so fortunate as to receive an income tax refund, we pay tax upon those "refunded" taxes that we didn't owe in the first place.

Private enterprise is strangled with paper and stupid governmental edicts. Government snipers put a bullet through a woman's forehead while she stands on her front porch holding her baby in her arms. Nothing happens. The FBI, out of sight of the news cameras is captured by their own infrared camera in an infantry-tank assault on Americans denied their constitutional rights under due process. They can be seen firing machine guns at women and children attempting to escape death by fire at the Branch Dividian compound in Waco. Most of our congressional representatives deny it ever happened. They never fired a shot; they used no incendiaries to transform tear gas into cyanide, yet we can see with our own eyes from autopsy films of dead children that they did just that. Children are gunned down in their classrooms—coincidentally by the very weapons our government wishes to relieve us of—by demented shooters who conveniently kill themselves at the end of their rampage. Do we dare suspect the forces behind gun control, the first step in disarming the populace might be behind such atrocities? Would the forces who assassinate their own president actually sacrifice the lives of a few dozen children or diners in a cafeteria in order to disarm the population? I shudder to think they might, just how is unclear, but there is no question they have the resources, motivation, and opportunity to do it. My suspicious mind suspects someone, somewhere, knows this to be true.

Our government sneers at us denying these and other atrocities have happened until they are exposed on film or by a witness they failed to take out. Uncle Sam is openly in bed with known criminals such as our own Francisco *the sleaze* Franco. Eventually the Captain Max Powers of society will get a belly full of it and take action, and by Jesus, I was doing just that! My conscience now crystal clear, my soul re-energized, I reached overhead to the flight attendant call button and rang it. Time for some good ol' shit airplane coffee and time to do some real flying!

CHAPTER 11

Johnston

"What!" he shrieked. "AAAAAH! You're fucking crazy! Oh my God! What are you doing!" Even before he said anything the minute difference in pressure and noise level told me the cockpit door had opened briefly and Blake was back. Now that we had left the fog behind, he had a clear view of the Gulf speeding by, seemingly close enough to touch.

"Steady big fella." The urge to strangle him was overcome by the breathtaking beauty of low-level flight. Our reflection on the water in the moonlight screaming silently under the nose and by the side windows from 100 feet above the surface was just flat *awesome!* The urge to pump her up to the barber pole was strong, but we couldn't afford the fuel and I didn't want to overstress the left outboard slat anymore than I already had. A fine salt spray was beginning to combine with the smoke trails on the windshield to further obscure our forward vision. Yes, we do have windshield squirters, but they spray a rain repellent that will totally obscure all vision unless used on a wet windshield. We'd need to find some rain or a cloud before arrival in Colombia, or it would be a mighty interesting landing.

Recalling my trips into Puerto Vallarta some years back it seemed to me that radar coverage in Mexico was sparse, yet prudence dictated we remain on the deck—a sharp eye out for mast lights—to avoid detection, salt spray or no.

I needed to do some fuel managing at the S/O's panel and have a look at the intake for No. 3 engine. I wasn't going to trust the autopilot, so it was time to give the only first officer I had some flight instruction. Back in the captain's left seat, I gestured to the right and said, "OK, Blake, time for your flying lesson."

"Oh . . . oh," the color drained from his face, "n—no! Why I—I . . . Me? Are you *crazy?* You are crazy! You're disturbed! Y—you, you—"

I thought by the look on his face that we might need to change another seat cushion. "Nothing complicated. I just need to get out of my seat for a couple minutes to balance some fuel and I have to take a quick run to the back to have a look at the No. 3 intake. Now get your fat ass back in that seat!"

He scowled, "You're a very rude person!"

I cautioned him not to bump his head on the overhead panel while sliding into the seat, but he did a pretty good job of burying a toggle switch in his cranium. I coached him on how to adjust the seat using the Boeing cross hairs, a small, international-orange ball used to place the pilots' eyes in the proper position. When he was settled I said, "Grasp the yoke with both hands, like this." Placing both of my hands on the controls. "It's the same principle as the steering wheel in your car with a couple of extra dimensions."

"I can't do this," he said, his eyes welded to the instrument panel.

"Nevertheless, you're going to."

I disconnected the autopilot with a tweak of the secondary electric trim, which produced the alternating, flashing red lights on the instrument panel. A result of Eastern flight 401 that crashed into the Everglades on Christmas Eve twenty some years ago, they are impossible to miss and I wanted him to know what he was to look for.

What I got out of him was a nasal "Ufda." With a name like Carlson, he had to be from Minn . . . Minne . . . Mmm—hell, I can't bring myself to say it. I've had a lot of fun there and it is true that they breed some of the most beautiful women I have ever seen. As the place is either frozen solid or boiling hot, there is every reason to believe it is a castoff chunk of another planet with a very flat surface. Their thought processes are based upon logic not known elsewhere on earth and they have this governor . . . . Their citizens, found in every conceivable place on the globe, are ambassadors of their heavily socialized state. They've adopted the Texan's attitude and improved on it, for everything in the world is better in Minn . . . Minneso . . . . The very utterance of the word makes my watch run backwards, rapidly heating to the point where I must remove it from my wrist or risk severe burns. After my years in Scottsdale, Arizona, where every other car has a Min . . . a Minn . . . one of those soft blue-and-white license plates that advertise their mosquito breeding grounds rather than the red ones with the cactus in mid-digit, I am not able to tolerate their accents well at all. If Blake's voice is chalk on a blackboard, theirs truly reminds me of large panes of glass shattering over my head combined with the cries of chickens awaiting their turn in the fowl death house. Geography is taught with the grossly-overrated Mall of America as the physical and cultural center of the earth. Little Frannie was from prestigious West Bloomington. Was. It hadn't sunk in yet.

When I took my hands from the controls, Blake had the jet in a death grip, squeezing the yoke as if he were trying to strangle a cobra. I tried to get him to relax, but that was beyond his capability. We practiced his maneuver several times where I'd simulate a spontaneous autopilot disconnect and he would initiate a gentle climb, then re-engage the autopilot and ring the flight attendant call button to get my attention as if that would be necessary. But remember, we love redundancy. The first time he pulled a little too hard and got the stick shaker that scared the hell out of him.

"AAAAAAAAAHHHHHHH!"

"Easy, big fella, er . . . that's only the stick shaker that warns of an impending stall. At our slow speed, we're flying just above a stall. You just pulled a little too hard, that's all. Don't jerk the controls, squeeze them tenderly as if you were, uh . . ." Over my right shoulder, the AFT STAIRS light annoyed me by flashing as the stairs trailed in the slip stream, but they had rescued me from an awkward moment. A quick scan of the panel seemed to me that all systems were as well as they were likely to be under the circumstances, but I wanted a closer look.

"I thought I was being electrocuted!" he said, sounding a lot like Richard Simmons.

When I felt he had the maneuver down pat, I extricated myself from the captain's chair and reseated myself at the S/O's panel, then ran a quick "U" check of the systems.

Airplane fuel gauges, like all fuel gauges, are not completely trustworthy. We rely on known quantities and burn rates to determine the exact quantity of fuel remaining. The fuel gauges are simply a backup, and yes we do love backups. Since poor little Frannie had apparently pumped several hundred gallons of jet fuel onto the ramp from the overflow vent, it was safe to assume the tanks were full on departure. If she had been standing under the vent . . . again I pushed aside the vision of her as a ball of fire wearing kerosene soaked overalls.

The No. 2 fuel flow indicator agreed with my calculated burn rate of 3,000 pounds per hour times two, that all added up to enough fuel to make Colombia—if we didn't screw around. Satisfied that all was reasonably well, I turned back to Blake who seemed mesmerized by the low level flying.

"Alright, Blake, you have the machine. If you need me for anything, ring the hell out of that call bell." I said pointing again to the button that I had marked with a piece of masking tape. Leaving my cockpit with an unqualified fairy at the controls was a definite first.

"Remember, Blake, pull up. Up, Blake. Push forward, or even let go, *even a tiny little bit,* and . . . we die!"

"Quickly," he said, his eyes glued to the altimeter as he squeezed the blood from his fingers with a death grip on the yoke. Telling him to relax, that a few ounces of pressure on the controls is all that's required, would be pointless.

"That's right. Now you've got the machine. Remember to look outside too. We don't want to run into anything." He flinched at that. "Don't screw up your fifteen minutes of fame."

"I had enough fame with the APU start, Captain." Then he started babbling something about a Rod Stewart concert, as if I gave a damn.

I stepped into a cabin untouched since the last flight. Few passengers ever see the unbelievable mess of the remnants from a full boat. Scattered everywhere lay peanut wrappers (their contents ground into the carpet), newspapers, magazines, blankets, spilled drinks, barf bags, cameras, a tampon, and the ubiquitous bulging diaper stuffed into a seat back.

Ducking into row 23 aircraft-right, I bent down to peer out of the galley service door window into the engine intake completely unprepared for the sight I was about to behold. An engine plug, melted like pulled taffy trailing off into the compressor section of our No. 3 engine and two F-18s sporting the red-white-and-blue emerging ever so slowly from behind said engine to form-up on our right wing.

CHAPTER 12

Johnston

Abeam Boca de Apiza, Colema, Mexico

"I'm glad to see you, Captain!" Blake was still concentrating fiercely on the instrument panel before him. Rather than insult him by telling him I wasn't particularly glad to see him, I gave a captain's nod while setting back into the familiar comfort of the left seat. I fastened my seat belt, crotch, and shoulder straps. Blake noticed. We wear the extra straps for takeoff and landing in turbulence and for movies. The air was satin smooth.

"Hell of a morning, huh?" My voice betrayed depression, because I could see no way out of this predicament.

"What's wrong, Captain?" He was still intent on the gauges.

"Might as well relax, Blake. You smoke?"

"I enjoy cigars," he said innocently but with a tweak of guilt in his voice that lead me to wonder if that was all he smoked, or if his cigars came from Cuba. There was something there, but I let it pass.

"You know there's no smoking in the cockpit?"

"Of course!" He seemed mildly incensed that I would question his knowledge on such a basic subject. "Why? Do you smoke Captain?"

I could hear the whine of the F-18s' compressor sections and no doubt Blake would pick up on it soon. While Blake and I have little in common, he is human and was about to get another horrific shock. "No, I quit about twenty-five years ago. Go ahead and light up, if you'd like."

"Smoke 'em if you got 'em?" He risked a mild grin and I guess I grinned stupidly back. Because I could see the tip of the nose on one of the fighters behind him and he couldn't.

"Yeah, something like that. And you might as well call me Max. Every time you call me Captain, I think something else is wrong."

"Thank you, Captain, uh, Max. Most of the pilots don't want us to call them by name. I think they hate us." I expected to see a Virginia Slim, but he shook out a Marlboro, that didn't look much like a cigar to me, then fished a Zippo lighter out of his pocket upon which were the globe and fouled anchor of the United States Marine Corps.

As he lit up I said, "There's some truth to that, I don't deny it. Most guys might wonder how you got that lighter." I envisioned it to be a souvenir from a sicko encounter.

Matter of factly he said, "I was a marine." My expression betrayed me. "*Was?* I know, once a marine, always a marine, Semper Fi and all that?"

"Well, Blake, yeah, that's the way I've always heard it."

Exhaling a cloud of smoke, he said, "My MOS was infantry." He had the build but I still wasn't buying it. "It's true, Captain, uh, Max. I loved the corps, but it didn't love me." He giggled stupidly, making me want to throw up. "Some of the guys suspected I was gay. They asked and I told. What can I say? I'm honest." The F-18s had backed down a few feet and were no longer visible, but I could still hear the faint whine of their engines.

"Alright, Blake, I gotta ask this one. How the hell did you ever get into the Marines with a voice like yours? I don't, uh, don't want to offend you," although I really didn't give a shit whether I offended him or not, "but the first word out of your mouth at the induction center, whatever it might be, would peg you on the spot!"

"I disguised my voice," he said, "like this." After only a few words, his flaming gay dialect and accent was completely gone. He took a deep drag from the Marlboro and had the courtesy to exhale away from me. It was a completely different person speaking, "I had a girl friend who was also in the corps in a similar situation. She was a lesbian and used me as I used her. You know, for appearances sake." I didn't know and didn't care. The F-18 had pulled up again so I thought this would be as good a time as any.

"Listen, uh . . ." I was at a loss for words, and didn't relish revealing that we were all but finished. "I, uh, well, marine, I don't want to have to tell you this, but it looks like the jig's up."

The fairy was back. He was shocked, sat bolt upright with his fists clenched effeminately against his chest, stabbing himself with a hot Marlborough. "What? What do you mean! What the hell's wrong now! W—we've, well, we've made it, haven't we? I mean this is Mexico, isn't it?" The transformation from marine to queen was magical. Black magic, I'd guess.

"Not exactly, we're over international waters right now, although that does give me an idea. Uh, take a look to your right." The two F-18s were from El Toro. Stenciled on the fuselage were the words *United States Marines.*

"Oh, my God!" He sounded a lot like a waitress I once knew who used that expression for an entirely different reason. Turning briefly to look at me, his expression was one of fright mixed with excitement. "Those are F-18s from El Toro aren't they?" I hoped they weren't from a nearby carrier battle group. "They're beautiful!" Excited, he turned back to the fighters and waved. No one waved back.

"Blake, they're here to shoot us down." He did a double take. "Bull shit!" he said returning his attention to the window.

"What, you don't think they will? How naive are you?"

"NO!" If there really is such a thing as denial, Blake was in it. "Those are marines!"

"That's what I'm talking about!"

"You're demented."

"Yeah, I probably am."

We flew along in silence for a few minutes longer, Blake and certainly myself, deep in thought. *Is there any way out of this?* I asked myself. While reviewing our position on the chart, I threw the transfer switch on the No. 2 VHF from the previous frequency to 121. 5, and transmitted: "One two two niner five?" The reply from the fighters was instantaneous.

"Switching." I changed frequencies also.

"Slick here, sir."

"Danno here too."

"Ah, good morning, gentlemen. You studs look mighty fine from here. You here to give us an escort?"

"Ah, yes, sir! Sir, we are here to escort you back to the United States of America." His voice through the oxygen mask mike was devoid of emotion, all business.

"Ah . . . well, we were thinking somewhere a little farther south. What, ah, meaning no disrespect gentlemen, but what if we choose not to comply?" I knew the answer.

"Sir, our mission is to return you, your crew, and the ship to the United States of America. Your compliance is not optional."

"What'd I tell ya?" But Blake still wasn't buying it. I used my pointer, "Blake, flip up No. 2 ADF, and tune it until you find a strong signal of Mexican music. Try to be innocent about it so they can't see what you're doing with your hands." Blake may be a lot of things, but innocent wasn't one of them. So, OK, it was a poor choice of words. I reached before me to flip the "killer switch" on my RMI from VOR to ADF. The switch is so named because if you have it in the wrong position when navigating with either system, you will likely die. The double needle swung lazily around the dial while Blake searched for a signal.

"Uh, either of you men hold a seniority number?"

"Uh, repeat that please?" It was the wingman's voice, that of Danno.

The flight leader, Slick, wanted to cut the subject off. I had only one card to play, and if we were going to be shot down, I might as well be playing it as we went down in flames. "You have a seniority number somewhere?" Each time he keyed his mike, I could hear the whine of his turbines.

"I had one at Eastern." So, Danno, the wingman was a victim too.

"So, you're a fan of Franco?" A little salt on their wounds.

"Belay that talk, Danno. Stockholm Syndrome."

"He knows!" said Blake.

"Of course he knows! And we're going to exploit him. Find a station, please. Try switching bands with that knob, yeah, that one, yes that's it. Now get me a strong signal! I need some landscaping music!"

"Yes, sir!" It was Blake, the marine.

"OK, marine," I said turning to Blake with a grin. Then I grabbed the hand mike, "We've all been trained in Stockholm so you don't have to worry about being affected by what I'm asking you."

"Sir, our orders are to return you to El Toro or to destroy your aircraft. Do not place us in that position, sir."

"What'd I tell ya?" Blake fiercely shook his head no. I heard music coming from his overhead speaker. You can hear that same music in the Southwest anywhere a lawn needs mowing or a tree needs a trim. A glance at the No. 2 ADF needle indicated the station was at our ten o'clock position. Knowing the fighters would be watching me closely, I kicked off my shoe, rolling the heading bug slowly to the left with my toes. The airplane followed the bug with an almost imperceptible bank. I kept talking.

"Uh, Slick? I believe you. I honestly believe you will follow the orders to shoot us down. So, can it hurt to hear the story? It'll be recorded on our CVR as well as yours to give the suits something to analyze. Sort of the aeronautical equivalent of last words of the condemned."

"I'm sure it's an interesting story, sir." The flight leader relented, knowing he would have to put a sidewinder into us in a few minutes. *Last wishes of the condemned.* I was banking on his conscience bothering him. It was all boiling down to the question of whether these guys would fire on their own kind? They might not want to, but orders come down from some pretty sinister places, such as the one who gave the order to machine gun the Branch Dividians at Waco who managed to escape the flames. And that brought disturbing thoughts of Frannie to mind again. In my book, an entity that would do those kinds of things could and would shoot down a stolen airliner, or at least give the order.

I continued rolling the heading bug leisurely in the direction of the number two RMI needle until it was at our twelve o'clock. It would be easy to kill time telling the story beginning with background on other carriers that had been swallowed by Franco's organization. Apparently the wingman, Danno, was a former Eastern pilot. The flight leader had a seniority number with us, but he had to come from some other carrier before that as Mariah was just an amalgamation of other airlines.

"Can you see land, Blake?" My vision consisted of air-roasted goose entrails.

"No, I, uh, wait . . . yeah, I mean yes, sir, I think I can see it . . . just barely, it's right off the nose." Blake's voice was a confusing mixture of queen and marine. I hoped the gyrene would prevail.

The flight leader broke in. It was better than I could have expected. Slick's bitter voice belied betrayal by Franco the Sleaze who had ruined a career for him too. "Uh, yes. Sir, I held a regular captain vacancy on L-1011s based out of Newark. By the time Franco bled the airline into chapter seven, I was thirty-three. I couldn't get another job—"

I interrupted him with a question that would hit home, "You ever figure out how they get by the EEOC rules on age discrimination?"

"No, sir, but the issue at hand has nothing to do with the EEOC rules. I must ask you to follow us. We will turn to a heading of three five five and climb to flight level three three zero for El Toro, and must insist again that you follow us."

"Well, Slick—sir—that does present a problem, because we are refusing your request. I'm afraid you're going to have to make good your threat, sir. I'd like to think that we are involved in a noble effort on behalf of the profession and to recapture my embezzled retirement and that of my crew. My conscience is clear. I am at peace with my maker as is my crew. Isn't that right, Blake?"

Blake wasn't so sure, "Are you out of your mind? You're telling these guys it's OK to shoot us down?" In fact he wasn't having any part of it. "You're fucking crazy!" He grabbed for the F/O's mike, obviously intent on screaming for help or exposing my insanity or both. I whacked him with the emergency checklist.

"Blake, if you don't play along with this, then they surely will shoot us down!" Keying the mike I said, "Say, speaking of the crew, the F/O here, Mr. Carlson, would like an opportunity to say a few words for the CVR. He's been Franco'd also, but his is slightly different from my case."

Blake was nervous, "He isn't gay."

"No shit! Start talking, Blake. Talk about anything you can think of that will buy us a few minutes. Remember, these guys don't want to hear anything about you and Kevin." I risked getting partially out of my seat to sneak a peek ahead. I couldn't make out any details, but land was definitely ahead, maybe 30 miles or so. Blake relayed most of the story of flight 266 when the flight leader broke in.

"Ah, Captain, this is totally irrelevant." His growing sense of irritation and the time we'd spent at low level, lead me to believe the fighters were getting low on fuel. I reduced power allowing us to slow to the edge of a stall. Every so often and with each bump we'd get the stick shaker and a plethora of flashing red lights. The fighters slowly began to creep ahead of us, then "dirtied up" by extending their leading edge devices. We were too slow for them to fly "clean." Extending flaps into the airstream would require more power and therefore more fuel for them. We struggled along a few knots below our minimum clean speed, the stick shaker going off every few moments. We had to reach land.

"You might think his statement is irrelevant? But the man is about to die. I mean, you're going to shoot us down, aren't you? Surely you can afford him the opportunity to say his last words?" Flight-leader Slick relented. Blake told the story from the perspective of a flight attendant whose pension fund had been raided just as ours had. Much of his story was redundant, so when it sounded as if Blake was running out of fresh material, I broke in.

"Would y'all give us a once over and record what you see on the CVRs? They might not find ours under water. We've got an old model voice recorder that's not pinger equipped." I couldn't see the approaching coastline, but Blake could. "How's it look?"

"Well, I can make out some detail . . . looks like a long, white beach with a cliff running behind it."

"Tell me when you think it's about three miles distant."

"Roger that!" Blake was getting into his role.

"Uh, sir, ah . . . what in hell have you done to this airplane?"

"Ever speculate as to what it would take to light off a fuel spill?" I told the story in as much detail as I could, stretching the moments, each second bringing us closer to the beach.

"Uh, Max." I didn't answer him. "Max?" Irritated, I acknowledged that I was listening. "You, uh, aren't thinking of, uh . . . landing, are you?" Blake appeared mildly concerned, peering into my eyes trying to assess my intentions as if I would ever be less than truthful with him. I shook my head no. He seemed vastly relieved. If he knew what was waiting for us in Columbia, he would have jumped out right there and very definitely been in better shape for it.

"Keep your eyes peeled for seagulls on the water and give me a clock position if you see any of them."

The lead F-18 moved up close on our left with the damage report. "You have a right main that appears to have been, *bent?* The right gear door is gone and the tires appear burned and flat. The inboard tire seems to be melted into the gear well. Uh . . . sir, how do you go about *bending* a main gear strut?"

"It's looking like about five miles, Max. I can't tell if they're gulls, but I see a large flock of birds just to our right . . . at, um . . . two o'clock?" I was picking up some of the shoreline on my left and bits of white water from the surf line through the captain's sliding window. The long, deserted beach was calling my name, but I had other plans for it.

"So, ah, how are you going to do it?"

"Do what, sir?"

"C'mon! You going to shove a heat seeker up our ass or kill us with the cannons? If you do use the cannons, ya'd make it a lot easier on me, at least, if you were to fire on the cockpit first. I'd like to get it over with as quickly as possible . . . I've got no desire to burn to death." All pilots share that phobia.

"Captain, we have no wish to cause you any harm! But we are under orders to either return you to El Toro or destroy your aircraft. Please, sir, please *do not* force us into that position!" There was emotion in the flight leader's voice.

It was time to play the only card we had. As we were close enough to see the printing under his canopy and the rank on his collar, I decided to make use of the information. "Colonel Lehman, you're about to shoot down a defenseless airliner with an unarmed crew. Are you also ready to do that over the sovereign shores of another country—with witnesses?"

From the corner of my eye I saw Blake turn towards me, "Birds are at twelve o'clock, Max, about two miles."

I fired our last defensive line at the fighters, "Gentlemen, we're well inside the Mexican three mile limit. You shoot us down now and our wreckage will be strewn all over the beach. While it's not a heavily populated area, there are enough people around to serve as witnesses, and there will be plenty of hard evidence to present at your court marshal!" There it was. It all boiled down to the basic question: *Will they fire on their own?* Whether they would or would not, the only opportunity we'd have to fire on them was at hand.

"If it flew in, it'll fly out!"
—*Unknown*

CHAPTER 13

Johnston

Abeam Puerto Madera, Chiapas Mexico
Near the Guatemala boarder

"Ah, Max those birds look nervous." Blake's eyes were focused on feathers while mine were on the F-18 leader. Slick's eyes were on our ship while his wingman's were on him. Aside from a momentary glance now and then, Blake was the only one out of the four involved in the drama who was looking forward.

"What do you mean, nervous?" *I mean, from where we're sitting, what's a nervous bird look like?*

"Well, they—"

"Sir, time is up. We have your statements on the CVR. In spite of the Stockholm Syndrome, I think we both have some sympathy for your cause. But, sir, our fuel is BINGO. The time is now. Sir, I am ordering you to come right to a heading of three—"

"Max . . . ah, CAPTAIN, THE BIRDS HAVE TAKEN O—"

Words from twin sources were cut off as we flew into the gulls. We took one under the nose. I felt several more sharp impacts reverberate through the airframe. The nose of the F-18 that I could see disappeared in a cloud of brilliant white feathers. The gauges for our No. 2 engine all began to fluctuate and there was the "Whomp-Whomp" of compressor stalls. More compressor stalls, but not from our engines . . ."Whomp-Whomp." The F-18 pulled up and disappeared from my sight.

"Eject—eject—eject!" I guess that's how you play hardball with a pair of F-18s—with seagulls. The irony was lost on me because with our No. 2 engine backfiring, I had my own hands full of yet another emergency. This had to be a record.

"Aw, shit!" No. 2's EGT was in the red and was going to have to be shut down. I complied with the first memory item on the engine shutdown checklist, *Engine Fire Handle: Pull.* This one I could reach. Most pilots never pull a fire handle except in the simulator. This was my third time, twice in just a few months. Meanwhile, I was picking up dialogue from the fighters on 121.5, the international VHF emergency frequency on our No. 2 radio. I picked up the mike to wish them well, but thought better of it. For the moment, I wanted them to forget all about Max Power.

"Ah, observe you down on the beach, are you alright, sir? Sir? Colonel Lehman, if you are able, give me a visual . . ." I wondered if Lehman even had time to unpack his transceiver. "Ah, roger—roger, have your signal."

I bumped the power up to 98% on No. 1. "Blake, do you have any idea how pissed those guys are going to be at us now?"

His head seemed to drop onto his shoulders, his eyes growing large again, "Max, sir? Those boys are going to be very, very pissed!"

"Yeah, at least that."

"W—well, what about us? Didn't you just shut off the second engine?"

"Uh, yeah, there's that, but at least we're rid of those two—for a while anyway. Uh, we're going to have to swap seats so I can see where we're going. How 'bout you shag us some coffee and I'll see how we're doing."

"Cream or sug—" I cut him off.

"No, dammit, black!"

"They say a 727 won't fly on one engine!"

"No, she'll fly alright, she just won't climb worth a shit." *Probably won't climb at all with all that crud hanging out.*

"B—but, well, uh, that place we're going to is in the, uh, in the, uh, well, it's in the m-m-m, uh, m—m—mou—mountains.

Isn't that what you said?" He was looking a little pale again. Meanwhile, the sporadic dialogue between Col. Lehman and his wingman began to fade in my ear. Sweet music!

"Hang in there, big fella." If Blake was going to lose his lunch I didn't want it to be all over me. "We'll make it." He extricated himself carefully from the F/O's seat, mindful of the cranium full of toggle switches from his last exit, and made for the galley while I settled uneasily into the warm right seat wondering just how we were going to make it with two engines out. The answer to that question was that we weren't. Somehow or another we would have to have at least one more engine. I dismissed landing on the beach to work on the engine on the grounds that we probably would sink in the soft sand and be there for the duration. Besides, we had no tools. I consulted the handmade approach plate to the Colombian strip. It lacked detail, though it did show the elevation to be 7,342 feet MSL and was a GPS approach that wouldn't be certified in the US for some time, if ever. If we could get one of the other two engines started, we could climb. If not, we couldn't, and we had no alternate airport. The white, sandy beach would have to suffice, and since it couldn't be banked on to last forever, we'd have to find out soon where to plant the wheels. And then what?

Blake was back with the coffee. "Cream or sug—"

"No!"

"Ca—uh, Max, why do you have to be so rude all the time? Just say, 'No, thank you!' It's a simple, innocuous question. For Christ's sake, all I asked was if you wanted fucking cream or sugar in your goddamned coffee!" He gave a shrug and a ladies' "ah—huggh" as if I'd come to the table in a dirty T-shirt.

"Forget it. Listen, we're going to have to get one of these engines started. Number two took one of those gulls—"

"I think they were pelicans or cranes or something like that"

"Who gives a shit?" The instrument bank for No. 3 showed about a 1% rotation. There was *some* air getting through the inlet. I remembered a chapter from Ernie Gann's classic novel, *Fate is the Hunter*, where the air intake scoop on a DC-3 had become iced over on a night that started out innocently enough. The ice was just a few inches away, but impossible to reach in flight. It was an impossible situation . . . but, hell, they made it. We had a similar situation with our No. 3. I reached overhead, engaged the starter for a moment, then terminated it when I didn't like what I saw, which was nothing. "Blake, run back to the aft galley and grab the interphone. I need to know if the compressor section of that engine is turning or if it's still frozen with the melted plastic." Blake scrambled out of the chair, head down, intent on following my instructions to the letter. "Ah, you don't have to actually run . . . just an expression." But he was gone. In less than thirty seconds, the flight attendant call rang. I answered it.

"Engine room."

"Ah, Max? This is Blake? "

"Well, who the fuck else would it be?"

"I'm looking into the engine—do you have to be so goddamned rude? That's the one aircraft right, correct?"

"It's my nature—yeah, that's the one . . . the other pod engine is running!"

"Oh, right. So, I'm looking—well it's my nature too! Uh . . . so I'm looking into the inlet, and I see . . . well, yes it's turning, you mean those blades, don't you? Wait! The first row isn't turning!"

"Yeah, those are inlet guide vanes. They're supposed to be stationary, cock sucker!" My patience was wearing thin. "What about the next row? They should be turning and that's what I need to know!" I released the push-to-talk button, knowing that his response would mean the difference between completing the mission or having to scuttle the ship on the beach. If we were really lucky, we might not be killed during the landing or starve while walking back.

"Uh . . . if you're going to be so vulgar, maybe you ought to come back here and see for yourself?"

"Do you really want me to?"

He clicked off, then in a moment was back on and seemed to have recovered some of his composure. "No, you stay there!"

"Is the damned engine turning or not?"

"Well, it depends on what you mean by turning?"

"C'mon, *marine*, you can do it! Just tell me what you see!"

"OK. The first section is not moving, but you said that's normal, right?"

"Right." Patience, Max, patience.

"Right. Then the next row is all gummed up with melted plastic. There are about, ah, about half, maybe two thirds of the blades covered with it."

"OK, got that, but is it turning?"

"Sort of."

Blake, it's round. Either it's going around and around, or it isn't.

"C'mon! Sort of?"

"Well, it's turning, but not . . . smoothly. It will turn, now, uh, I mean the whole section, it will turn, say, a third of a revolution and then it stops. There! Now it's started moving, but . . . wait, now it's stopped again! That's what I'm seeing. It's turning, but not freely. It seems to be all gummed up with the plastic, and that's what appears to be hampering its rotation. Is that what you wanted to know?"

"Yes, marine, it is! Now, I'm going to operate the starter for another few seconds, tell me just what you see. Ready?" I reached overhead, engaged and guarded the starter.

"Ready. Oh, uh . . . go ahead, I'm watching it now and it's turning erratically just as before. Oh, wait! Wait! Now it's turning! It's turning faster, and faster, but—"

I released the starter. "But what! Dammit, just tell me what you see!"

"Oh, right. Well now it's slowing down, but before, just a second ago, it was turning quite a bit faster, and the movement was smoother than it is now. See, now it's almost stopped, no, it is stopped—wait! There it's turning again, and it does seem to be smoother!"

The RPM indication for No. 3 on the center instrument panel hadn't changed. But this was a better bet than the No. 2. We were definitely asking for a fire on that one. The EGT had gone into the red as a result of shredding up a couple of large birds into taco filling just before I shut it down. "Alright, Blake. We're going to attempt an air start of number three. What I want you to do is to get as far forward as you can get and still be able to see that inlet. There's a—"

"I'm as far forward as I can go now. I'm afraid I'll pull the wire out if I pull any harder on it!"

"Ah . . . shit. Ah, OK . . . hmmm, OK. You'll have to use the megaphone. There's one at row—"

"I know where the emergency equipment is, Captain!"

"Yeah, Blake, I didn't mean to imply that you—"

"Just 'cause I'm gay, doesn't mean I don't know my job, Captain!"

"C'mon, Blake. Park the emotions! All things considered, you've done a great job so far . . . for a girl." I thought a compliment might put him back at ease rather than on the defensive where he didn't need to be.

"All things considered? What does *that* mean, *Captain?*"

"Blake, you're doing a fine job. Now, cut the crap, Shirley. Use the megaphone to tell me exactly what you see when I engage the starter. I'll use the PA so you can hear me."

"It's just that I'm so used to—"

"I understand."

"Do you? Wha—whaddya mean *Shirley?*"

"Blake! We've got an engine to start! Stay with it, dammit. You can ream me later!" I stepped into that one. And there was another one. Ahead, the beach was taking a turn to our left. I couldn't see if it continued on as a long, soft runway or abruptly ceased at the base of what could be cliffs in the distance.

I picked up the PA handset, punched the round combination transmit button and in-use indicator. "Alright, I'm going to turn it now, just start talking and tell me what you see."

"I'm ready."

"Turning three."

"OK, the blades are turning now, the motion is kind of jerky . . . it's spinning now, much faster. I can see big pieces of plastic breaking loose and, uh—oh, they're being sucked down into the engine! It's turning real fast, now, I can't see the individual blades anymore, it's more of a blur."

We were getting 23% N1. I allowed the starter to motor the engine for a full minute hopefully clearing most of the plastic out before I set it on fire.

"OK, Blake, move as far away from that engine as you can, and still see the inlet. I'm going to torch it off now and she is probably going to backfire, you know, compressor stalls."

His response came through as a tinny one from the battery-powered megaphone. "Alright, I'm up to row 17."

Too bad to waste a good fireworks display. I wondered if anyone on the ground was watching us because this could really be spectacular. Oh well, no guts, no glory. I raised the start lever up and over its safety gate. For a heart beat and a half, nothing happened.

"It's spinning at about the same speed . . . ah! There it goes, it's turning much faster now!"

The EGT rose smartly into the red as N2, then N1 accelerated fairly rapidly. "Whomp-Whomp-Whomp!"

"Ahhh!" screamed Blake. "There's fire and all sorts of crap shooting out of the front of the engine!" We needed a good old-fashioned backfire, a good one. I shoved the No. 3 throttle forward about a foot, and we got one. "WHOMP" and an airframe shuddering "BANG!"

"Holy shit!" I heard Blake from clear in the back on the airplane. All traces of his homo voice were gone in an instant of genuine fright. The far row of engine gauges went berserk. Both RPM indicators went past 105% into the red. EGT was pegged, but would take instantaneous dips into cooler territory. Plastic in the burner cans? I was banking on that, and let 'er burn.

"Oh my God!" Blake thundered up the aisle and was back. "I don't know what you did, Capt—uh, Max, but you blew the shit out of that engine, and I mean literally! There was fire and chunks of burned plastic and smoke shooting out of the front of the engine!"

The No. 3 fire warning sounded, its bell clearly audible to the naked ear in Paramas, New Jersey. "Oh shit! Not another fire!"

"Ah, maybe not." I silenced the bell on the overhead panel and pulled the power back to idle to allow the engine to digest its meal of charred plastic. After a few minutes, the EGT slowly returned to green territory, the red light in the engine fire handle extinguished on its own. The RPMs were sitting at 55% each. Sinus rhythm for a jet engine. We were back in business. I coached Blake on putting the No. 3 engine generator on the line, re-arranged our fuel burn profile and allowed my head-stereo to play. High on flight, I applied climb power to our two good engines to scramble up into the flight levels for better fuel economy to the reggae music of Jimmy Buffett and Barometer Soup.

"Don't get mad—get even."
—Unknown

CHAPTER 14

Johnston

We were living! Even with just the pod engines operating, we had 35,000 pounds of thrust to push an essentially empty airplane. I fought the urge to roll her again. But why? In the galley, Blake never knew it.

I clicked off the autopilot, punched out the disconnect lights, and shoved both throttles to one point nine five EPR for climb power. I let her accelerate to 300 knots, then eased in mild back pressure on the controls, putting her into a gentle 2,500-feet-per-minute climb. The ocean fell away, and soon the 5,000 foot cliffs were behind with only jungle and distant mountain tops before us. Fog lay in the valleys where no doubt our airport would be located while the 727 climbed like the proverbial homesick angel.

In the high flight levels of rarefied air where the big airplane is king, man cannot survive. But he can enjoy a cocktail. Behind the heavy red drapery that says "First Class Passengers Only" and far above the sea, there are meals to rival the fine eateries. Creativity in the blue rooms and under blankets in a darkened cabin spawns new life on the red-eyes while others' last breath is of cool pressurized cabin air. "Biffies" or "blue rooms" see to our biological needs. First run movies are screened while some sleep and all the while the Boeing keeps going. And going and going.

And so it was that Blake and I punched through a thin overcast, rocketing through 15,000 feet rolling inverted again to level off, and en route to a rendezvous with the bad guys. My head-stereo began to sing in cockney accompanied by the "wop-wop-wop" from the blades of a Huey:

"We don't need no regulations . . .
We don't need no flight control . . .
No dirty dealings in the boardroom . . .
Hey—Franco—leave those planes alone!"

Pink Floyd's modified music and the memories that seemed to fit our situation flat got to me, sending shivers down my spine. I couldn't resist it, uttering the words to poor Blake that no fellow crew member *ever* wants to hear from their captain, "Watch this!" Adrenaline coming to me not in sharp jolts, but a smooth flow of energy and power. Max Power!

Up one octave, roll in right aileron, roll in some more. Flight spoilers coming up on the right wing, heavy beat and cool blues guitar.

"Hey . . . Franco! Leave those planes alone!"

Past 60°, then inverted, a little forward pressure to round out the top of the roll, hanging us by our shoulder straps for just an instant, and the predictable shriek from the right seat. Not of terror, a shriek of joy, of exhilaration and excitement. It was the first moment of life that Blake and I truly shared together.

When we came *smoothly* to the bottom of the roll that I'd wanted to do for twenty-five years, I looked over at Blake. He was energized, as was I. The risk from our moment of play was worth it. "Wanna do it again?" I joked.

He surprised me by saying, "Yes!" And we did. I'm not much for that sort of thing, but when Blake held up five, I whacked him with five of my own. Really high five.

And then it was upon us. The familiar part of flight. Throttles back to cruise, one point eight six EPR, 3,300 pounds of fuel flow per hour on each engine at 15,750 feet that would theoretically avoid both VFR and IFR traffic, was giving us a smart 320 knots over the ground thanks to the thin air and subfreezing temperatures outside. Slower than usual, but fast enough to get there, and thank God we'd left our reason to hurry behind on the beaches of old Mexico.

Unfolding the charts, I marked our present GPS position, drew a line to our destination representing our new course, noting a few checkpoints along the way, then punched in direct on the little hand held unit. I thought of Manny back on the *Dogfish*. Was he awash in grief, believing me to be slowly undulating to the currents at the bottom of the Pacific? Or, was he sharp enough to have figured it out? I decided to try the "Call Home" feature that would send our lat/longs and a three-word message to my home computer on the submarine. If somehow the feds were there, their options would be limited. I punched the CH button, and using the up, down, left, and right arrows composed the message. A simple "OK for now." Maybe he'd see it.

For the next hour and a half, I reverted to the comfort of the role I was born to play, Airline Captain. Keeping a good instrument scan, and a sharp eye out for traffic, I spied a line of buildups marching up over the horizon in the natural northeast to southwest orientation. They appeared small at first, like puffy clouds on the horizon. But as we progressed over the curved surface of the earth, more and more of the clouds appeared until we were face to face with the massive forces of nature, standing tall in their full height. Tuning the radar from STBY to ON, the circular sweep began across the green screen of our ancient and beloved "C" band radar. From our ten o'clock to infinity on our right, a line of buildups extended well into the flight levels, 390 at least, maybe up into the 50s. The tops were brilliant in sunlight while their bases, from which poured tons of water, were still in the surface predawn. Their interiors were lit by the orange lightening of a dying thunderstorm. Indeed fortunately for us, these monsters were dissipating. In the right seat now, I turned over my left shoulder to Blake.

"I, uh, figure we ought to wash the windows before landing," pointing at the line of thunderstorms. Flight attendants are for the most part well aware of their dangers. Next to unscheduled contact with the earth, a thunderstorm is, at least in my book, the most serious hazard to flight.

"Ah, Max, uh, aren't those suppose to be rather, uh, dangerous?"

I smiled and nodded yes, then pointed at the F/O's windshield that was nearly opaque with salt spray and some gull guts. "But I can't see!"

"Oh, uh, Max . . . uh, isn't there another way? I mean, we don't *have* to fly through those, do we?"

"Blake, if you've got another way to clean that windshield off in the next forty-five minutes, I am ready to hear it." He couldn't think of one. And neither could I.

"Aw, b—but . . . but, sir! Do we really have to—"

"Remain calm, Blake." Washing the windshield would cancel out the need to deviate around the line of storms, but was still risky. Why stop now? I used the autopilot turn knob to make for the center of one of the storms that had a lot of water in it. "Strap it in." I didn't have to tell him to use the shoulder straps.

I set the Boeing up for heavy turbulence penetration and the ingestion of massive quantities of water. Inflight ignition—ON. Autopilot altitude hold—OFF. Set 80% N1 on both engines. Lower chair to the stops. Overhead whites—ON. Teeth—GRIT. Respectful as I am of the buildups, I am also in awe of their beauty. The clouds seem to glide silently toward us in air as smooth as a prom queen's thigh. The anvil head rose up and up until I could no longer see the top. Switching down to the 25-mile radar range, I steered us towards the *contouring* portion of the storm where the highest concentration of water would be. This was something completely contrary to our way of life—we just don't fly through thunderstorms. I didn't want to do it at all, but there was no other way. One time would be plenty.

Blake leaned against his shoulder straps with his arms on the F/O's chair bending his neck backwards looking up at the storms. He couldn't see the tops, even when he leaned back and looked through the overhead eyebrow windows. The white, boiling surface of the cloud came closer and closer, its speed increasing upon itself with the decrease in distance until we were swallowed in the flash of an instant. The world turned dark, the windshields were plastered with unbelievably heavy rain. The cockpit environment transformed instantly. At once it was extremely humid and I could smell the faint rot of the jungle from surface air the thunderstorm had sucked into the high flight levels.

FLASH—BANG! Lightening! It's very close indeed when you can hear it. Rain beat upon the windshield with the force of a thousand pressure washers and ice crystals were our sandpaper. The air had been totally smooth to that point, but my attention was drawn to the rate of climb indicator that was sagging through 500 feet per minute, then more until it pointed straight down to a 1,500-feet-per-minute rate of descent, the result of a downdraft. The smell of steamed gull guts was sickening, yet the left side of the windshield remained opaque. But the salt spray and some of the smoke trails began to stream aft from the first officer's windshield before me. The rain intensified to fire hose proportions. I wondered for the thousandth time how the engines can make fire while drowning in all of that water. No. 1's RPM dropped a few percent, but recovered nicely. At that moment in the fashion of a projectile, we were spit out the back side of the storm into brilliant day light with a light kick in the butt, the only turbulence we'd encountered in penetrating the line of storms. As its parting, final shot, the storm rained down hail upon us, making it sound as if we were flying though a storm of ball bearings. Thankfully, it was brief, and caused no further damage to our machine. "That wasn't so bad, was it?" Blake looked around for a moment, concluding that it wasn't so bad, when we were soundly trounced with a series of sharp chops that ended as abruptly as they began.

My GPS clattered to the deck. If it had broken, we would have been screwed. But it had not been damaged. When I picked up the unit, it displayed a single word on the screen: Pendejo.

"Never underestimate the therapeutic values of water."
—*Captain Max Power*

CHAPTER 15

Johnston

In Range

There it was. Colombia. Thick, verdant jungle clinging to sheer cliffs rising abruptly from the Pacific. High on volcanic peaks, rivulets flow into creeks that turn into streams, then to rivers that rush to waterfalls. And steam. Plenty of steam in the valleys along with stagnant smoke and early morning thunderstorms dumping tons of water into the jungle, preparing to start the process all over again. We got a few bumps on the descent as we neared 10,000 feet in a long, smooth glide. Out of habit, I used my pointer to tap on the sterile cockpit switch that the crews have labeled "Bring Food/Stay Out."

"Sterile cockpit?" The company would prefer I answer him with a "That's correct. Sterile cockpit switch, affirmative." But I just nodded. We do a lot of nodding. Blake threw the switch, and I reached overhead to ring the flight attendant call button. "Under normal circumstances, that would be your cue to leave the cockpit."

"Well, let me tell you, I've had captains throw that damned switch when we were still six hours out," he said looking up at his panel. Except for his hair, he looked like a real pilot.

The faint scent of smoky rot, common to tropical jungles everywhere, permeated the cockpit. The increased humidity condensed on our skin to form thousands of small droplets. Even the heated windshield gathered condensation, framing the jungle that stretched to the horizon before us in a soft corona.

An invisible beam stretched from the nose of the airplane GPS direct to our field, now 163 miles distant. Its location was obvious because there was also a thunderstorm throwing orange bolts of lightening into the trees very near to the spot where the mains ought to meet the mud. According to our crude approach plate, proceeding inbound on a bearing of 175 °, while following a series of altitude restrictions would theoretically lead us to the imaginary spot just short of and slightly above field elevation we call "minimums." The elevation is 7,342 feet MSL. How many times have I questioned the accuracy of the little hand held unit and come up with the same answer: It's all we've got! And then I ran the other question through my mind: What's going to happen when we get there? Would they just shoot us? I hoped the seed I planted about being able to deliver more airplanes had taken root.

We'll find out sometime after we land.

Turning in my chair, it was time to brief Blake for landing. "Yo, Blake!" He was engrossed in the second officer's panel, a feeling I know well. Know each system, be able to find it blind-folded, what each switch, dial, button, and indicator does both under normal and abnormal conditions and how it affects other systems. Memorize the location of key circuit breakers. Be able to find them in a hurry, when it counts.

"Sir!" Blake was all concentration, his brows knitted. Blake had had a pretty full morning, yet the fastidious fag's hair remained in place. Composed and at ease his face shows no age, unlike mine. Smooth of skin, tanned and very clean. Unlike Buckie Don, he bore no trace of makeup.

"Time to wrap it up and land this beast!" He took a deep breath, exhaled politely away from me and then was ready.

"OK, Max, what do I do?" Blake the enigma. Captains love an eager, positive attitude and he had one. I'd had him studying the checklist, abnormal gear extension, how to crank the gear and where the crank is stored, asymmetrical flap extension and others.

Apparently Blake was trying to keep this as close to a normal flight as possible by serving the food on descent when we don't have time to eat it. "Time for a quick last meal?" A good sign—gallows humor.

"Any pastrami?"

"Turkey's good for you. You'll have turkey." He sounded like my mother.

"OK, Turkey, a turkey for the captain!" Having called him every name I could think of, I didn't think he would take offense.

"OK, turkey for the captain, and . . . pastrami for the Turkey!" Where food is concerned, the flight attendants win every time.

"You remember what little Frannie used to say? That it took very little to amuse a pilot? Now you see it for yourself." I shouldn't have reminded him. Or me. In a few moments, Blake pulled out what appeared to be an expensive silk handkerchief *and blew his nose into it.*

"When we get on the ground, I'm gonna have a good cry over her."

I felt the tightness at the back of my throat again. "I may join you. We'll sure as hell hoist a few in her honor tonight." I hope.

"*Hoist* a few. That's not very politically correct. Cap, uh, Max . . . when are you going to learn that you have to conform to PC to get along in life?"

"Blake, haven't you figured this out? We are the Flagship, the Spirit of the Politically Incorrect! And we don't conform to *anything*! Anyway, we need to brief for this landing. It's been a fairly gentle flight so far"

"Ufda."

"But now we're going to turn the heat up a degree or two."

"Oh, shit! Please, don't say that to me."

"The good news is that one way or the other it'll all be over in less than a half hour." Blake didn't like the way I put that and frowned disapproval. He was trying to put up a good front, but I sensed he was truly frightened. "Steady . . . ."

"Oh, steady yourself! You need a new word."

"OK, get hold of yourself then—you ought'a like that."

"Oh, fuck you, Max!" He said holding back a laugh.

"C'mon, Blake . . . we'll make it. The 727's the best airplane ever built! You've seen her do some unbelievable things yourself. She's built like a tank. We take care of her, she'll take care of us."

He sat bolt upright in the S/O chair, "But, CAPTAIN, y—you, I—I mean we've, uh . . . ha-ha, well, uh, we've practically, uh, well we, uh, we've practically *destroyed* this airplane . . . haven't we?"

"Well, hell, it's a figure of speech, anyway. Don't worry, you're as safe as if you're in your mother's arms."

"Mom's dead."

"Aw, c'mon, Blake, you know what I mean? Stand up there, son, have some respect for yourself for cryin' out loud! You don't think this airplane is built? Go bump your head on it sometime! That'll make a believer out of you! Jump up and down on the deck. You won't fall through!" Blake was the picture of skepticism. "Naw, I mean it! If we were in some other kind of airplane, there might be cause for alarm. You can just thank God these guys didn't want an Airbus! Listen, pard, we don't have time for any further discussion. Just believe it. We'll be hashing this over on the ground over a cool one before you know it."

"We don't have any . . . *beer*," he said with a mild look of distaste towards my all time favorite liquid, but then he brightened up quite a bit, "but I did bring some miniatures from home."

"That'll work." I realized that at least for the moment, Blake and I were having a conversation like two normal people. I'd set the galley queen issue aside. Apart from his effeminate shrieking once in a while, Blake's performance on the flight had earned my respect. "Yeah, that will work just fine, even if we have to mix it with river water!"

"*Mix* it? You want to *mix*—"

"What'd ya bring?"

"Well, Remey Martin." He said as if his citizenship were being questioned.

"*Cognac?* That's it? Yuk!"

"Yuk? At Cognac? And you say this from the perspective of a *beer drinker?*"

"Alright, alright. Cognac and creek it is. Let's run the In Range Check. Those are mostly your items, so I'll read to you. He turned to the panel, ready, confident.

"Circuit breakers?"

"Oh, I know they're OK, I've been studying them for the whole flight!"

"Check 'em again."

"Right." While he checked the thousand or so breakers on the P-6 panel, I looked over the few breakers on the forward panels.

"Checked."

"Checked. Annunciator Panel?"

"Uh . . . we've got a DOORS light, but you said that's redundant?"

"Yeah, see here?" I pointed to the comparatively large, red, DOORS light next to the gear handle. "Col. Lehman said the right gear door is history, and that the gear itself is twisted and probably melted into the wheel well."

"You going to belly land it?"

"US, Blake, WE! But, no, the conventional wisdom is to land with whatever gear extended you can. It doesn't sound good, but . . ." Just then the annunciator panel flashed while Blake was looking right at it.

"Look at that, Captain, The AFT STAIRS light has been quiet for a while but now it's flashing again. I don't understand it . . . sometimes it blinks, and sometimes it doesn't."

"It's just bouncing in the slip stream. When we slow down, it may come on steady, and might even, no, it probably will drag on the landing roll and make a hell of a racket, so be ready for that. With the right main in the well, we'll be dragging the right wing and will probably skid off the runway to the right. It's going to be a memorable landing." It was obvious that Blake was frightened, but he was handling it well. We moved onto the next item.

"Hydraulic pumps? Go ahead and marry that toggle switch there on the "B" system to HI." I whanged it with my pointer. "Yeah, that's good." Blake beamed.

"No, that's not good, dammit!"

"What?" Instantly his smile was gone. Blake was biting his nails and looking like a kid in the principal's office.

"See those twin amber lights under the switches?"

"You mean here?" he said gesturing with a diamond equipped pinkie finger.

"No, these two ri—" And with that my beloved pointer skittled off under the S/O's panel. "Shit!" There was no time to look for it. "No, it's to your right, uh—no, there!" He'd found the lights. "That means, ah, yeah, take a look at the "B" system quantity gauges." I glanced at the brake pressure indicator on the lower F/O panel. It was reading 3,000 pounds. I recall there was something significant about that . . . accumulator pressure? "I'm pretty sure it's reading the accumulator pressure which means we have one or two shots of brakes and that's it."

"You mean brake."

"One wheel, one brake . . . Yeah, that's about the size of it. We'll need the alternate flap extension procedure there in the abnormals. It's that red plastic—"

"I'm ahead of you, Captain . . . I've been reading it. Ah, there, yes, that's the procedure, isn't it?" he asked while pointing at the orange-and-white bordered checklist.

"Yeah. We'll need the one on brakes, too. Actually, brake like you said. We're only going to have brakes on the left main, nothing on the nose wheel because Mariah, or who ever ordered the airplane from Boeing, was too cheap to buy the nose-wheel brakes or the taxi light." *Belly landing, huh? Hmmm . . . the suits say not to, but they're not here.* "You know, uh, maybe we'd better, ah, yes, let's do hold a bit here while we sort this crap out. Besides, maybe it'll give the thunderstorm holding over the airport time to move off."

"Or time to move directly over it."

"Positive thinking, Blake!"

For reference, I'd set the inbound course to 175° on the HSI, an instrument that graphically displays our airplane in relation to desired course and magnetic heading. For the moment it would represent our relationship to the runway. "To give us some time, we'll hold on the inbound bearing with a tear drop entry at the one-hundred-five mile fix. Might as well give ourselves twenty-mile legs." The last thing I wanted to do was hurry. When I hurry, I make mistakes. We couldn't afford any. I started the holding pattern entry with a 30° right turn when the little GPS read 105 miles to destination. "We're in the hold at," I glanced at the large clock mounted on the F/O's panel, "three five. Now would be a good time to make an IN RANGE call." One of the few advantages of the right seat over the left is that I can use my right hand for the mike, and to write with on the small clipboard that is mounted on each pilot's sliding window frame. Actually, that's the only advantage. I brought the mike to my lips, keyed it and sent the prearranged message. "Ah, in the blind—in the blind, Mike Poppa in range, estimating oh five." They were adamant that this was the only message I was to send. Considering our situation, and as I rarely do what I'm told, I thought perhaps a little "PS" might be in order. "Requesting emergency equipment standing by." No response, so I sent the message again. I had a rough idea of where the airport was supposed to be, somewhere in fog enshrouded valley before us. We were both quiet, listening for any response to my transmission, however weak. But the only sound in the cockpit came from the rush of air from the eyeball vents, the tap-tap-tapping of the "dildometer," a small vibrator that keeps the STBY barometric altimeter from sticking, and the thousand or so small individual electronic hums that blended into a single high pitched tone.

"There! There it is!" Red was oozing through the fog precisely where the little GPS said the airport would be, and by the radar three miles from a contouring, or in other words just plain nasty thunderstorm. Not good. Green smoke would have been better. I keyed the mike, "Have your smoke," and just in case, "roger the rojas." I couldn't remember the Spanish word for smoke.

"Ah, y—you said to watch for any amber, uh, amber . . . uh *fuel* pressure low lights? We're getting some." I turned to look over

my shoulder at Blake. He was really nervous. "Uh, Ca—uh—
Max . . . sir . . . are, uh, are the, ah, say, Max, are the . . . the . . .
the, uh . . . *engines* going to uh, to, ah . . . to, uh that is to say are
they going to uh . . . quit? They're intermittent. The lights, I mean."

"OK. That's a normal indication when low on fuel, and I guess
by now we are." I was a bit uneasy with that report, 'cause guessing
has no place in the cockpit. According to my fuel calculations, we
should be fairly fat. I don't like it when things don't agree.
Wondering if we had holes in our fuel tanks was unsettling. *I don't
like holes in my airplane!* "Turn all of the boost pumps on and open
the number three cross feed valve," I said grieving for my pointer.
"There's no time to waste, so we'd better dirty up and get on in
there." Cussing my descent planning, I turned partway in the seat
so Blake could hear me. I turned a little more. "Collect our three
million bucks and see about hitching a ride home, right!"

He was trying his best to be a good sport, but Blake's smile
fizzled. "I wonder if we're ever going to see home again?"

"Belay that shit! Here goes." *Another poor choice of words.* "Flaps
two." I moved the flap lever into the 2° detent. Acting on my
instructions, Blake had pulled the prescribed circuit breakers for
the damaged No. 1 LED, then read the lengthy abnormal
procedure to me. Either his lisp was gone, or I was getting used to
it, which was highly unlikely. It took a few minutes to configure
the flaps using the alternate procedures and electrical rather than
hydraulic power. The thought occurred to me that I should be
wearing two wristwatches . . . one for the flap procedure that went
so very slow, and one for the fuel that burned so very fast.

"Gear down." I swung the big lever into the down position.
Except for the right main, Mrs. Lincoln, the in-transit indications
were normal. Two green lights, one for the nose gear and one for
the left main, red for doors and the right main gear. As I was
coaching Blake on how to read the step down altitudes from the
scrap man's approach plate, I sensed a minute difference in sound
and wondered if it was really a mild sense of deceleration I was feeling.
It was.

"Aw, shit! Gear coming up." At least we had a hydraulic system for gear retraction.

"What!"

"Look at your number one engine generator."

"Uh-oh, we lost it!"

"No, we lost the whole damned engine! You're gonna get your belly landing."

"Oh, shit!"

"Really. We'd better get our asses on the ground! Turning inbound!" Normally, I use the autopilot in cruise flight only, but when loaded up with emergencies it's an extremely valuable tool. Rolling in a 700-foot-per-minute rate of descent on the autopilot pitch wheel, and reducing the power on our remaining engine to 70% N1 to compensate for heading down hill, I ran the mental calculations for a normal 727 rate of descent through my mind. It's a continual process. The machine will descend one foot for every three feet it goes forward, so at least in a "steam gauge" cockpit, it's a relatively simple process of arithmetic all the way down. But I know from experience just how difficult it can be to do 3:1 glide ratio problems in my head when there are a ka-jillion other things to think about.

"Transmitting in the blind, we are inbound with multiple emergencies, requesting your fire equipment." Still no answer. We could be descending straight into the jungle. Maybe there's no airport there at all? Maybe we've been had from the start? The airplane isn't behaving normally. *Crap! The gear isn't coming up! Ah, with No.1 out, we have no "A" system, you idiot! Hydraulic pumps on engines 1 and 2 only!* If No. 3 flames out, we've had our last drink, sung our last song. Stolen our last airliner. The gear lights were all red now. With no hydraulic power, the wheels would remain down when the gear handle was commanding up. We also had only one shot of pneumatic brakes, but as it turned out that wasn't a problem.

"What do you, uh, what do you, uh, that is to say, think, Max?"

"Aw, hell, everything's peachy! Piece of cake!" Her damaged wing required right aileron trim. With the No. 1 engine out, she took seven units of right rudder trim to keep my leg from shaking. "You'll be sparring with the Los Angeles Vice Squad before you know it!" Right on our imaginary glide slope, I clicked off the autopilot and rolled in a quarter turn of secondary elevator trim every few moments as the Boeing slowed, our single engine at idle power.

"Captain, you—you're . . . you're an asshole!"

The mist shrouded jungle rose slowly as the altimeters unwound, until at 3,000 feet AGL, "Smell that?" Since even Mariah tests for illegal substances suspended in our bodily fluids, I was pretty sure Blake could smell, although he does smoke."

"Yeah, I do! It smells like Guam!"

I made a mental note that smoke from what looked like a fishing village on the coast would be on a bearing of 270° and about 30 miles, mostly straight down. "Standby with those altitude calls. They will be important." The thunderstorm appeared stationary, looming high above our heads, its interior constantly changing color by electric fire . . . blues, orange and black, with the tops of the storm a brilliant white. An awesome, staggering sight. Not awesome like a cheeseburger, or a bowl of avo, awesome as in a cloud of unimaginable power, rising straight up from near the ground to perhaps 60,000 feet! Right before our eyes. Its desire is to kill and eat us and it can easily do so. *That's awesome!*

"I'm ready. You're leaving ten thousand five hundred now."

"That's twenty-two hundred and change over the ground—that's what I want you to back me up with. Remember to cross-check your figures with the radar altimeter. We'll use the higher of the two unless the baros are obviously off.

"Right, I remember. Leaving two thousand seven hundred now."

"Alright, from now on you talk, I'll fly. I don't want to hear anything but altitudes *unless* something really important comes up, like we're going to hit something. Use your good judgment."

"Understand."

It was whisper quiet in the cockpit. The whine from our remaining engine was distant, far behind us. Slightly left of our inbound course, I pressured the right rudder into a 2° turn.

"Out of two thousand five hundred, you should be seven miles out."

We were at eight miles, slightly low which, on one engine, is not acceptable. I added some power, while pressuring the elevator for a few seconds to level off and get us back on profile, then set the power at 83% N1. A beautiful sight as always, the pristine white tops of the mist were sliding silently by, just below us. "Leaving two thousand, you should be at six miles." We were at 5.8 when we submerged slowly into the goo, now slightly high. I used my peripheral vision to search for a thickening in the cloud that would mean ground contact, but it was solid gray. On speed at 128 knots, sink was 800. The machine shuddered, or was it me? We could easily be flying into a brick wall.

"Out of one thousand five hundred, you should be at about four miles."

"We." I risk a glance forward with one eye, but the view is a solid, opaque gray. This is taking forever. I muttered the word "we" to myself, thinking how ironic it was for Blake and myself to function as a team

"Leaving one thousand feet. Three miles."

Whine of engine, silence in the cockpit. Airspeed 129, sink 700. I spooled up to 90% N1 on No. 3, our "good" engine, 2.9 GPS flaps at 15°. Gear down, auto spoilers . . . uh, we don't have any auto spoilers. It'll have to be manual deployment. There may be enough pressure in the systems to operate them once . . . *have to hold the right wing off 'til the last instant.*

"Five hundred feet, mile and a half."

Another glance forward. Flicker of lightening, nothing else. Radar was ugly! Nothing down either. How far does the fog go? The zero zero landing in Anchorage was with three good engines, full avionics, a flight director, and experienced crew using a precision instrument landing system on an 11,500-foot-long runway. The little voice that lives inside my head was screaming at me, "This is nuts!" and it was right! I should pour the coals to her, holler out "missed approach" and climb out for our alternate, call flight control, request fuel and provisions. Stomp into some airport coffee shop for a cheeseburger and bitch about the state of aviation today. But we had no alternate, and we couldn't climb, not even one foot. We were going to land, very soon and there was a very definite possibility our lives might come to an abrupt end in the next second. I was getting real tired of that sensation.

"Three hundred . . . one mile! I don't see anything!"

Don't tell me what you don't see . . . tell me what you DO see!

"Two hundred feet!" The cockpit lit up like daylight, thunder following right on its ass. The deadly thunderstorm cell was close. Real close!

On speed, sink seven, gear down, well sort of. Time for the final commitment. "Flaps twenty-five!" As I moved the flap lever into the 25° detent, Blake comforted me by repeating the command, bless him, before motoring the flaps down with the alternate electric extension system as I had coached him to do.

We were looking for 100 feet when "WHAM!" Simultaneous lightening and thunder! Even though partially blinded from the strike, I thought I could see a thickening before me. Still partially blinded by the lightening, I split my vision between the gauges and outside.

"One hundred feet! We should be there!"

No energy for speech. I had to concentrate 100% of my strength, focus all of my flying experience on this final moment of descent. If we were hit by a microburst or wind shear from the nearby storm, on one engine we were without defense. I searched for runway lights. There were none. Quick cross-check of GPS course. No highway flares, no coal lamps, auto headlights, nothing. My radar altimeter showed us at 50 feet when I first saw a for sure thickening in the gray. Yellow, possibly the yellow chevrons of a displaced threshold painted at the end of the runway? We may be a few feet too low. I cross-checked with the radar altimeter. It showed 42 feet. It ought to be enough.

Jesus, are there power lines? I am sure the approach plate said no. No time to look at it now. Using the yellow for a target, I aimed the Tri-jet directly at it. No more than a second or two flying time from the runway the yellow formed up with black to make a man made shape. I allowed myself a momentary release of pressure on my shoulders . . . until . . . .

Yellow with large black letters. Form of Cheshire cat fits the insanity of the moment perfectly. It is a huge bulldozer parked in the center of the runway.

The voice recorder captured Blake and I uttering the customary last words of the dying aviator in two-part harmony, "Aw, shit!"

CHAPTER 16

Johnston

As I saw the word "Kubota" disappear under the nose, I recalled the time back before everything was illegal, riding to the airport with Lee Hunziker's mother. I guess other people see their whole lives pass before their eyes. All I saw was that damned '63 Rambler Ambassador trying to chug over the Interstate Bridge as it tried to get across the Columbia River to Vancouver. Mrs. Hunziker had a unique way of shifting the automatic transmission. She'd floor it, producing actual ounces of thrust to the wheels for approximately four seconds, then release the accelerator completely. She'd learned the only way she knew how, through multiple trial and error sessions that such a technique would result in forcing the machine to shift from first to second prematurely, which, in her feeble little mind, would make each 27¢ per gallon of gas last just that much longer. Mrs. Hunziker, ahead of her time, was an adamant believer in the theory of the parabolic curve, rocket type thrust lasting for a few seconds followed by the long coast out into space where her mind was.

Those were the days when there were still American cars on the road, the year of the first Stingray. As badly as I wanted to get to the airport, I was embarrassed to be seen in Hunziker's car. I hated that car, and for that matter, Wayne Hunziker who came along with the car. The tradeoff was worth it in some ways but not in others. While I would actually arrive at Pearson Airpark for my day's work towards the left seat in which I was having this flashback,

Mrs. H. was rid of Wayne for the day. But mine was full of him. While laying on my back cleaning the exhaust scum from the bellies of the small airplane engines literally held together with Elmer's glue, oil, and solvent that dripped up my nose and into my eyes, Wayne was off merrily stuffing pitot tubes with pea shooter ammunition.

Perhaps remembering Hunziker was a lead-in to recalling the theft of my first airplane with Wally the F-106 pilot, the recipient of one of Wayne's peas. Wally found out the hard way about the spark plugs being held in by the Elmer's glue when one came through the cowling of his Aeronca Champ. We were flying in formation at the time with two other rented junkers and by that I do not mean the fine airplanes produced for the Reich. No, those were real junkers, as in pieces of junk somehow held together for the purpose of one more flight. Having survived our first combat experience together, we became fast friends that ultimately lead to some nocturnal airplane liberating designed to avoid the customary rental fee of $6 per hour. And that was wet. We were apprehended at once, since our instructor lived in the traffic pattern and could easily differentiate the sound of his crummy little machine from the nearby noise from the still-under-construction Interstate-5, passing DC-3s, 6s, 7s, and the occasional jet.

What that had to do with a bulldozer had frankly escaped me. A shrink would have a field day at my daydream during such a critical moment. It was a time of intense concentration for me, but my role was changing from that of captain to spectator. I was sure the solid report I'd heard was the left main gear shearing off on the dozer because when I began to reach for the ground with it, there was nothing there. I quickly pulled the speed brake handle up, aft and up, killing the super efficient wings' lift. The effect is identical to sticking a 12-inch knitting needle up a two-year old chicken's ass. It's all over. Then, counting on the accumulator pressure, I grabbed the No. 3 reverser, and pulled it full up to the 12 o'clock position and reefed on it. I was asking too much.

"Whomp-Whomp!" I felt the bursts of reverse thrust on my

left foot as she tried to yaw right. It was still dark enough to see the orange reflection from the flames shooting out of the engine. All the while, palm trees and a few parked airliners where whizzing through my field of vision.

The flaps contacted the runway first. After minimal protestations, first the inboard, then the outboard flaps were carried away, as they are designed to do. Boeing thinks of everything. The airplane settled to the ground at the same time the nose wheel began to spin up. The 727 sank to the mud runway like TJ's Beaver on Morro Bay.

The wings were through lifting, but their job wasn't over. For Blake and I, the wild ride continued. The nose-wheel tire, apparently pneumatically challenged, began to dig up steel runway matting which brought with it copious amounts of mud. My forward vision was gone again. But out of my peripheral vision, I could see chunks of it standing to a 45° angle, just right for the wings to slice them off like the lawnmower I wish I were back pushing now, looking up at the airplanes and wishing I were there instead of here.

"Oh shit! AAAAAAAAAAAA!"

"For Christ's sake, Blake!"

The machine began a slow turn to the left, allowing a brief preview of what was hurtling out of the fog at us. The most interesting was a 1965 Lincoln limousine with a large man in white suit and a Panama hat standing next to it. His eyes were open wide, but his mouth was a slit of grim determination. He made no move to escape, but had assumed the posture of a quarterback looking for a place to go. A smaller man dressed in work clothes was vanishing into the tree line on his hands and knees, leaving behind a rooster tail of mud. I glanced at the airspeed indictor. It was reading 120 knots, broken. Or, inoperative, as we have come to say, our multiple airspeed probes undoubtedly plugged with mud.

"NOOOOAAAWWWWSSSHHHHHIIIITTTT! We're going to hit that man!"

"And his car!"

For the next few leisurely nanoseconds or so, the machine continued to plow up the runway, depositing dumpsters full of red-ochre mud that we would soon learn to hate, over the nose and onto both sliding windows which are the cockpit emergency exits. Through the tiny opening remaining, I estimated we would impact the Lincoln amidships. The man was standing his ground as if daring the airplane to strike him down.

It did.

With a hollow thump, the radome caved in the suicide doors on impact. Wearing the Lincoln like a hat, we continued for another hundred yards or so, sliming to an abrupt, squishy halt. I guess Blake and I both held onto our last breath. We looked at each other, then exhaled, "Holy shit," in two-part harmony. There was a two-syllable chuckle celebrating our arrival, then training kicked in again, and we scrambled from our seats. Blake had the main entrance door, aircraft left, open by the time I reached the cockpit door just as the morning twilight was violated by a near-by lightening strike. A clap of thunder reverberated inside my lungs. It seemed the perfect opening to my own personal horror movie. The storm that had been hovering over the airport, waiting, chose this very moment to dump on us. Next to mobile home parks, airports are their favorite spot to hang out.

Blake made the short hop, following his duffel, to the ground. "Careful, it's real soft and slippery." He held out his arms to help me deplane in deference to my advancing age, but I declined the offer.

"Yeah, you would say that." Jet pilot Max Power was not about to be helped to the ground by a swish. As I stood in the doorway, I marveled at the contrast. Inside, space age, first-class technology, comfort, and of course plastics. Outside, stone age, mud, vines, sections of WW II era runway matting. I made the short jump and sunk painfully to my hands and knees in the slimy, gritty, ochre mud.

Any ramp rat will tell you that it never rains until their flight is on the ground. The sky opened up, and I found myself studying the effects of what I thought at first was a micro-burst. But there was no wind, it was utterly calm. Tons and tons of freezing cold water crashing down on my head, fresh from the upper atmosphere. We were quickly soaked. "Blake, I need a hand," I said flashing on the life-like rubber one I carry in my flight bag along with a pair of fuzzy dice I hang from the mag compass on every flight.

"I'm stuck too. Hang on a sec—" Blake grabbed a vine to help him get unstuck, but it broke landing him on his face and elbows.

"I'm a little busy right now, but if ya's can wait a second, I'll give youse a hand." Chat with a few hundred thousand people throughout the country, and pretty soon you can gauge within a hundred miles or so where that person is from. Queens? Brooklyn? Maybe a transplant to Cicero? I picked out the voice coming from the nose of the airplane from the chattering of monkeys and tropical birds. There was also the low, guttural cry no doubt from a hairy animal I didn't recognize, nor wish to meet. I turned to look up at the large man with the now normal sized dark brown, piercing eyes. He was framed by a dense stand of dark-green bamboo and some broad-leafed plants I didn't recognize. Bananas hung in clumps from several trees. I guess he'd tip the scales somewhere around five hundred pounds. He wasn't fat; he was *big*. His Roman nose was the size of my fist, but in perfect proportion and caked with mud. It seemed that each of his fingers were larger than my wrist. Rain poured from what remained of his Panama hat while heavy, black, curly hair flowed freely from under it, dotted with the ochre, volcanic mud. The front of his white linen suit was caked with it. He finished urinating on the nose of our airplane, stowed his cargo, zipped, then wiped his hands on the little fellow's shirt who had returned from the jungle as he mushed through the gluck at our feet.

"Ah, thanks," I said, reluctantly taking his proffered hand. He caught me low, around the fingers and applied pressure. Too much pressure. The broken thumb from high school began to speak to me. It was painful, motivating me to climb quickly out of the hole I was in.

"Bab Tomassi," he said still vice gripping my hand, his eyes cold as he grinned. "I'm just gonna guess dat youse is dis shit head Max Power. Wheah da hell did you pick up a freekin' name like dat?" Here we were, standing around a just crash-landed airliner in Colombia, probably still all over the network news. We should be painting small seagulls, geese, and one F-18 on the nose, and this guy asks a question to which he already knows the answer? And, it was absolutely and completely-totally irrelevant. *Who gives a shit?*

"Nice bulldozer."

"Youse asked fer da equipment."

I turned to look at the airplane. She was a pitiful sight. The once proud bird lay pitifully on her right side and down by the nose, her T-tail high in the air. Her left wing was nearly buried in mud. She was steaming from the heat caused by the slide home and the runway matting she'd plowed up left a trail of wreckage and destruction that lead into an infinity of fog.

"Ah, this is Blake, my F/O." Blake nodded politely and said hello. At first Bab's didn't say anything, but he did seem to be studying Blake intensely. I moved towards the right-wing root to inspect the landing gear. Never having had a landing gear malfunction, my natural curiosity was strong. Approaching the leading edge of the right wing, I noted two bloody areas where we'd taken bird strikes that had caved in the leading edge. From the movement of the voice, I could tell Tomassi was keeping me in sight.

"Pilot my ass, dis guy's a queen. Youse a maricon too, asshole?"

"Asshole? Hold on, *Bab,* you don't know anything about me! I brought you the jet like you asked." I turned around to face the wreckage and held my arms out like Milton Berle, "Here it is!"

Bab's was studying the wreck, not paying much attention to me, as if he was assessing what would need to be done to get her back in the air. "Yeah, some kind of pilot you are."

It was necessary to get on my hands and knees to gain access to the wheel well. Glucked up as I was, it didn't matter. I reached in to the claustrophobic space and found a prize. I held up the battered piece of aluminum for Blake to see. On it painted in what looked like fingernail polish was a single word: Garcia. It had been a lunch pail. "Bizarre," said Blake. He stopped swatting mosquitoes shocked by the sight. At some point when whoever was going to work on the airplane gained complete access to the wheel well, he might find something even more unusual. And fragrant. I turned to Tomassi who was fiddling with a new cigar.

"She's a little, uh . . . shopworn, but hell, you're, uh . . . gonna scrap it anyway, right?"

He chuckled, his chest jiggling like a topless dancer in heat. "Yeah, dat's right, we's gonna scrap her. Right after youse fly it back ta where ya's came from with a little cargo." *Ah, so that's it.* "We'll even give it a tune up fer yas."

Line—Jerk. Hook—Set.

He caught me studying his empty shoulder holster. "Yeah. Gonna need a good cleaning. It's got dat freekin' mud jammed into da barrel. Magazine's fulla it too, see?" He took the Glock from his waistband, ejected the clip and showed it to Blake and me. "Yeahr, this baby needs a bath, for friggin' sure. Probably won't even fire!" I felt somewhat relieved to hear that. He broke into a broad smile, "But dis one heah is nice 'n clean! Woiks great!" He jacked a round into the chamber, and fired into the mud where I had been standing. He apparently had his backup piece loaded with hollow points; the single round made a crater two feet across and a foot or so deep. "Don't 'chas tink?"

Blake gave an involuntary, "Eek."

"I told yas guys once dat I freekin hate queens, didn't I?" Blake looked up at him with an expression of defiance, as if he knew what was coming.

"You shouldn't hate anybody." Then the bang. Though deafening, I could hardly hear it over the downpour.

"Oh, no!" I cried. "Aw, Jesus, aw Jesus!"

"I doubt it." Very cold, Tomassi. Very cold.

After whirling around to his left from the force of the 9 mm hollow point, Blake sunk like a stone into the mud, straight down. His eyes were wide open, devoid of any expression, and had rolled back in his head oblivious to the downpour. His jaw was hanging open, blood coated his tongue and ran from the corner of his mouth. He looked pretty dead to me. I was thunderstruck with instant cotton mouth. I was scared. As I felt sure my turn was next, and soon, I decided to find out a few things to chew on during my descent into hell.

Feeling pretty stupid and naïve, I asked Tomassi the question, "You, uh, you never had any intention of coming across with the money, did you?"

"Ay! I, unlike youse, is man of my woid! Geraldo! Geraldo, ya little shit, wheah ahr yas?" Blake must be dead. I moved to find out. "Watch it, pal. Just hold it right der!"

"Fuck you, fatso!" I slogged towards Blake. Other than satisfying my own curiosity, I didn't know what I could do. And there was all of that flaming red blood.

"Fatso? Foist of all, maricon, I ain't fat!"

"Look, I, uh . . . it's, well, we didn't expect this kind of reception. And I'm no fruit! We went through seven kinds of hell getting here, then you shoot my accomplice for nothing! What the hell kind of deal is this? I guess it's true that there is no honor among thieves."

"Wait a second, wait a second . . . Just whose ah' yas callin' a freekin t'ief?" What I thought had been a 9 mm auto now looked more like an S&W .357 magnum in my direction.

"Hey, *Bab*, hold on there!"

"Name's Bab."

That's what I said! "Bob?"

"Yeahr, Bab! Das' whad I said, shit head."

I felt for a pulse on Blake's carotid artery. He was alive. His pulse was weak, his breathing shallow. His color was gone, expressionless eyes half-open, hair plastered to his skull with mud. His white shirt was nearly all red, blood oozing from the entrance wound high on his chest. It was good that I couldn't see the exit wound.

The jungle sounds were violated by a heavy diesel approaching from the far end of the runway. The chattering monkeys, birds, and insects retreated into silence. Moments later, I spied the flashing blue-and-red lights of a modern, state of the art, airport crash truck. It pulled to within twenty yards of our position. The operator set the air brakes, the heavy engine was at idle. On the door was the official State of Arizona seal, combined with the words *City of Tucson Airport Fire Department.*

I hollered towards the truck, "Anybody in that truck know first aid?" I didn't get the answer I wanted.

"I got 'chur foist aid right heah, asshole." Babs was grinning as he held the .357 up for me to see, leaving no doubt as to his intent.

The small man who had disappeared into the tree line returned. "Señior Tomassi?"

"Yeah, Geraldo. Show dis miscreant da money."

He's calling me a miscreant?

Meanwhile, Blake was having trouble breathing. It was tough for me at first, but I held him upright in my arms, cradling his head on my shoulder. While it seemed to help his breathing, I could feel the warmth of his blood soaking through my shirt and even I knew that the rattle coming from deep in his lungs wasn't good.

The small fellow named Geraldo labored to remove three suitcases from the trunk of the Lincoln. Babs had to blow the lock to get it open. The frame was bent, the car totaled. Tomassi noted me studying the car. "Dem tings is hard to get down heah's, y'a know?!" Geraldo slogged through the mud, bringing one heavy case at a time. They were gold Halliburtons, one size larger than my carry on. Geraldo dialed in the dual combinations, and one by one opened them. They were stuffed with machine counted and banded used hundred dollar bills. "Go ahead, grab a handful. I want 'chas ta see I wasn't going to cheat ya's."

"But you are now."

"Hey, asshole! Youse was ta deliver a Seven Two Seven! Dis ting is a pile of shit!"

"Well, you're gonna scrap it anyway, *right?*"

"It would seem dat's already been handled, dick head! I got no more use for youse, asshole." He raised the pistola with both hands pointing the weapon directly at the bridge of my nose. I wondered if it would hurt, or if it would be over so fast that I wouldn't feel anything. Would I be able to see the round coming?

"Max! Max Power, you shit head!" The shrill sound of a banshee came from behind me. It was the voice that man fears most: a pissed off woman. I heard the voice plop into the mud. "Max Power, you asshole!"

"Ay! Who da fug is dat?" screamed Tomassi, his eyes focused on a target behind me.

"I truly will be damned if I know."

"Max Power, you asshole!" But I did know.

"Ay! Dat's what I calls him!" Tomassi beamed at the sight of a female, and a fairly good-looking one, usually.

Wait a minute! I turned. I tried to run in the mud, but it wasn't going to happen. First one shoe was lost in the cockpit's black hole, then the other was sucked from my foot by the mud, but I didn't care. Frannie? Whoever it was knew my name and was cussing worse than Tomassi with a toothache. My God, "Frannie?" I slogged on towards the voice and away from Tomassi. Not only was I glad to see her, but she had possession of our only fire arm.

"You BASTARD! How could you leave me back there? You fucking idiot, you fool! She was but a few steps away now. I could see that her hair and eyebrows were singed, her eyelashes all but gone. I mouthed, "GUN?" She ignored me.

"Hey, youse come back heah. We's ain't finished yet!" Even though I expected a bullet in the back of my head, I found the courage to tell *Bab* to go fuck himself.

"Yeahr? I got a better idea." He said leering at Frannie.

And then she saw Blake. "Oh my God!" She bent down tenderly to wipe the rain from his forehead. "I heard shots." She looked at me accusingly. "You! You shoot him?" The intensity of her voice was rising with each word. I shook my head no, but she wasn't buying it. "You *did* shoot him! *You shot him just because he lisps?*"

"No, I did." Tomassi was gesturing at his chest with his stogie.

"Where's the gun?" I whispered to her.

"Gun? What gun?" she said out loud.

"Gun?" Flecks of cigar dotted Tomassi's chin. I smiled at him. He smiled back. Fran turned towards him. It appeared that things were gelling in what seemed to me to be her partially-filled head.

"Watch it!" she said to me, as if I would be studying her behind at a moment like this which of course I was. Then, returning her attention to Tomassi, she began to walk slowly towards him. He moved his aim from me to her.

"Think you're going to need that big gun against me?" she asked in mock innocence.

"Year, well youse know a guy gets a little tired of dese Colombian broads. You bein' as small as you are . . ." he said, his eyes locked on her crotch. She walked up to him showing no fear. I would treat him as a cobra, ready to kill instantly and without warning. Judging from what he did to Blake, I knew he could and would.

"Yeah, it is." She said with an expression of seduction only a woman can have. "And as big as you are . . ." She let Tomassi fill in the blanks. It was working. No one could be that stupid.

"Well, ah, dis ain't exactly a good spot, but what the hell, let's get started." He began to unzip with his free hand.

"Here, let me," she said continuing where he left off. "Oooo, what do we have here?"

He began to make guttural sounds from deep within his chest. "Ah, dat's nice."

Frannie had him by the frog, then she grabbed the que ball and squoze hard. "Drop it, fatso!" I couldn't believe it was going to be that easy.

Color was draining from his face. "Fug you, twat!" Each time he tried to raise his pistola, Fran would squeeze harder. At that moment, her attention was diverted to Blake as he groaned. I thought Tomassi would use the diversion to pump a round into someone, but it didn't work out that way. Little Frannie squeezed with everything she had, while reaching over his big belly with her left to relieve him of his weapon. He tried to fight her for it, but it was no use. When she had the gun, she let go, retreating from his reach quickly and gave him a shove. He ended up on his ass in the mud.

"Now, fatso, where's there a doctor?"

"Uh . . . doctah? You'se got ta' be kidding!" You tink I'm gonna tell youse anything? Youse a' fuckin nuts!" Frannie knelt down next to Blake. She placed her ear at his mouth, her hand on his wrist for a pulse, then turned to the huge man.

"C'mon, just tell me where the doctor is. It'll be much easier that way."

"Hey, fug you twat!"

"You said that already. Where's the doctor?" She used one of his own tricks on him, holding up the .357 for him to see.

Some of the color had returned to his face. He grunted, slipping while trying to stand up. "I hate dis fuckin' mud." Having regained his standing position, he turned to me, "Dis your woman? You put up with dis shit?"

There was no time for me to reply, Fran shouted, "No, I am not his woman or anyone else's!"

"Oh, one of *dem*. It figures."

"The doctor, fatso, where is he? You're going to tell me one way or the other. Start talking!" He gave her the finger instead.

"I ain't afraid of dying, gash. I ain't telling youse nottin'. Maybe next time youse is blowin' me see, you'se won't have any teeth to bite wid! Maybe we'd bettah break yure freekin' fingahs so youse won't be tempted to try anythin' else cute. Den we can have a real good time, dat is 'til I get tired of ya's." He turned his attention to me. "Max, ya know how it is wid old pussy. Ya gets tired of it after a while." He turned back to Fran. "Den we'll feed your ass to da sharks. We got some real big ones down here." He made a gesture. I memorized the direction.

Frannie turned to me and shrugged. Babs made a move for her, but she saw it and pointed the pistola at his nose. He stopped. "Doctor?" He stuck his tongue out and did his best to flick it like a cobra. Fran lowered her aim and matter of factly put a hollow point through his right knee cap. The unexpected deafening roar sent the birds to flight and some of the crowd back into the jungle where they would be safer. The blast reverberated in my lungs and set my ears to ringing. Some things are worse than death, and this was it for Tomassi. He fell back in the mud with a scream that would curdle a vampire's blood.

"Now, where's the doctor, slime bag?" She had to shout over his screams.

"Jesus H. Christ! Frannie!" I've seen pain, and I've been in pain before, but nothing like that have I ever seen. Frannie was still holding the pistol and was using it as a pointer in the general direction of my head. "Frannie? . . . uh, Fran?"

"What did you do to him, you idiot!" she said gesturing towards Blake with the pistola.

"I didn't do anything. Ever since I got out of the airplane, people have been pointing guns at me," I said, gesturing to hers. She still had her finger on the trigger. I wished she wouldn't do that.

Her face pinched with rage, she screamed at me, "You, you fool! You—you stupid idiot!"

"Where the hell have you been?" I had to raise my voice to be heard over the downpour, but Frannie continued to scream at me.

"Where have I been? You stupid nincompoop, I've been locked in the aft stairwell, that's where! Don't you even know Morse code, you stupid shit?" She didn't give me time to answer. "I've been signaling ever since the fire!"

"We thought it was just the stairs trailing in the slip stream. I had Blake look in the stairwell, he said there was nothing there."

At the mention of Blake's name, she lowered the piece. "Max, did you—you did shoot him, didn't you?" With Blake lying in a mud hole I thought it might be polite not to mention my ongoing thoughts of strangulation.

"No, Babs did. Just like he said." I turned to look at my would-be captor writhing in pain, then back at Frannie. "Jesus, Frannie."

"Nope. Lucifer."

*"Any flight worth commuting on
is worth running like hell to catch."*
—Commuters' credo

CHAPTER 17

Johnston

An airplane crash draws a crowd, even in the jungles of Colombia, especially when someone is screaming in pain. At first, everyone including Tomassi's men had disappeared, but then people began to appear at the jungle's edge little by little until there was a crowd of perhaps a hundred people. They all appeared to be native Colombians, and seemed to be no threat to us. They watched intently while we manhandled Blake who was in and out of consciousness, into the back seat of the fire truck. Somehow we managed it without killing him, the crowd letting out with a group "ooo" each time he cried out in pain. While I was loading our gear, Frannie, who is almost fluent in Spanish, went to the crowd to see where we might locate a doctor. People shrugged as they lied to her.

Just then, I felt the solid unmistakable sensation of a rifle barrel sticking in my ribs. "Oh, ah, good morning," I said feeling stupid. My courtesy was rewarded with the rifle butt in the back of my head. I saw stars as I went down face first into the mud. It had been a little attention getting tap. When I was kicked in the ribs, I heard Fran shriek.

I lifted my head to see what had happened, but someone's boot mashed my face back into the mud, then stood on my head. I was doing a good job of holding my breath when someone kicked me in the ribs again. I was already seeing stars, but that was the end of my lung full of air. They pushed harder on my head, forcing me further into the mud. I needed to forcefully expel air from my lungs through my nostrils to blow out chunks of impacted mud, but there was no air. Someone was killing me.

Choking on water and mud, I could hear the muffled sounds of a struggle with Fran's voice mixed into the commotion. Suddenly, someone lifted me out of the mud by the hair on the back of my head. I was coughing, gasping for air when I was punched, refracturing my broken nose. More stars, another rifle butt in the gut, or maybe it was a club. It's funny how the mind works. I was thinking that no way was this worth three million bucks.

When I heard Frannie scream, I rolled onto my back, and opened my one remaining eye. My assassin was slapping her around. "Hey, asshole!" I said. My reward was another rifle butt to my stomach that knocked the air completely out of me. My vision went dark. Another of assassin's men kicked me in the ribs. At first, all I could see was a spit-shined jump boot. Then macho man grabbed Fran by the ear as one might a small child, quickly covering the 30 meters between us in spite of the mud. Having torn some of Fran's clothing off, I was afraid he might rape her on the spot.

"Doctor, we need a doctor!" she pleaded. "Your own man needs a doctor badly as you can see!" She pulled her ripped blouse together. "He's in terrible pain!"

Assassin pulled a large pistola from his belt. I'd guess it was a .44 magnum. "Pain?" he asked as he leveled the weapon at Tomassi. "It is easily cured." He thumbed back the hammer, then fired. "Now," he said coldly, "there is no more pain!" The .44 hollow point left a stump, just a bloody mass of bone and tissue where Tomassi's head had been. At that point, I was ready to concede that we were in serious trouble. Under the circumstances, I felt it better not even to mention Blake.

Having heard the shot that had taken off Tomassi's head, the crowd took refuge in the jungle, but I could see a few peasants watching us from the tree line. It looked like little Geraldo, the dead thug's man, might be hiding among them, but I couldn't be sure. Then I wondered if what was happening to us would turn into a legend to be handed down from generation to generation of little Colombians.

The sound of a jeep gearing down to second jerked me out of my reverie as I lay stupidly in the mud, hoping the pain would go away at least someday. The jeep stopped in a puddle of, what else, mud. "Geet eento the cheep, osshole!" The driver had a truly intense expression on a face with skin stretched tight over the skull. He smoked a black, very crooked cigar. Assassin turned to Fran, still clutching her blouse, "Eee ooostead, bonita señiorita," he said with an evil smile.

I knew what Fran was about to do. I'd had enough of the rifle butt, so I stopped her from telling the guy in Spanish to go pound sand, with a scowl and a very slow shake of my head and by mouthing the word no. She looked at me with disgust, as if I was some kind of coward and said, "Caca del pollo!"

Assassin, in the right seat of the jeep, heard it. As we trundled down what was left of the runway, he turned to me and laughingly said, "Cheeken sheet?" Apparently it struck him funny. He'd giggle to himself, mutter "Cheeken sheet" to himself, occasionally turning to share the humor with me. "Cheeken sheet."

When we pulled up next to an idling Huey with "New Mexico Air Guard" markings. The pilot goosed the turbine and the big wing overhead began to spin. "Geet een there, asshole," said assassin, then motioned for Frannie to follow as he helped her down from the jeep in exaggerated chivalry. He made the mistake of copping a feel when her back was turned. Frannie, apparently fearless, turned around and gave the guy a solid kick in the balls, doubling him over. I jumped back out of the chopper thinking he was going to shoot her and that maybe this was our opportunity to make a get away, but it didn't work out that way. In a few minutes we were all onboard and ready to go.

A glance at the chopper crew did little to inspire confidence. The command pilot couldn't have been much over sixteen. He had thick black curly hair and bad teeth and wore jungle-camo fatigues with mirrored sunglasses. To his left in the copilot's position sat a lovely little thing greeting us with a defiant expression. "Eh, Quixote, where we goin'?" He didn't hear me over the sound of the turbine engine, but Fran did.

"Ooof! Dammit, Frannie, I hurt all over as it is, quit hitting me!"

"He hears you call him Don Quixote and we'll really be in trouble."

"What? You don't think we're in trouble now?" The rest of the helicopter ride was a relief. It was too noisy for Fran to sling insults and ridiculous ideas at me, so I did my best to find comfort. We lifted off from the enshrouded field, flying at treetop level with forward visibility nearly nonexistent, not so much from the fog but from the sun crazed windshileld that seemed to have been washed for the last time in 1967. After only a couple of minutes of sliding over the jungle canopy we slipped over the edge of the mountain in a rapid descent to the beach 7,000 feet and change below.

Our destination became apparent right away, obviously a small village with a marina, several fishing vessels, and one large yacht. It was only a short flight, but each rotation of the rotor stabbed at my injuries. I had vision from only one eye. As bad as our predicament was, I thought that attempting to escape from the jungle on foot could have been worse.

The ride on the way down was fairly smooth, since the rotors were essentially gliding. But as our teenage crew leveled the helicopter as any teen age crew would, all at once, the rotors loaded up, the heavy "wop-wop-wop" stabbing at my injuries. The pain got worse as the sand flew until we landed with a thud on the beach, a hundred yards from the marina at the bottom of a hook turn. The young pilot turned to me, his initial sneer replaced with a broad smile, apparently looking for my approval. Remembering what it's like to be a hot-shot, sixteen-year-old pilot with a girl friend onboard, I gave him the thumbs up. His girlfriend saw it and we were friends for life. One little round of applause goes a long way, and we could use all the friends we could get. Unfortunately, it didn't help a bit.

Moored amidst the few small stinking fishing boats was a huge yacht, the *PC*, homeport San Francisco. I didn't recognize the design, but it was a beautiful ship of at least 100 feet in length and was apparently where we were being taken. It hurt to walk. Frequent proddings from assassin's rifle barrel didn't help. It hurt. It hurt to do anything. With blood running from my nose, and smeared across my face, I knew that I was not presenting the image one should when boarding a yacht for the first time.

"Welcome aboard the *PC*, Captain Power." A short, bald, and dumpy man with a bland smile held the swim-step door open. It was Bob Adoni. When the shock wore off, things fell into place and everything fit. My gears were still grinding when someone grabbed a handful of my hair, jerking me backwards off my feet. "When I was in the Air Force, I was taught ladies first. *Asshole!*" I vowed to do a little introspection at my first opportunity to see if there was any validity to being called an asshole by everyone I met. It was the same Bob Adoni alright—but he was somehow . . . different? *What the hell . . . is . . . going . . . on?* But as I was mouthing the question, the answer stood to. Adoni's performance at the meeting with Buck made perfect sense. A look into his eyes told the story. A good guess was that Adoni was flat-assed, pathologically insane!

He seemed genuinely happy as he spoke. "We're all going for a boat ride. A nice long one." He looked from one of us to the other for a reaction, but didn't get one. "You'll enjoy it," he laughed again, almost giggling, "at least part of the way."

"Jesus, Bob, I hope you're not going to drive!" Adoni laughed off the insult.

"C'mon aboard and meet Mr. Franco. He's the man you've been stealing from!" He wore a mean *get even* type smile and used his rich bass voice for emphasis. "He really wants to meet you!" I went to enter the cabin through French doors. "Oh, no, Captain, not there. He gestured towards a stairs with his eyes, "You two will be quartered on the flying bridge, up there.

"It's fly bridge, moron. You're obviously the same kind of sailor that you were a pilot." Adoni laughed as we climbed the stairs to the fly bridge . . . actually it was more of a guttural giggle, something I'd never heard before, but then I'd never been around a certified nut before either. Well, maybe Frannie.

"Were?" He giggled again, then turned to face me. "Eh? Come on, sir, surely you don't mean that?" He held out his hand as if for a truce-making handshake. Automatically I reached for him, but caught myself in time. I caught a glimpse of what might have been a *stun gun* concealed along the inside of his wrist. "Idiot?" he asked. "Moron?" He giggled sickly at me again, "Not so stupid now, am I, Captain?"

"I'll say this, Adoni, you may be a piss-poor second officer, but you've definitely surprised me."

"You're going to *suffer* a lot of surprises on this voyage." And this time it was him using emphasis. "Like I said . . . for a while." Grinning like a smiling bowling ball, Adoni gestured me towards the fly bridge that was to be our prison for the voyage. After negotiating two decks, I opened a small gate and stepped onto a spacious sun deck. The first thing that struck me was the height above water. We must have been a good 25 feet above the waterline. The deck was several times larger than most living rooms. Adoni saw me studying the controls at the top-side steering station, "Ah, too bad, Captain. Those controls have been locked off below! You still have your GPS with you?" Apparently my eyes gave me away. "It's alright, Max, uh . . . Captain. Go ahead and keep track of where you are. It's a fun way to pass what time you have remaining in your lives! We're going to slip you in at about north twenty-five and one forty-three west . . . up around the Channel Islands where there's plenty of big, hungry sharks! Give you an idea of how much time you have left . . . rather like little Nell tied to the tracks watching an hour glass, isn't it?"

"You are a greedy little bastard, aren't you?"

He stood up straight as if he'd been insulted. "Yeah, I am! And I'll be sitting in *your* left seat on my next trip. You see, Captain Power, crime does pay! We've got two of your suitcases full of money here. Care to tell us where the third one is?"

"Third one?" I asked. I didn't have to play stupid—I really didn't know—as I looked around casually for a weapon.

"That's alright, Captain. You'll tell us before this is over." He broke into a genuine smile, a wide grin showing off his perfect teeth, "Uh, I have some . . . toys, you might call them, below. And remember, this time when it's over, it's really all over for you and Fran Olson."

"How about I tell you now?"

"OK, tell me."

"Where's Fran?" He stopped at that one, turning his head as if listening for something.

"Fran is, uh, busy right at the moment, Captain."

I noted a mild vibration from the deck. Someone was starting the engines. "Yeah, well you get her unbusy and we'll talk about that third bag."

This time he really laughed out loud, "You don't give the orders on this deck, Captain! I do! And, uh . . . Miss Olson? Well, she'll be up when she is . . . finished. She's having a, uh, well a sort of conference with Mr. Franco." The little weasel. Frannie would be able to handle him all right. "Ah, we'll be getting underway in a few minutes—"

I cut him off. "Right after you run down there and untie the lines. The world needs deckhands, Bob, and you'll always be a deckhand." That dig hit the target.

Seething, he hissed at me, "But I'll be a live deckhand . . . unlike yourself, *Captain!*" Adoni opened half of a locked French door, then disappeared down a spiral staircase. Right after the lock went "click."

I made a quick assessment of the situation. Other than the locked door that Adoni had used, there seemed to be no way off the bridge other than over the side. That would most likely be our escape. The area was large enough to host a medium sized party, with soft white leather seats paired off around the bulwarks. There was an impressive array of antennas amidships near the set of controls forward with the entire bridge protected by a smoked-glass windscreen.

As I suspected, Adoni shouted a few instructions to the dock committee, then hauled the two-inch, double-braided, black nylon lines aboard. After stowing them neatly he disappeared into the wheelhouse. The *PC* was bow thruster equipped, so she moved sideways, away from the small pier with ease. Then as the ship gathered steerage way, she took up a westerly heading for open ocean. After clearing the small natural breakwater, the *PC* began to rise and fall with the long ocean swells.

I heard a commotion below—the unmistakable sound of Fran's voice in anger, sounding like a chicken locked in a cardboard box with a wolverine. The French door opened and Fran was thrust through the opening by Adoni whom I could see had blood running down from his forehead. Fran didn't look so good either. She seemed pissed and focused on me.

"You alright?"

"Max? You are an asshole!" All previous doubts were dismissed. Fran was pissed! But, hell, like most women I've known, she was almost always pissed at something. Now it was my turn. "How did I let myself get talked into this? Max, they're going to kill us!"

"*Talked into?* You and Blake *blackmailed* me to come along!" Fran slumped down in one of the leather deck chairs. The mud that had been cleaned off her body left no doubt as to what had been going on below.

"Max, they tried to rape me! And what the hell is that little weasel Bob Adoni doing here? Where are we going, what's going on?"

"Never mind that crap! We've got to get real creative if we're going to get out of this. We're already too far from shore to swim, or at least I am. Could you make it from here?"

"I—I don't think so," she said studying the distance to shore.

As the shoreline retreated the turquoise waters of the shallows changed to the deep blue of the Pacific. The shore behind us grew smaller and smaller until all I could see was water.

*"A screwed up flight will get progressively worse
until the flight number changes."*
—Captain Max Power

CHAPTER 18

Johnston

On the high seas

I've skippered my share of boats, ridden a few more, but never have I seen a craft like the *PC*. We were at sea, but might as well have been in the lobby of the Los Angeles Airport Marriott. Through the skylight I could see thick carpet with in-floor track lighting, atmosphere subdued through heavily tinted windows. Fran said the soft elevator music in the background completely eliminated the sounds of being underway. The *PC's* stabilizers eliminated the sensation of being at sea. Why anyone would want to do that to a perfectly good yacht escaped me but then these people obviously think differently than I. We were enjoying a moment of peace on the spacious fly bridge when Adoni returned, welcome as an industrial strength case of diarrhea. They were going to let Frannie off the hook on this one . . . I'd be the star of the show.

"This way, Max," he said as we descended the stairs. "You're going to be meeting some interesting people soon. I'd suggest that you avail yourself of the shower here." He opened the door to a large dressing room that could hardly be called a *head* even though it did contain the correct plumbing fixtures. "There are clean clothes in this closet. Please help yourself to whatever you like."

"It's a locker, numb nuts"

"I'll be waiting for you just outside the door."

"Swell."

The shower was equipped with twin heads and plenty of room, suggesting some delightful possibilities for another time. Like most people I come up with some pretty good ideas under a blast of hot water. "Never underestimate the therapeutic values of water" I always say. Try it on your next hang over, when you're tired, or just don't feel good. It's amazing stuff.

Sabotaging the boat seemed like a good idea, beginning with the area of the ship I now held. Marine toilets, or heads, usually have some sort of a cutsie little plaque over them stating that nothing is to be placed in it unless that object has first been eaten. I thought the *PC* might be above basic bathroom humor, but apparently shit is shit regardless of one's station in life.

Marine heads are notoriously cantankerous, often stubbornly refusing to perform the job for which they were designed. Since a mere additional square of tissue has been known to gum up many a head, a wash cloth ought to plug things up quite well?

I hit the flush button expecting to see the beginnings of a flood, but instead the washcloth was sucked through the opening at high speed. Equipped with the same computerized vacuum powered toilet flushing mechanism that is present on the newest jets, it could suck a full-grown pig though the inch-diameter opening without clogging, so sabotaging the head was out.

I picked out a pair of khaki cargo shorts and removed the price tag from a forest-green polo shirt complete with horse from an amply supplied locker. Franco shops Nordstrom. As I stepped outside, I was expecting a guard to be stationed outside the door and wasn't disappointed. It was Adoni, fondling what looked like a .380 automatic. "Enjoy your shower, *Captain*? It could have been your very last one."

"Lead on, mouse." That got to him too. His face seemed to dissolve just long enough to mouth the word mouse as if he were chewing on a live one. That wouldn't surprise me. That Adoni was insane was no longer in question, but how insane and how dangerous? It was interesting to observe a crazy man. But lead on he did, mouthing the word mouse to himself. From our position aft, we moved forward through the spacious, beautifully appointed cabin, then up a small circular stairway to a deserted wheel house and the helm. The ship was on autopilot. "Who's on watch?"

"I'm the captain of this ship," he said as he dabbed at the drool that had dribbled onto his chest. He stared out at the seas silently for perhaps thirty seconds then said to no one in particular, "I'm the captain . . . it's like when I was in the Air Force. I'm always on watch."

"Well now, that figures. Your watch, but no one's looking out for traffic."

He turned his attention casually to me as he dabbed again at his shirt with a handkerchief, "Oh, *PC's* radar is equipped with an alarm that will warn us of any vessel within a fifteen-mile range." That's our Adoni. Place your faith in the autopilot and hope for the best. "Don't worry, Captain, you won't die from a mid-ocean collision," he said as he switched the radar to the 50-mile range. I watched the sweep intently for other traffic, but the only image displayed on the screen was the static of sea return. "But why put off the highlight of your trip?"

Adoni stayed behind me as he directed me back down the spiral staircase to the main deck where we were greeted by the smell of expensive liquor and cigar smoke. It had the aroma of a seasoned saloon. Passing through a pair of French doors into what was a floating boardroom, several men were seated around a huge monkey pod table. They looked vaguely familiar to me. I'd seen some of them somewhere before but couldn't place them. At the head of the table was one man I did recognize from his photos. The infamous Francisco Franco, himself. He was a small man, olive complexion with high cheek bones, his eyes jet black, his persona utterly devoid of expression. He wore what I'd guess to be a $2,000 blue pin-striped suit *and tie*, on a boat if you can believe that, and hard sole shoes that were totally out of place at sea. What would he care? He wouldn't have to deal with the marred decking. Adoni would.

"Captain Power. Please be seated." He did not rise nor extend his hand. I felt as if I was in a pit full of rattlesnakes, docile, but capable of a lethal strike at any instant. I took a chair at the opposite end of the table. "Gentlemen, this is Max Power." I searched for a trace of accent, but I couldn't detect any. "He was, I emphasize was, a captain at Mariah Air Transport, but decided to take matters into his own hands, something we can admire but not condone. Isn't that right, Warren? Captain, meet Warren Francis Langdon, Senator from Ohio. Out of the corner of my eye, I noted properly displayed portraits of the Clintons on the bulkhead forward.

"Cah . . . I—I, I . . . uh . . ." The man was drunk. Not the .08 breathalyzer nor the imaginary "impairment to the slightest degree" law enforcement uses as an excuse to relieve citizens of their cash, but real, actual commode-hugging, drunk-on-his-ass drunk.

Franco interrupted the good senator's attempt at oration, "To his left, Congressman Phil Bowles, representing the great State of California. Perhaps you voted for him?"

"I apparently made a mistake." Duly insulted, he glowered at me saying nothing but made a note in a pocket diary that I supposed was designed to intimidate me before they threw me to the sharks.

"And this is the Secretary of the Department of Transportation, the Honorable Howard Edward Erickson." His eyes were dilated, and he seemed agitated.

"Call me Howie-Ed," he said smiling. There was a small glass pipe before him and at the center of the table, a Jack Daniel's mirror with a mound of white powder explained why. Franco caught me looking.

"Oh, we've plenty more downstairs should we run out. You see, this is a working trip for us but we do enjoy our comforts now and then. Your presence is an added bonus to us. We haven't met. I am Francisco Franco as you may have guessed. Would you care for some cocaine?" I almost fell off my chair not from the invitation, but from the sight of two more portraits behind him in matching pewter frames. Hitler and Dr. Joseph Mengele.

"Beer man, myself," I said studying the portraits. The authorities frown on that sort of thing, you know?

"We are the authorities, Captain Power." Perhaps thirty seconds of uncomfortable silence while Franco stared me down.

"Which one of you *gentlemen* molested my flight attendant?"

No one answered my question. "Captain, we are very much interested in what motivated you to steal one of our company airplanes?" He saw me studying the likenesses. "You must have known that it would be the end of your career, and that there would be great danger involved? Your chances for success were dismal from the start. I understand you lost one of your men to violence at our jungle overhaul facility?"

"And you lost one or two of yours."

"And while we have many more, you are to lose your remaining accomplice in the waters off Southern California. Oh . . . as well as yourself." He might as well have been talking soybean futures. There was no reaction from the men seated around the table. A herd of sociopaths.

"I take it these *gentlemen* have something to do with the Mariah/North Air America merger? That's how you get around all of the regulations, the union contracts, and so forth?"

"It's really very simple, isn't it?" At that moment, Adoni appeared with a tray of hors d'oeuvres and presented the tray to Franco. He helped himself to a grande-sized chilled prawn from a serving tray of crushed ice and dipped it into a chunky, red cocktail sauce. "Yes, Robert," he said pandering to the madman, "those will be adequate." Adoni placed the tray next to the mound of coke. "Help yourself, Captain Power," he said without a trace of expression, "to either." The last thing I'd eaten was Blake's turkey sandwich. It seemed a lifetime ago, and I was very hungry. If Adoni had prepared the tray of prawns and little salami stuffed with a chive-cheese, olives, and peppers, I had underestimated him there as well. As I chewed the delectable morsels I thought again of Blake. I'd finally reached the point of admitting to myself that I hoped he'd made it. I knew he would understand my giving the men before me my full and complete attention and I wished like hell the marine side of him was there with me.

"Gentlemen, this gives me a unique opportunity on behalf of all the airline employees in the country to ask you just what the hell it is that you want? You've got everything as it is. You're all rolling in dough. You can't possibly spend what you have much less any more. Why the hell are you raiding the kittie and running everyone else into bankruptcy? What motivates you to destroy the finest transportation system the world has ever known?" Then I recognized one of the men munching on one of the delectable tidbits. "And YOU! You, sir, are singularly responsible for destroying our communications system. Mr. "Push one if you have a touch-tone phone."

Marten Charles Smith, the man responsible for countless hours of irritation and who single-handedly was responsible for the loss of thousands of jobs through his telecommunications empire sat up straight in his chair, offended by my remark. "Why, it's a simple labor saving device! It reduces the labor force by thirty-five percent! Wall Street loves me!"

"Yeah? What about the rest of the world? You've nearly hamstrung the country! No one can get through to anyone else, or at least I can't. I do not fit into options one through five!"

"Our goal, Captain Power, is to eliminate voice communication altogether by the year 2010. It will speed the transfer of information by several percent."

"Yeah? But . . . why? Why would you want to eliminate voice com?"

"Well . . . uh, because written word is so much easier to categorize and manage." The men exchanged glances, their expressions were of complete innocence.

"Well, why the hell do you want to do that?"

"Well, it's . . ." The men looked at each other again as if I were a complete idiot, as if I were the one who was insane. Like a bunch of kids, they all spoke at once making it difficult to understand any of what was being said.

"I'd like to respond to that—" Howie-Ed tried to stand but fell back in his chair.

"Congressman, I hardly think we need comment—"

"It's who we are!"

"WE are in control."

Franco waited until the commotion had died down, then stared me down with those eyes of darkness. "Why do you fly airplanes?" He paused using the silence as a weapon. "Excuse me . . . why *did* you fly airplanes?" I gave him some of his own silent medicine, staring him down. It was like peering into the eyes of a viper. "It's the same with us." He looked each member of the group straight in the eye, holding their gaze for perhaps fifteen seconds each. It seemed to make them very uncomfortable. "It's what we do," he said to me.

"So, you're the guys pulling the strings?" I asked. The honorable senator bent over and did a line of coke. I suppose it should have shocked me, but it didn't.

*   *   *

It felt good to be back on the fly bridge, away from the sea of human garbage below. The air smelled fresh and clean. Fran was curled up in a semi-fetal position in the shade of the antenna mast. "Fran? Fran! Frannie, wake up!" I shook her, but she was out. Women do not drool unless they know for certain they are not being watched. While I stared at her, she was far away, whimpering, her digits jerking. She was having nightmares, live.

I bellied up to the bar—hell the whole ship was a bar. Around the fly bridge had been installed a brass rail for your feet with a small table space just right for one's elbows. It seems that throughout the ages that man has gained wisdom from the sea so I took up a position of comfort and studied the water. I needed wisdom badly.

*"You will have plenty of time
to make your connection."*

—*Gate agents*

CHAPTER 19

Johnston

At sea on a clear, warm,
and moonless night.

Looking for answers I was bellied up to the rail, breathing tropical, salty air. The hiss of seas was white noise for my mind as the *PC's* bow cut through the troughs at 14 knots. The big turbocharged 550 CATs that were rumbling two decks below were barely above idle. I couldn't hear them, but I could feel them under my feet. If you set a glass of anything down there would be little tidal waves radiating out from the center that matched the frequency of the engines. It's the same on every boat, but these were oh, a little healthier tidal waves.

But the biggest attraction was the stars, especially when you think they're the last you'll ever see. With no light pollution at sea, the carpet of stars that stretched from horizon to horizon, from for to aft, was simply awesome. Not cheeseburger awesome, either. To me, this was the mirror reflection of flying at night. Captive or not, it was a magnificent sight I would never forget. The *Bible* had to be written under skies like these. It was a sight to inspire! All you had to do was look up to imagine philosophers composing the Great Thoughts. Their symphonies began to play in my mind. Then . . .

In the distance I heard the faint but unmistakable rolling, growling, round sounds of a DC-6 in climb. Then I saw her. The flickering tongues of exhaust from four Pratt & Whitney R-2800s, 18-cylinder, turbo-supercharged engines that powered the *Six* and the music they make is unmistakable. Not so long ago, she was the queen of the skies. Climbing into the Pacific night, her nav lights blink-blinking like the good old days before the jets came. No strobes on her wings or tail, she would blend in well with ground clutter, but what a romantic, really wonderful way to fly! Salivating for a San Miguel, I watched the old liner climb across the sky, remembering the cantankerous old Western Airlines bird, cigar in beak, resting on the tail of a DC-7C with a glass of champagne. "Western Airlines, The oooonly way to fly!" Barney Keep's voice. And Barney Keep was right.

I remembered because that was all there was to do on the bridge of the *PC*. Think. Picturing the cockpit, warm and cozy in the nest I made for myself in a real Sky King's left seat, a thermos of rich Colombian coffee straight from Colombia resting on my flight bag, a pair of fuzzy dice hanging from the mag compass. Charts folded and stowed just right, jack box and radios set the way I like it with the clearance taped to the glare shield.

In terms of history, the round engine airliners were just a flash on the scene, their prime lasting only a few decades but like *Old Man River*, they just keep rolling along, hauling meat, auto parts, guns, and yes, plenty of dope for the bad guys.

Peering into the seas kept my eyes busy, as my mind saw the view from the cockpit window. Enchanting. Hypnotic. Spinning silver propellers slashing an arc through the top of the clouds. Flight instruments, gauges, switches, and gizmos glowing a soft red. A dim-red overhead coating everything it touched with a little magic, and beyond the windshield the stars and the ocean. Little droplets of oil making trails over the wing and along the cowling, and all the while the engines and propellers creating their powerful music of flight.

And then came the jets, and with them the likes of Franco and the Harvard MBAs. Colon cancer to an industry. And the seed of that cancer and other cancers to other industries were below on the yacht, *PC*, with a belly full of government cocaine, and there wasn't a damned thing I could do about it.

We couldn't be that far from land, obviously still in South America where the round-engine airliners continue to ply the skies, even if they aren't wanted back home in the land of voice mail. I watched the *Six* first losing the sound of the engines in the throb of *PC's* diesels, and then sight as her exhaust flames blended in with the stars as she climbed into aviator's heaven.

* * *

The yacht rode well, her bridge level with the top of the rollers in the troughs, then as she climbed the next wave sent me towering above the sea under the stars. With no sight of land in any direction, I guessed we were at least forty miles out. Judging by the lack of hits on the depth finder, we were in deep water, over 300 fathoms.

Fran was sleeping as I should have been, but how could I sleep on a night like that? Having been given the freedom of the fly bridge for the trip to San Francisco, and even head calls below, they were actually treating us quite well in view of what I had done to them. That Adoni steadfastly refused any inquiries of Blake, of course meant that he was dead—or maybe he just didn't know and was playing poker with me. I'd never seen anyone die before and I hope I never do again. From the look in Blake's eyes the last time I saw him it seemed his lights had just faded to black, and then it was all over.

I was numb to it by then, still in half denial. All the shit I had given Blake who turned out to be a really decent guy, was coming back to haunt me and now the poor cock sucker was dead. Better to just gaze at the sea then to review what had happened in the space of just three days, and certainly better than to speculate as to our eventual fate.

Just then I caught movement out of the corner of my eye. Fran was stirring. I wasn't so sure what kind of mood she'd be in this morning. But these were circumstances that gave her every right to be pissed at me or for displaying any of the unexpected emotions a woman can throw at you. We were still prisoners, our lives very much at stake, and who knew how she'd react to that? There wasn't much doubt that our financial future was as bleak as ever. Money. What a stupid thing to trade our lives for, what an insignificant thing it is when compared to life, but it was of course at the very heart of the matter. Route of all evil; it applied well.

"G'morning," I said trying to be cheerful. No sound, not a good sign.

"Hi," she finally said. And after a few minutes with the basic necessities, she emerged from the small biffy with the suggestion of a smile but there was no sincerity in it. Just being polite. "Any coffee?" she asked. I rattled around with the contraption and in a few minutes I poured her a cup of excellent Honduran coffee from the topside espresso maker. Nothing too good for Franco.

"Anything in it?" I asked knowing before I'd shut my mouth that my foot was in it again. She just looked at me with this really bland expression. We'd already torn the bridge apart and there was nothing to put in it. No cream and no sugar.

Our environment included all the best: wet bar, espresso maker, any number of items except for booze or an icy San Miguel. No weapons either aside from the espresso pot. I ruled that out figuring that a man has got to have some pride, and it would do little damage anyway and not terribly intimidating against Adoni's stun gun or the automatic weapons below.

"Any idea where we are?" Fran's singed hair stood up, defiant to the breeze.

"Not really," I said. "I estimate we're at least forty miles offshore, but it could be a hundred and forty. By the course shown on the repeater, we could very well be headed for SFO like they said. We're definitely headed northwest making good fourteen knots in the water. I saw a ship an hour ago, headed northeast across our course. Could have been bound for San Diego or maybe even San Pedro, just south of L. A. I don't recall there being much in the way of deepwater ports in Northern Mexico. We've only been underway for a little over twenty-four hours, so I'm guessing San Diego. If I'm right, we should see some traffic moving in or out of Los Angeles in about six hours or so. If we really are bound for San Francisco, that would take about twenty-five or more hours at this speed.

*   *   *

After another day had passed we heard it together. It was upwind and distant. "Didja hear that?" Fran asked excitedly. I held up a hand for quiet, and closed my eyes using my cupped hands as an extension of my ears. The hollow, golden tones of R-2800s again . . . but this time only two. No mistaking the music made by those engines, amplified by the cowling and floating on the wind. Not just an airplane, and not just an old airplane. I was electrified. I grabbed Fran by the shoulders, unable to contain my excitement. "Snade!" I cried.

"What's a Snade?"

"Never mind that, I'll explain in a minute, but do you have a mirror?"

"Well, yeah," she said. There seemed to be some life in her again. "There was one in the RON kit they gave me." Just then she caught on. With a shot of her own adrenaline, she sprung like a fawn, silently to her purse and extracted the RON, or Remain Over Night kit, airlines used to hand out when passengers and their luggage took separate flights. Franco had thousands of them.

"Rats!" I said. "I know SOS, but that's about it in terms of transmitting anything quickly."

"Give me that!" said Fran. "I'm a Navy brat, remember?"

I didn't. I hadn't paid a hell of a lot of attention to her life before. I hadn't cared. For that matter I still didn't.

"Well, I am," she said. "My dad was a Chief on "Tin Cans" in the war, and he taught me Morse when I was just a kid. Other girls were playing with dolls and I was playing with a code key. I used to be able to transmit twenty words a minute." It doesn't sound like it, but that's fast.

"Well, if that airplane gets near, hit him with SOS and give him my name, MAX POWER. I know Snade pretty well. He'll figure the rest out. 'Course, I don't know what good it will do, but it's worth a try."

Fran was already working the sound. She was flashing in the blind in the general direction of the golden tones that sound the same now as they did when the airplanes were new. The rich, powerful, golden, music of round engines! And these engines, like all of the old liners, had a definite individual sound. It was a Martin 404.

"Jeff gives champagne flights in his Martin 404. We fly it around California to air shows each year. Her palatial interior and rich history draw big crowds and produce a lot of mist in the eyes of old timers fortunate enough to have flown her, or ridden on them, or even the Saturday afternoon airplane watchers. He's probably got a group on board treating them to some real flying. The purr of the engines tends to put 'The Folks' to sleep as soon as the gear is up."

"I know what you mean," said Fran. "I used to fly on the C-54s a lot when my dad was still alive. They do put you to sleep." She continued to work the sound; maybe someone on board would see it and tell the captain. Maybe someone had, for the sound was growing stronger. They wouldn't be able to hear it below, this might be our only chance for rescue.

Fran continued to flash SOS towards the sound as I searched the horizon. I saw the dot that was the airplane and told Fran it was at eleven o'clock. I think we felt the same surge in our veins as survivors on a raft. Then the airplane showed a landing light. I wished he hadn't done that. "Did you get Max Power off?"

"Working that right now," said Fran. She hadn't done this in quite a spell, but it was coming back to her.

"I'll take that," boomed Adoni's voice from behind us. I hadn't heard him climb the stairs to the bridge. She tried to get off just one more letter when he floored her with a single blow. I charged him delivering a blow to Adoni's solar plexus, spraining my wrist in the process. Short, bald, and dumpy but also very frigging solid. It was kind of token defiance; I could have hit him in the chest with a baseball bat and it would have bounced off and saved me the sprain.

His grin vanished. "Now you wave, real cordial like when that airplane comes over head, or I'll slip the both of you over the side right now."

The 404 with its distinctive cantilever wings appeared on the nose, waving his wings in greeting. "Wave real nice like," is how he put it and I did. He had his arm around my shoulder so that we'd look like real pals. Fran was out cold on the deck. The picture they were creating would look like she was sunning herself while the two friends waved back. He could make me wave, but he couldn't make me smile. At that very instant Jeff snapped the picture with his Nikon 8008 and 300MM telephoto lens.

The airplane thundered by overhead no more than fifty feet off the deck in a 30° bank. I was looking directly into the captain's eyes, and I was sure it was Jeff. So close our salvation.

She kept going, straight as a preacher's . . . uh . . . Adoni released his grip on me, then he wound up delivering a nose-breaking blow. That's the third time. Or was it fourth? Blood from my nose splattered onto his white sport coat and white bucks and was dripping onto the nonskid of the fiberglass deck.

"Great Whites like blood, and there are lots of them between the Channel Islands and the Farillons." No more pretension. No more pretending. I guess he could see the look in my eyes. I'd seen *Jaws* and it scared the hell out of me.

Adoni was cold and seemed to be getting meaner, "Yeah, that's right, asshole. You and your girl are goin' for a swim. Mr. Franco sort of insists. Groove on that for a while, you fucking scumbag amateur. You embarrass me in front of Mr. Franco. You insult me in the cockpit. Fuck you." I thought of Adoni like a rabid dog,

thinking that if I made a move he would strike. "You make a fool
of me in front of my employer and have the audacity to expect
humane treatment from me? It's people like you who give crime a
bad name, you and your woman." I was about to tell him she felt
sort of the same way about me, but he wasn't going to give me a
chance to talk. "You think you're cute with the mirror and the
airplane. Well, we see that airplane all the time out here, so don't
think you got some kind of message through. The only kind of
through is YOU, asshole," he said, "and the only place you're going
is nowhere. Straight down for a swim with the Great Whites. And
we'll make sure they know you're coming, asshole." Adoni was
nearly frothing at the mouth. "I've got two buckets of chum below,
just for you. Full of globs of blood and plenty of guts. So sleep on
that for a while, asshole, and, oh yeah, uh," he chuckled, "have a
nice day." I wondered if he'd picked that up in the Air Force.

After another night, boredom was well settled in. Fran, I had
concluded, must be suffering some kind of mental breakdown,
because other than an occasional head call, she rarely moved. There
were the seas to watch, and the stars at night, but that was all. *PC*
was a flush deck design, meaning there were no outside decks for
me to climb down. The entry way below was secure. Other than
vandalizing some antennas, which would only serve to piss off our
host, there seemed to be nothing I could do. Fran was worrying
me, she seemed to be slipping away, so I sat down beside her and
began to talk to myself aloud, hoping, then pretending she would
carry on the other side of the conversation. She didn't move, no
flinch, no nothing. I finally said more to myself than to her, "Well,
Fran, I guess that's it. There's . . . nothing else we can do."

As woman has done to man throughout the eons, she shocked
the hell out of me. She turned lazily over on her back towards me,
and in her naturally husky, sexy voice said, "Well . . ." Lazily shaking
her head, she began to unbutton her blouse. "There is *one* thing
we can do."

*"Runway's short and wet;
I'm turning the anti-skid off."*
—Former airline captain

CHAPTER 20

Johnston

"Uh—Ahh—Uh . . ." It had been a while for me. Little Frannie. Ha, I guess for that I can call her Fran. And I almost lost her twice. She was like the first time all over again. Completely awed at just how smooth, soft, warm, and all enveloping a woman can be. Our beginning, awkward scramble soon gave way to a comfortable rhythm of pure unashamed lust that traveled to the very end of every nerve in our bodies.

We super stallions are not designed to think or analyze at such moments, merely to perform. To get the job done. And when the shot is fired to immediately get on with life by changing the oil or mowing the lawn, or whatever the hell needs doing. And so it was that my warped mind couldn't help wondering if we were making love, savoring our last moments on earth together, or were we just having one last, good old-fashioned roll in the hay? You use me, I use you. A little of both? Whichever, in my entire world there was nothing but tight, little Frannie whose natural scents blended with a little of her intoxicating gardenia perfume that smelled so tropical, so sensual, that she actually smelled good enough to eat . . .

So . . .

Together again, I felt the stabbing heat of the afternoon sun on my sunburned back. We were close to mission objective at full takeoff power. So close, so very close, reaching for that most magic of moments together, steam from her sexy little flight attendant grunts and gasps condensing in my ear, *"Lift-up-on-the-silver-buckle."* Then rolling down my neck in little randy rivers of lust.

The cannon was loaded, I was ready to fire—but she was delaying me, raking the skin from my sunburned back with what passed as her nails that brought out cries of mercy from me, "Jeee-sus, Frannie!" Half of me was in heaven, the other half in hell. One part of me yelling STOP! The other saying "I'll kill you if you do!" Then, she was there. It was *the* moment. She was just starting to arch her back releasing an incredibly sexy, guttural moan in my ear.

Oddly enough, it was at that precise instant the Boston Whaler motor launch was blown from the davits. A terrific explosion sent a chunk of what would test out later as fiberglass shrapnel deep into the right cheek of my ass. It didn't hurt yet, but whether it was love or just plain desire, any physical abilities to, ah . . . well, it was just over.

Beneath me, Fran was breathing deeply in the steam of passion. There was the explosion, then an extra moment where I could tell she was thinking something. She opened her eyes, just barely. Her expression was . . . well? Heavy in the heat of lust, my siren of the seas slowly transformed to that of a housewife from the Great Depression in a burlap dress, hair up in curlers, arms immersed in a sink-full of slimy pots and greasy, corn-pone pans. Complete and total frustration of she whose shapely tanned legs were still wrapped around me.

"Sorry, Fran."

As I tried to leap up to investigate the source of the explosion, she held onto me at first, then gave me a little shove and said in a very tired voice, "It's OK, Max."

That wasn't what I expected her to say. "It is?"

"Yeah." She closed her eyes, lay back, and let out a long and very deep breath. "I'm used to it."

I let her have her dig at mankind, thinking to myself that it was a damned good thing. If she'd had a great sex life, we'd never have had the battery power to transmit the call home messages out on the GPS.

When I stood up, I was aghast at what I saw. Slicing through the seas, with a *bone in her teeth*, stood the sleek profile of a United States Submarine, SS 379, the Submarine *Dogfish*. She was about a thousand yards off the port quarter coming up fast at what must have been 20 knots.

"HOLY SHIT!" I gave a jump, deciding quickly from the pain in my ass that I would not do that again soon.

"What?" shrieked Fran, gathering her clothes around her.

"YEEHAW! Get ready! Something's going to happen! You can swim, right?" I got the same deadpan look as when I'd asked her if she wanted something in her coffee. "Well, let's before Adoni shows up with his tiny little machine gun!"

"Max, you can't, you're bleeding! It's all over you!" She was right. My right leg was covered with blood, a fresh river of it flowing from my right cheek. I thought of the bucket of chum and of the sharks, then of the machine gun. Adoni. He was coming. There was no time. We had to get away!

"GO!" But she wouldn't. "Go on, I can make it!"

With one hand clutching each shoulder, she yelled in my face, "I'm not going without you!" Then her expression softened and tears formed in her eyes. With a tiny sympathetic sting at the corner of my own eyes, I felt a tug at my emotions I had not felt in a long, long time. Damn.

"Git!" I hollered, "Go on, dammit, JUMP!"

Weight Check, something most flight attendants have never heard of and, being a thing of the past, flight attendant uniforms these days are designed to hide a lot of pork. It had certainly been hiding little Frannie. Her treasures highlighted by the briefest of tan lines, strong back muscles, and long, solid legs stood out to define the most perfectly formed body I had seen in quite a while. She leapt upon the three-inch teak cap rail holding her small handful of clothes—that barrier having been set aside earlier. She turned to me, a defiant expression on her face and mouthed a quick, "Fuck you, Max!" I flashed her a grin and nodded with enthusiasm. Standing on her toes, holding her arms straight out to the sides as if this were the Olympics, her firm 36Bs jiggling lightly to the rhythm of the seas, she released her clothes, mostly rags by then, to drift off in the wind as so much chaff. As long as no one could hear her talk, Frannie was Venus as she dove over the side. I etched the vision into my mind.

I thought the wound in my south end must have reached the bone or maybe a nerve bundle as I hobbled painfully over to the belly-high rail. I tried to roll over the side, but any pressure on my leg brought a heavy, throbbing pain. There was no doubt in my mind that Adoni would be here in seconds to end all of my pain permanently unless I got my bleeding ass over that rail, so I climbed with my left leg and arms, keeping as much pressure from my right as I could. I am not a screamer, and I do not "oof" over football, but when I made the big roll over the side it came from the diaphragm.

"AHHHSSHHHHIITTTTT!"

It was a long way down from the bridge to the water and I screamed all the way. Not smart. The comparatively warm water felt like solid ice, knocking what wind I had remaining from me. With no air, I knew I was in trouble. The thunderous "swish-swish-swish" sounds from the PC's propellers that would slice me to pieces were close and I could feel their suction pulling me towards them. Swimming under water as hard as I could in the direction that I hoped was away from the boat's propellers, I wanted only one thing: Air!

I saw stars.

My body cried, begged, then screamed for air and when I would not give it any, it involuntarily abandoned the wishes of its master in favor of a lung full of fresh, cool air. But it wasn't air; it was salt water. Drawn to the spinning choppers, I coughed it out and drew an involuntary and potentially deadly breath under the sea.

Slowly, a lazy thought came to me that I was drowning. I didn't seem to care. I was no longer cold and didn't seem to give much of a shit when the PC thundered on by until I erupted out in the troughs, tumbling in the churning wake of the *PC*. I could see nothing but water and taste nothing but salt. I was coughing, choking, vomiting, breathing salt water and diesel exhaust. I gasped for air as the next roller lifted me high. The receding *PC* was just a couple hundred yards or so away, and though I could see Bob Adoni on the fly bridge, I couldn't hear what he was screaming at me. Little puffs of smoke were coming from what appeared to be an Uzi or some other toy machine gun that he was pointing at me. Tiny projectiles kicked spray high into the air as they impacted the water around me at 600 knots. I'd never been shot before, so I was surprised at what little I felt when one had found a home in part of my right shoulder. Making an irregular pattern around me, the rounds made a flat "pfft-pfft" sound as they shot past my head. Still choking on salt water, I was unable to get back under water when I heard another "pfft" and felt a searing sensation on top of my left ear. I thought of the sharks as I risked another glance back at Adoni on the *PC*. A tight pattern of small holes appeared in the decking next to him, followed rapidly by another, then the teak rails exploded into toothpicks. A moment later, I heard the distant staccato report from one of *The Dog's* beefy .50 caliber Browning machine guns. By the way he was jumping around and the expression on his face, I could tell Adoni had been hit and that he was furious. He screamed something, raised "the finger" high in defiance, then sprinted below.

I was dead in the water, unable to swim in the churning wake. As lucidity began to return, my right leg was throbbing and my shoulder began to pound. I saw Fran about four swells ahead, when the seas lifted me high into the air. She seemed to be looking for something when she raised a hand in the air and shouted something, but I could hear nothing over the sloshing, gurgling of the seas. I was having trouble keeping my head above water with my useless right leg when out of nowhere came my little nemesis from Fergus Falls. This time, I didn't care what she sounded like, she was someone to hang onto. Like the drowning man I was, I did. When she began to scream at me her flat, nasal Minnesota dialect that she apparently tries to hide, became more pronounced. I would have laughed at her, but she slapped me hard!

"Dammit, stop that! Quit thrashing around or you'll drown us both!" I shook my head that I understood, but I guess I continued to thrash, 'cause she slapped me again, but as my head was mostly submerged, it was a glancing blow of mostly water. "Max! Dammit, listen to me!" I coughed in her face. "Relax, you son of a bitch! I'll do the swimming! Stop fighting me!" I didn't know I was.

So, still coughing and choking on the salt water, I forced myself to let Frannie swim for both of us even though it seemed that she was intentionally trying to drown me with her arm around my neck.

Through a watery fog, questions began to come to me. The *Dogfish* could never make way again, we all knew that, and yet somehow she was here. Who was manning the deck guns? And who the hell was conning the boat? Manny knew the boat's systems backwards and forwards, but piloting the sub was never his bag. *Whose bag was it?*

Submarine *Dogfish* was moving slowly now, only a hundred yards or so to go. Then what? A submarine's "tumblehome" creates a nearly round hull at the waterline. Slippery, difficult, if not impossible to climb, even without injuries. With two-thirds of her structure below the surface, it would still be like climbing a giant greased beer bottle. In the war, to take on survivors, the crew would lower heavy cargo nets over the side for footing. But this wasn't the war, there was no crew, and there would be no cargo nets. Without a shadow of a doubt, *The Dog's* slimy hull would also be festooned with muscles and barnacles. Neptune's little razor blades.

Never having seen the boat underway before, it was a *Twilight Zone* apparition of a submarine from another era that blew me away. 312 feet of black killing machine, low and sleek against the seas that raked her deck, trimmed by her fairwater and bridge, and topped by twin periscopes, spinning radar, and communication antennas. The air around me was reverberating from the power of four huge diesel engines. Tropical seas continually washing over her mottled decking and whitewater cascading from her limber holes, created the roar of a small waterfall. Marine growth clung to her hull, long streamers of kelp trailed from the lifelines that encircled her deck. She was a ghost boat, one that looked as if it had been on the bottom for fifty years—because it had.

I could make out people on deck, some I recognized others were strangers. It's times like these when you find out who your friends are, and apparently we had some. Manny himself was nowhere to be seen, probably below in the engine room. Exhausted from the swim, and weak apparently from the loss of blood by the time we reached the boat, I was still choking on salt water and felt like I was ready to pass out. Someone threw a heavy life ring and hit me on my bad shoulder causing me to utter a string of unkind words towards my rescuers.

I was aware of a crowd on deck above me. "Careful, he's wounded!" I knew that voice, Margaret from Tyee Marina. And once more Fran was around me, helping me to stay up, so to speak, until they could haul us aboard. Those on deck didn't seem to understand that I was hurt and she wasn't. Chivalry prevailed.

"I got her! Here now, miss, give us your hand!"

"I'm OK, but Max needs help!" She was holding onto a line and to me, but the boat was still moving a knot or two and the drag was tremendous. Two of the men, also from Tyee jumped in the water to help us.

"We've got you, you're safe now, young lady. Oh. Oh, my goodness!" Whoever belonged to the voices swimming beside us finally noticed what she was wearing. Nothing.

"Uh, ah, ah . . . you've been, ah, cut, you're, uh . . . bleeding!"

"Jea—sus, luuk, dey've got cuts all over dem!" They hauled Frannie out first, probably because she was a lightweight. There was more commotion on deck. I thought I heard someone holler *shark* in the bedlam of the moment.

"Here, here! We need a blanket for this young lady and right now!" And as an afterthought, "One for him too."

"Grab heem!"

Someone did. "AHHHHHHHH!"

"Easy—easy! Watch his arm, he's got a nasty shoulder wound!"

"Someone get a blanket for this lady!"

"Vatch hees leg, vatch hees leg!"

"AHHHHHHSHITTT!" The fiberglass shard was dragging along the hull. They were having a hard time getting two hundred pounds of Max Power aboard. I was hearing lots of familiar voices. How they—and for that matter the submarine—got there would be a real interesting story in itself.

"Easy, dammit, he's got a wound back there too!"

"Watch his shoulder too, there might be a bullet in there!"

"I think it went through the other side," Frannie's voice in the crowd.

"Here, give us your hand . . . that's it, that's—watch it! There . . . good!"

I don't think I lost consciousness from the excruciating pain, but memories of being hauled aboard are a little vague. My leg was not responding, and my shoulder was pounding. A good sized roller, probably a seventh wave, came up depositing me the rest of the way on the deck with a painful, scraping thump on the slippery deck.

"We got him!" As I regained my feet, I leaned on the voices around me who seemed to be having a discussion as to how to get me below. A blanket came from no where.

"Crack the aft torpedo room hatch. We'll lower him down that way."

"Belay that! Take me to the bridge!" My rescuers, mostly tough, burly men looked skeptical. They had to be Manny's pals from the fishing fleet in Morro Bay. "I can make it, dammit!" Although I wasn't sure I could.

"Like hell you can, mister! You've got a piece of a boat sticking out of your butt and a hole in your shoulder. Smarts, I'll bet!" Manny's pal, Dirty Dave, the hard-hat diver.

"Oh, you don't have to worry about that!" It was Frannie. "He'll tell you all about it!" It was a playful insult from Fran, but it hit home. I vowed not to complain of the pain and then broke the vow. Uttering the foulest words I could think of and that naturally came to me in moments like that, I hung onto *The Dog's* handholds as I made my way unsteadily toward the bridge with my arm around Frannie's shoulder. "Do you have to use such filthy language?"

"Yes!" If a woman can put on make-up, as the saying goes, when boarding a lifeboat, then a man can swear at his pain, at his suffering, or even at his car. We mean nothing by it. Any mechanic will tell you it is highly effective when making repairs.

A thousand yards off the starboard bow, I could see that the *PC* was maintaining course, but with spray from the oncoming seas reaching the fly bridge, she seemed to have increased speed. Their dinghy was shot, and the antenna mast had been destroyed by the deck gun. "Are they going to get away?" asked Fran.

"Not hardly."

The Dog's deck was in poor condition and very slippery. Though she rode well, I nearly fell twice on my way to the bridge, once against the barnacle encrusted five-inch deck gun. I could see rusted, broken iron members under what was left of the teak decking supporting the superstructure beneath us as we made it up the three long steps to the cigarette deck, around the periscope shears protected by the fairwater, to the bridge. The lookout positions were manned by two of the marina workers from Tacoma, Bob and Jerry who had flown as part of a group of twelve when they got the news from Manny. Hearing my groans, a slender figure wearing a *Dogfish* ball cap and a Navy flight suit, poised at the TBT using the optics to track the *PC*, stood upright, and turned to me. "About time you got here!"

"TJ! For Christ sake!" He took my hand and Fran in his arm for a hug.

Over her shoulder he said, "No, for your sake! Welcome back to the world, buddy!" He threw an arm around me while hanging onto Fran and pretty soon we all had our arms around each other. Only bad part was that she fussed over him and hung on a little longer than I would have liked. Why should I care?

"Ahhhh!" Everything hurt.

"He's got a couple holes in him," she said. Little Frannie looked pretty good, even sopping wet in a blanket. Her hair was beginning to dry, trailing in the warm breeze like little, dishwater-golden pennants glinting in the sunshine.

"Sorry. You've definitely opened a few cans of worms, pal, and there's one of them," he said looking off the starboard bow towards the hundred-foot yacht. "The feds are all over Morro Bay looking for you."

Hmmm. So they know it was me. "You con the boat?" I asked, though the answer was obvious.

He gave me a sideways glance, then bent down peering over the tops of his half-frames into the TBT, high-powered optics used to pass target bearings into *The Dog's* computer. "So far it's been fun, but we've been real lucky not to have been spotted. One of them has a cell phone, but it's not working for him—we're too far out. The bad guys are trying to outrun us."

"Can they?" asked Fran.

TJ stood up straight, turning towards me. "Not *even* in their dreams."

"Where are we?" This time it was me asking where we were.

Pulling a folded marine chart from his flight coveralls, he pointed to an empty spot on the chart he said, "GPS wise, we're right here at thirty-three north and one nineteen west, around two hundred sixty miles southwest of Santa Barbara. I've plotted their track, and they seem to be bound for the island of Santa Rosa in the Channel Islands."

"That one's privately owned, isn't it?"

"Yeah, and I'd say that's their destination."

"Those bastards were going to slip Frannie and I along with some chum over the side just offshore to have lunch with the Great Whites. Shit, TJ, do you know who's on that boat? Fucking Bob Adoni! He's been working for Frank all this time!"

Frannie piped in, "Yeah, well that's not all. They've got that asshole Senator from New York aboard too."

"One of Hillary's boyfriends, isn't he?"

"Yeah. And there's others. Two more congressmen and that shithead, Marten Charles Smith. He's the guy who improved on your favorite system, the push-one-for-this-and-two-for-that guy." What little blood remaining in my system began to boil as I thought of the hundreds of wasted hours listening to his fucking menus and bastardized elevator music. I thought of the big button in the conning tower I'd like to push for him.

"Yeah?"

"Yeah! And they've got a thousand pounds of coke along for the ride, and two suitcases that are very dear to my heart." And then I couldn't help it, "My ass hurts."

TJ turned to look over my shoulder, "Yeah, well, you've got a piece of a Boston Whaler sticking out of it. Why don't you go below and get taken care of. We've got Doc on board."

"Doc Myers?"

"Yup. He insisted." He took another look through the TBT at Franco's yacht. "We did their antennas, so they won't be calling in any air strikes."

"Who's we?"

"When word slipped out about what was going on, I had no trouble with volunteers. Brian Foreman got the antennas with the deck gun. He and Mike Carmegetti—both ex-Eastern—are having a great time with all this."

I turned to look aft at *The Dog's* boiling, white wake against the blue Pacific. It looked like the No. 4 diesel wasn't running too well, trailing occasional puffs of black smoke from the starboard side, aft. "What are we doing, around fifteen knots?" I asked.

"Seventeen over the water. We're matching the bad guys' speed. They've picked it up five knots since you bailed out. I think they're flat out now." It was impressive with the deep blue seas breaking white over the bow, occasional cool spray flying in our faces.

Frannie pulled TJ down, and gave him a quick—I am glad to see you—kiss. "I'm going below now," she cooed.

"OK, one coming down," he hollered into the opening forward

of our feet leading to the conning tower. "Someone will help you down the ladder," he said.

"Oh," she said clutching her blanket around her, then thought better of it. Women. They're always thinking someone's trying to peek up their dresses, or in this case blanket, and of course they're right.

Having figured that out by herself, this time she gave me a peck on the cheek. "I'm going with Nels," she said with a grin. "He warned me about that earlier!" She turned aft and bounced down past the cigarette deck and the five-inch deck gun to where the old gentleman from Manny's favorite saloon was waiting. I wished she'd be more careful on the rotted deck—we had enough injuries already. If someone fell through the teak, the rusted iron and steel could cut them to pieces. I watched Manny's pal spin the dogs free on the hatch to the aft torpedo room's escape trunk, then raise the hatch for Fran who, with her blanket clutched around her, scrambled quickly below. Then it was my turn to duck under the fairwater to the conning tower hatch, TJ steadying me with a firm grip on my good arm.

"Stand aside, I've got him!" I definitely recognized that voice coming from below. Mike Carmegetti from Camarillo. We'd flown many trips together, and both belonged to the Confederate Air Force. "Here, Cap'n, try to use your left foot going down the ladder," he said in his signature staccato voice, his vice grip hands lowering me into the opening. After transferring ladders in the conning tower, he hollered below, "Heads up, compadres, here he comes! Cap'n, Try to use your feet on the ladder," he barked again. "We don't want to drop you!"

"Ey, El Capitan *Pendejo!* Como esta?" And that voice too! At the bottom of the ladder in the control room, I intended to boom out a greeting and crush his hand in friendship. I was shocked to hear my weak utterance. "Como esta frijoles, yourself, you old bandito." My handshake was as limp as . . . well.

But the old guy was in his element, refreshed, renewed and happy. Mexican lawn mowing music was playing over the antique

speakers. The familiar strong aromas of heavy machinery, the deck
moving beneath my feet, and throbbing from the huge diesels
made the boat seem alive. This time it was my arm around the old
master chief's shoulders as we shuffled forward towards my bunk
in officers' country. "Ju have made the federalies berry, berry angry!
And who are theese *vatos* pendejos on that bonita barco?" I had to
rest, leaning on the chart table.

"That fits 'em pretty well, amigo. They're just plain assholes.
Frannie could use an issue of sweats."

"Señiorita Fran say not to call her dat. She hit me when I deed!
She has some cuts from the, uh . . . como se diese . . . varnicles? Si,
varnicles!" He beamed at the right word. "But jes, she ees fine.
Dees woman ees . . . ees . . . deeferent."

"Sure she is."

"Do ju know dat ju have a piece of a boat sticking out of jur
ass?"

"I've noticed." The water tight door separating the control
room from officers' country in the forward battery that I have eased
through so many times was now a barrier to me, and I understood
at once what Manny had been going through. It was agony getting
over the lip of the hatch. By hanging my weight from the grab bar
overhead, I was able to get half of me through the oval doorway
into the forward battery compartment with the injured-half
remaining in the control room. I could go no further, and then the
lights began to dim. My lights.

Brian Foreman, who'd also flown many a trip with me, his
arms the size of small trees and hands of iron, lifted me through
with a "hup" and a flourish. "Look out, Doc. I've got him!"

"You're in the way, Brian, now please, please! I'm a doctor.
Move out of the way, I'm a doctor!" Doc was fidgeting around
examining my wounds and, as yet, had not spoken to me. "He can
walk!" He was fairly shouting at Brian, then he turned to me and
asked conspiratorially, "You can walk, can't you, sir?" Doc and
Brian get into good-natured arguments frequently. It's sport to
them. I nodded my head yes, but only groaned as I attempted to

get into my bunk, knowing for certain I would never live this down. "Just lay down there on your stomach, sir. How was Colombia? Can you lay face down on the bunk?" Doc's string is pulled just a bit tighter than the rest of ours. He didn't give me time to respond before he was back in Brian's face, "Help him into the bunk, would you please?" The two were nose to nose for a moment, then Brian turned to me with another "hup" and loaded me onto my bunk as if I was a toothpick. He'd been a captain with Eastern for twenty years.

He turned back to Doc, "You call yourself a doctor?" There were a couple of whispers, then he huffed out of the tiny cabin. And came right back to watch.

"Sir, I've got a little something for you!" I turned my head painfully—everything was pain—and there to my astonishment were the five of them, TJ, Doc, Brian, Manny, and little Frannie crowded together with a camera pointed at the shard of fiberglass sticking out of my bare behind. As I raised my eyebrows in protesting astonishment, the strobe went off.

"Aw, shit!" Then I saw it. "Oh, shit! No, aw, c'mon, Doc!" Grinning, he was holding a syringe with a very long needle. I don't like needles.

"Now, just relax, sir. You won't feel a thing, but take a deep breath just in case." We've been friends for twenty years and he still calls me "sir" when he lies to me.

"Yeah, right." I felt cool alcohol being swabbed on my butt, and I knew what was coming.

"Max, you're chicken!" Someone snapped another picture. Lying on my stomach, I couldn't see her, but there was no mistaking her voice. The little chicken hawk. And I was even glad to hear her sing-song, Pollyanna-style, Fergus Falls voice.

"Hi, babe!" I said over my shoulder. I don't like sounding weak. "Babe?"

"Aw, c'mon, Frannie, not now . . . please? Ow! Damn it, Doc!" Airline pilots do not get stoned, but in a few minutes I was ripped, and all was right with the world, at least until Doc jerked the piece of the Boston Whaler from my aft bulkhead. "Sweet Jeeeeeeeeeeeesus, Doc!"

"Now just relax, sir, I have a little sewing to do. You may feel a little discomfort." *Their favorite word. Discomfort, my ass!*

Brian said, "Other doctors might consider the use of tape."

"Not this one. Now, take a deep breath, I have to clean the wound."

"AHHHRRRRRGGGGGHHH! Is that muratic acid, for Christ sake?!"

He uttered an evil chuckle as he began to sew. "No, sulfuric for your sake."

"You're a sadist!"

"At times—especially considering all of the trouble you've caused. How was Columbia? I'm missing *Star Trek*, you know." Doc is a complete *Star Trek* nut and was enjoying my pain as would Dr. McCoy when patching up Captain Kirk. As ripped as I was, I didn't seem to give a shit. With one wound taken care of, he started on the other and this time it didn't hurt much.

"That's gasoline, right?"

He chuckled, "Yes, it is, sir! You're a lucky man." And there was an understatement. "The bullet went through your shoulder, but I think it's bruised your clavicle, so you're going to be pretty sore for a few days. A little nick on your ear too."

After the bandages were on, the voices around me evaporated. Someone drew the heavy, green curtain over the doorway, then I heard the snap of industrial-strength rotary switches as the whites went out and the soft-red night lighting came on. Vaguely aware of gardenia perfume, I dropped off into a deep sleep in the comfort of my own bunk, massaged gently by four huge Fairbanks-Morse diesels and the sensuous touch of Frannie's magic fingers.

"Rougher than a stucco bath tub!"
—*Ride report from Braniff Pilot, circa 1980*

CHAPTER 21

Johnston

Muffled voices through the fog of an opiate induced sleep. It sounded like Doc, and he was pissed. "Sink that son of a bitch to the bottom of the sea!" I rolled up on my shoulder raising an eye to glance at the repeater gauges at the foot of the captain's bunk. We were still on a northwest heading, doing 17 knots.

"You can't do that! That's cold blooded murder!" I knew that one . . . Fergus Falls chalk on a blackboard.

"Lady! They tried to kill you!" Sounded like Brian was pissed.

"Maybe they didn't mean it?" *We gotta be from different planets.*

"Hijo de puta, señiorita!" *Atta boy, let 'er have it, Manny!*

"Those are real people on board!"

Are they, Frannie?

"I say get 'em with the deck gun!" said one of Manny's pals.

Fishing sounded good to me, as in an MK XIV "Fish" doing 45 knots aimed at the *PC's* waterline with a 750 pound Torpex warhead.

My favorite restraining bar to keep the skipper from rolling out in heavy seas was acting like a hospital bed rail to me, but I had to get out. It would truly be a major pain in the ass. Reaching for the intercom, I selected the wardroom.

"Wardroom." Chalk, but lovely chalk, in my ear.

"Frannie?" My voice was raspy from sleep and lack of coffee. The line went dead, and in a second she was hovering over me in a pair of black *Dogfish* sweats, the uniform of the boat, smelling

174

fresh, clean, and carrying the scent of a field of gardenias but no coffee.

"Nice nap?" I was expecting her to hit me over the head with something for calling her Frannie, but this time she didn't.

"What's happening?" I was working up the strength and ambition to move.

"In the wardroom?" I raised up on my elbow and gave her the deadpan look. "Oh, yes. Well, we're just sitting around having a discussion about Franco and the boat. The men want to sink it!"

"Don't you?" It was painful, but I rolled out of the bunk, wearing only a couple of bandages, making a feeble attempt at dragging my blanket around me for cover. Frannie didn't seem to mind. "I gotta have some coffee. And a shower. Never under—" Frannie interrupted me and finished my own Max Powerism. I took advantage of the time by grabbing some clean skivvies from my locker.

"I know, I know, 'Never underestimate the therapeutic values of water'—I've heard that a hundred times—but, Max, you can't seriously be thinking of just killing those people?" The captain's cabin has barely enough room for two people to stand, making for some interesting collisions. "Here, let me help you get into those. Don't you have a bathrobe?"

"I don't wear bathrobes or name tags and I'm not just going to kill them. I'm going to sink their boat. What happens after that is up to them and the Great White Sharks to whom they were going to feed us and, of course, THE Chief Pilot in the sky."

I maintain that a hot shower is the best temporary cure for jet lag there is, and I definitely needed one. For whatever reason, Frannie was looking pretty good to me. Perhaps it was the isolation at sea or the bond created by our ordeal. I thought to myself, *what the hell*, so I asked her: "Wanna go?"

"At ease, mister!" she said with a playful look that said she wouldn't ever do such a thing, especially on a submarine with other people on board.

I thought she would.

"Argh!" It was a little embarrassing and a painful struggle, but the clean skivvies and sweats felt great. Now for some coffee. "They tried to kill you, lady, and they stole your million dollars. Mine too. Frannie, these are the *real* bad guys. You want to just let them steam away?"

"They're saying *we're* the bad guys!"

"Yeah, well. Badder than us. Just think for a second of the constant scandals and cover ups, the quote "*War on Drugs*" unquote. Confiscatory taxation with zero representation. Kids being murdered in their classrooms, the assassins conveniently killing themselves after each attack to be whisked away by the coroner never to be seen again . . . until the next shooting. Not to mention killing a few airlines, like ours for instance. It all started by giving you the vote." She hit me again, this time almost playfully.

"Oh, come on, Max . . ."

"What? You don't think the bad guys would sacrifice a few hundred kids to disarm the country? Looks to me like there are sinister forces within the government that are trying to do just that and they've got a lot of people believing their bullshit! Don't you watch the *X-Files*? It's those kinds of entities that burned women and children, not to mention thirty or so men to death at Waco, live with the whole world watching, and got away with it!"

"B—but, those people shot first! They were criminals!"

"Were they? Are you *really* sure about that? Someone got hold of the FBI's own airborne infrared surveillance video that shows automatic weapons fire being directed at those who were trying to escape from the flames and cyanide gas. I've seen it with my own eyes and yet the federal government's position is that it didn't happen. It's a little technique they borrowed from Goebbles, Hitler's Minister of Propaganda, and it still works. And one of those bastards behind it all is aboard the *PC* with Franco and that fucking Adoni. Yes, I'm going to sink that boat!"

A case of cotton mouth got me to salivating for a glass of freshly-squeezed, Arizona orange juice, right off the tree, but since that wasn't going to happen, I'd settle for a cup of Manny's swill. "Don't forget, Franco and the good Senator from New York have a ton or so of coke on board . . . and they were going to kill us, Fran. They were going to feed us to the damned sharks!"

"What do you mean about Hitler?"

"You know, tell lies to you until you believe them. Mariah does it all the time," I said from inside my sweatshirt. Frannie helped to steady me from the motion of the sea and to get my bad arm through the sleeve. Even with doc's pain medication "on board," it hurt like hell. Worse. I felt like a kid getting dressed by his mother. "And you do believe them, don't you?"

"Max, those are some pretty wild assertions. People will think you're crazy if you talk like that."

That figured, and she was probably right because it sounded crazy to me too. "Well, you just sit your sweet little butt right down here in this chair. We'll see how you feel about that in a few minutes." I snapped on the small 12 volt TV/VCR combo I have in my cabin, and hobbled one compartment forward to break out the video, *Waco: Rules of Engagement* from the radio room's video locker. Wondering what effect the autopsy photos of dead kids, murdered by our own government, and the self-righteous denials from a herd of the *honorable* members of congress would have on Frannie. I loaded the video. "Now, you sit right here and watch this video from beginning to end—"

"But I—"

"That's an order, miss."

"You can't order me, Max Power!"

"Dammit, Frannie, just watch the video! How else are you going to know?" I held her in the chair by her shoulders. "And while you're watching, don't forget that one of those bastards is on the *PC* with your money!" And my money.

Wondering to myself how many people besides the IRSS might lay claim to *our money*, I hobbled aft through the water tight hatch into the control room where Margaret, who was also dressed in a set of *The Dog's* sweats, was keeping track of our position at the chart table. I gave my old friend a hug. "Margaret, I don't know what to say. You may have gotten yourself into something fairly sticky."

"None of us would have missed this. Besides, we needed a break." We stepped over to the SD radar. Maintaining a position 3,000 yards astern of the *PC*, each sweep of the radar antenna revealed the *PC* maintaining her course for Santa Rosa Island. I could visualize Franc, the *honorable* senators and congressmen, and—my faithful crew member—Bob Adoni yucking it up, having another laugh—while snorting taxpayer-funded cocaine—at constituents Blake, Frannie, and especially Max Power's expense. I have known for a long time that our system is broken. Yes, we all know that the *honorable* senator and those like him are a lethal grade crook, merrily stealing our tax dollars through the administration thereof, totally and completely disregarding the will and directions of his constituents, but what the hell can we do? Vote him out at the next election when the choice is once again Senator Foghorn Leghorn or Senator Leghorn Foghorn? Voting no longer seems to matter. But aboard the Submarine *Dogfish*, we had the power to make some changes and actually do something. *Max Power!* I reached overhead, rang the alarm and on the 1MC cried out, "Battle Stations Torpedo!"

"Control room?" came an electronic voice on the overhead speaker. It was TJ calling on the battle phone from the bridge.

"What the hell, Max, you ring the alarm? What's going on?"

"Let's play submarine," I said. I could see Manny struggling through the hatch from the forward battery.

"Wait a second, I'll be right down."

Manny plopped his hands on the chart table and was invading my personal space, "Ay, are ju crasey? Bottle T'sashions, Torpedo? Vat torpedo?"

"What the hell do you mean, what torpedo? You've got a full load of the damned things." I struggled to remember, "What twenty-two of them? Hell, you sleep right next to one!"

The old sailor took his *Dogfish* ball cap off, revealing a shiny pate that he scratched vigorously to demonstrate the depth of my ignorance. Plopping the cap back on he looked like himself again, peering deeply into my eyes to make sure I got the point. "Jes, we have plenty of torpedoes, mark fourteens, but dey can't fire! Dey need to be t'serviced and fooled!"

"Well? You've been telling me for twenty years about your damned Double Dolphins?" His expression changed to a scowl, knowing something was coming. "You're qualified at every man's position on the boat, are you not?"

"Jes, ju know damn well I am, an' ju and I are going to tangle eef ju don't show respect for the Double Dolphins!"

With my hands on his shoulder I said, "I've got all kinds of respect for the Double Dolphins," softening his expression until I said, "but what good are they if you can't service the torpedoes?"

"Pendejo, we got no fuel! Dey need alcohol to run, an' we don' have any!" I thought for a second we were shot down, but I hadn't watched all of those submarine movies time after time again for nothing.

"Alright, we'll ram the bastards!"

Manny planted his feet and with his eyes open wide fairly shouted at me, "Bool t'sheet! Ju ain' rammin' notheeng weeth thees boat!"

"John Wayne did it in *Operation Pacific!*"

"Jes, and de boat went to Mare Island for an overhaul too. De bow vas focked, and we damn near deedn't get back! Dat vas weeth a full crew! I don' hafe enough hombres to help mee weeth the whole boat!"

"You were on that patrol?"

"Jes I vas on dat patrol! Dat vas my patrol number ocho . . . uh, eight, I have told ju thees story before, ju were not leestening? Why don't 'chu just e—tshoot them weeth the machine guns? I'll tell ju why! 'Cause ju would see all of thee blood and goots up close, and ju wouldn't like it." I thought about that. Normally he'd be right. Just then, TJ slid down the ladder from the conning tower as Mike and Brian came through the forward hatch followed closely by Frannie. "What are you doing here, miss? Did you finish the video?"

"I've seen enough."

"Mike!" I put both hands on her shoulders, "Frannie, video tape, rapido!" He clapped his hands, then rubbed them together as if ready to demonstrate a few hundred one armed push-ups.

"Aye, aye, sir! Right this way, young lady!"

"But I don't want to miss anything!" She was whining and didn't want to leave, but Mike escorted Frannie back to my cabin to finish watching the exposé. He was back in a minute, and she was right behind him.

"Dammit, woman!" I said. Jack looked at me with an expression that said she was my problem and shrugged. "Look, we've got some serious planning to do and you can't help! Please just go finish the video or bake a turkey or something. Ooof!" She punched me in the gut.

"Well, I overheard your problem, no alcohol, right?"

"That's about the size of it."

"Well, how about all of that Cuervo in the exec's cabin? Margaret and Bob found it last night when they went to turn in. They drank some of it."

"Now just a meenit, jung lady! Dat is Captain McLehney's tequila and beesides, thee torpedo wouldn't run on tequila! Maybe Max ees right about you? Hee says ju are crazy and I theenk hee ees right!"

"Who's Captain McLehney?"

"Hee ees the other pilot who belongs to the Tequila! Hee eesn't here now. Off flying the avion, I theenk."

"Yeah, he flies for JAL, shows up sometimes—helps with the expenses."

Mike smacked his hands together, "It's worth a try! Maybe we could distill it! That would give us pure alcohol, wouldn't it?" Without waiting for an answer he barked, "C'mon, Manny, let's go boil up McLehney's booze!"

"Folks, welcome to Owl Falls where
we've arrived twenty minutes early.
Unfortunately, our gate is occupied and . . . ."
—The captain

CHAPTER 22

Johnston

Several of the crew from the marina—Brian, Mike, Manny, and even little Frannie—worked all afternoon and into the night on the MK XIV torpedo, servicing its components, adding the alcohol that Doc had distilled in the galley, and moving it out onto the skid to prepare for loading into the No. 1 torpedo tube.

With some of Doc's painkillers on board, I'd spelled TJ on the bridge so he could get some sleep, dividing my time between the bridge and the SD radar in the conning tower. We did not need to be spotted. While we were defenseless against satellites, I hoped no one was watching. And if they were, would not notice a black submarine against the deep blue Pacific.

"Bridge." Manny on the battle phone.

"Hokay, señor, eet ees time for ju to help us weeth these sheet. We weel need everyone, TJ too." I roger'd his call, then took a good sweep with the attack periscope for any other traffic. We'd kept our distance astern of the *PC* at 3,000 yards, close enough to track easily on the SD radar, yet far enough away so that they couldn't see us from the *PC* and would think we had abandoned the chase. I made a one legged descent to the conning tower, then swapped ladders for the descent into the control room on the main deck below. My leg having loosened up from use, it was now considerably easier transiting the watertight hatches, but ladders were a bitch with a bruised clavicle, painkillers or no painkillers. Reluctantly, I parted the green curtain at the chief's cabin where Manny ought to—but refuses—bunk, and gave TJ a shake.

"Reveille, reveille."

"Uh?" he groaned. "What's up?"

"Time to load a torpedo. It's going to take all of us. Sorry to wake you."

"Ah, that's alright," he said bleary eyed. "Let's go," and rolled out of the bunk.

Manny could have any of the three empty officers' or chiefs' cabins, but chose to maintain his bunk high on the starboard side of the forward torpedo room that was assigned to him in 1945. The crew, consisting of Manny, Bob and Jerry from the marina, and a couple of Manny's pals were visibly weary from their nocturnal torpedo maintenance, full of grease and sweat. The effects from lack of sleep showed on Manny who was a bit irritated at the whole thing, and especially at me.

"Ju gonna get us all sent to focking Kansas!" He mopped his forehead with a white handkerchief, "An' I don' wan' to go!"

"Aw, quit stewing!"

Frannie was at my elbow. "Kansas? What does he mean, Kansas?" Her head was cocked about 15° to port and had a puzzled look on her face.

"Means nothing. He's just rambling." Manny's eyes went wide.

"Rambleene my ass! Theenk of all those focking maricones in the preeson!"

"C'mon, dammit, let's get at it! Set torpedo depth at the surface, high speed!"

"Ju have to load her in thee tube before wee can make thee settings shanges. I don' like maricones!" His mention of maricone, Spanish for fruit, reminded me of Blake who had been a pretty fair copilot. His death still weighed heavily on my mind and would no doubt haunt me forever. I guess that's why they frequently call me "sucker!" If I had any idea . . . I mean, I'd strangle his ass again myself!

"Let's get this damned thing in the frigging tube!" I was anxious to get this over with, and still concerned about being spotted. If we were, there would be little we could do. We didn't have the manpower or the balls to submerge the boat. I mean, it would go down all right, but . . .

Using 1943 armstrong technology, it was the four of us on two heaving lines while Doc took a much needed rest in his cabin. Twenty minutes of straining saw the fins of the MK XIV securely inside the tube and along with it a new appreciation for the way the WW II crews made it look easy. It took muscle too, to close and dog the breech, but finally it was done.

"Alright, now set torpedo depth for the surface, high speed and stand by to fire manually in the event the electrical mechanism doesn't cooperate after fifty years of neglect." There's always time to tease Manny.

"Jew are an osshole! Thee mechanism, shee ees brand new! She has never been fired!" We'd fix that soon enough.

"We'll need flank speed to catch 'em, Chief." Manny took off his ball cap and threw it as hard to the deck as an arthritic seventy-three year old can throw. He let out a string of rapid-fire Spanish that was beyond my ability to keep up with.

"Ju jews dee steenkeeng engeen room telegraph, *Capitan*! Das what eet ees for! Do ju remember where thee engines are, pendejo? Dee eengene rooms are on dee other end of dee boat, if ju can remember dat. Dose guys back der don' know what dey are dooeeng without me der to help dem." He gave me a dirty look, then turned to shuffle aft, slinging a burst of Spanish at me over his shoulder. I made for the conning tower with Manny's parting shot stinging in my ears.

On the SD radar, the small, green blip representing Franco's yacht was maintaining a 12-knot cruise now, an indication they thought they had lost us. We were trailing them by a good distance, but as I rang-up flank speed it would soon be "surprise" time for Frank, Adoni, the good Senator from New York, and his pals. Eventually after traversing four and then five hatches, Manny answered up flank on the engine room telegraph. The vibration under my feet increased to a frenzy, and the boat surged ahead. I rang the engine room on the battle phone. "Jes? Whad dee hell do ju want from me now, Capitan?"

"Uh . . ." The chief was still pissed. "TJ says the No. 3 engine is puffing out some pretty good smoke, amigo. Anything we can do about that?"

"Don' amigo me, señior! I know who ees we! If ju want *flank* speed, ju gonna geet e-smoke. I need to cleen the injectors and dat ees a beeg job! Why don' ju come down heere and do dat and I weel come to the breedge and dreenk café weeth the bonita seniorita an' watch thee booteefool ocean?" No one was hunting us, at least not yet, but the smoke trail could give our position away if someone was looking. I thought again of the satellites.

"Hmmm . . . better just shut that No. 3 down, Chief. We should still be able to catch 'em." More rapid fire Spanish, then the battle phone went dead. In a moment, the smoke stopped and there was an almost imperceptible sensation of slowing. In a few minutes, we'd slowed to 18 knots. We'd have to live with it.

By pressing a button, I raised the attack periscope to its full extension. The relative bearing was 010, just off the starboard bow. At full magnification, the dark silhouette of the *PC* was barely visible on the now dark horizon. As the periscope hissed into its hydraulic well, I loosened the friction lock on the conning tower steering station and gave us a few more degrees to port. Using a technique perfected by the *Wahoo's* famous skipper, Mush Morton, we would make an end run around the *PC*, lay in wait and then, when she crossed our path, we would kill her. I secured the friction lock on the steering and climbed back to the bridge where TJ and Bob Stipp were on duty.

"Hey, Cap," Bob looked like a kid with a new bike on Christmas Morning, only his bike was the bridge of a submarine. "How's this . . . pretty neat, eh?"

"And how's you ass, Boss?" Mike was glued to a pair of 7 x 50's.

"Sore . . ." The small talk trailed off as we each took in the majestic sights. Surrounded completely by water, far from the sight of land, the *Dogfish* cut through the seas with a huge, orange sun dipping into the Pacific off our port bow. Even at our reduced speed of 18 knots, spray occasionally lashed my face to keep me awake. It would be dark soon, but if we were going to fire any ordinance, it would have to be before we got any closer to land and an audience. I asked Margaret, our officer in charge of navigation in the control room below, to double-check the plot on Adoni's course against the coordinates for Santa Rosa Island. According to her, there was no doubt the *PC* was bound for the island. There was also no doubt in my mind Franco's yacht would ever reach that or any other port.

Some of the newness of being underway in the *Dogfish* having worn off, I found my self at ease on the bridge. I think I could watch that bow cut through the blue water forever, imagining what it was like to see the bow planes rigged out, the lookouts scrambling below, ringing the diving alarm and making a dash for the conning tower as the seas closed over the hatch. As I do often on the boat, I reflected on how it had been back in the war, before our country lost its mind. As an occasional wave broke over the deck, I imagined what it had been like in a country where values prevailed and where we were still The People. A nation truly united against two clearly definable foes in the days when the skies were full of round engines and the houses full of two-parent families. And I speculated on how men like those on the yacht we were chasing—and the white powder in her hold—were responsible for the big change. Or the big coup.

We closed on the *PC*, and soon were five miles ahead, laying perpendicular to her projected course. Without a full, qualified crew to operate the torpedo data computer, I planned to fire the fish from nearly point blank range. Our lethal killing machine would show no nav lights, but the *PC* already had to believe the *Dogfish* had abandoned the chase after picking Fran and me out of the water. Mike Carmigetti and Bob Stipp had taken care of Adoni's toy radar when they blew the shit out of their mast with the five-inch deck gun, so there was little chance they would know we were laying in wait. In fact, there was no chance at all.

Hearing voices below, I dropped back down into the conning tower. TJ and Fran were hunched over the SD radar, intent on the small, light-green return. "You really going to do this?" asked TJ. "You're in a fair amount of trouble now, but it's manageable— maybe." Bob and Margaret piped in from the control room below, "You sink that boat and the shit's going to hit the fan!"

Manageable—maybe, my ass.

The *PC's* course was 280° following the west coast of the Estados Unidos. I rang up dead slow and was turning *The Dog's* steering wheel hard over to starboard when Fran appeared at my elbow with coffee. "Frannie, can I—ouch, dammit, that sh—stuff's hot— can I put you to work on the helm? Steady up on zero nine zero. Start your roll out by a good thirty degrees."

"Translate, please."

"Yo, TJ, show Ms. Olson the helm, please." Steering the boat is not difficult, but does require some practice. Frannie would get plenty of it in the next three days. Using the indices I raised the attack periscope on a bearing of 105°, and there she was. White over red, her nav lights confirmed her direction of travel to be perpendicular to our course. With a full crew, sinking the yacht would be a matter of plotting geometrical mathematics, feeding the *PC's* course, speed, and angle on our bow into the Torpedo Data Computer that took more training than we had under our belts to operate.

"Here she comes." I clicked down to a magnification four with the periscope's twist grip. The *PC's* dark silhouette was trimmed with red and now green nav lights, with the cabin lit up cheerfully as if it were Christmas Eve. In a way it was, 'cause Francisco Franco was about to get his. "Down scope," I said to myself. I scrambled back to the bridge as fast as my injuries would allow with TJ and Fran in trail." The *PC* was about three miles off and closing rapidly.

With the fish in its tube and ready to shoot, and without the complicated mathematical calculations, the plot and especially teamwork that goes into firing a torpedo, there were only two things left to do. Aim, or in other words guess, and hit the firing plunger. "Where are we, what's going on?" Doc asked negotiating the ladder to the bridge. With the four of us on the bridge, it got sort of togetherish standing shoulder to shoulder. "Hey, Doc. You're about to see something. Or maybe nothing if the torpedo doesn't fire."

"Chief Burruell says it'll fire. I've just come from the torpedo room, and he says everything is in place for it to fire. Have you thought about what you're doing?" I certainly had. And it's *Master Chief.*

"You gonna just eyeball this?" asked TJ. "I've got her on the TBT at two thousand eight hundred yards. Their fly bridge is a mess."

"Someone better go wake up Mike and Brian. They'll want to see this." Things were beginning to roll up, to happen with increasing speed. I considered ringing-up all stop, but we would need steerage way to aim ourselves at the *PC* and I wasn't sure how the crew in the engine room would do without Manny. We were going to be close, perilously close to the boat. A shot from 500 yards in the war was considered point blank range and that was about what we were going to need considering the size of the target, shooting from the hip.

Like the Titanic approaching the iceberg, the *PC* closed inexorably on our position, the geometrical equation changing each second. Fire too soon, the torpedo would pass in front of her bow, fire too late and it would pass astern of her. This was all coming down to eye-balling, like playing billiards. Mike and Brian squeezed up from the conning tower to join the action, but everyone was quiet in the tension of the moment. I rang up the forward room on the battle phone. "Jes, what ees eet ju want from me now?"

"Manny, stand by that manual firing mechanism!"

"What the hell do ju theen I am dooeng here? I steel don' like thees." I didn't feel like bantering. I was going to have to just guess at the firing point, and since I had only a vague idea of the torpedo's speed it was going to be a lucky shot—either good luck or bad.

The diesels were barely above an idle, we were making good about three knots, just enough to give the rudder authority. It was a beautiful night with the carpet of stars. We were riding the six-foot-long ocean swells easily. The constant sloshing of seas against the hulls, some washing over the decking and back out the limber holes, the only sound until just barely at first I heard the *PC's* throaty CAT diesels, then as she drew closer the hissing of her bow wake. The angle on the bow decreased slowly, then faster towards zero. "You gonna lead her a bit?" asked TJ.

"I'm guessing about twenty degrees. Damn, I wish we had another fish!"

"Yeah, well wish in one hand, boss. You miss with this one and they get away unless we ram 'em, and I guess that's out. I wish we had more rounds for the five-incher."

"Well, we don't." I was getting a little irritated from the tension, and I think TJ and everyone else knew it because it got real quiet as I debated in my mind how to make the shot. Shooting from attack periscope in the conning tower would be more accurate in terms of number of degrees to lead her, and the distance, but from the bridge the entire picture would be in play—better for shooting from the hip. "Fran," I was careful to say, "I think the honor should go to you to hit the firing plunger after all you've been through."

"What? You want me to go to Kansas with you? Forget it! I'm not about to kill anyone."

"Neither am I. I'm going to sink the boat, and what happens to them is between God and the sharks.

"Max?"

"Dammit, woman, we don't have time for this shit! TJ, you feel like hitting the plunger?"

"You're the skipper, Skipper. The rest of us aren't all that sure about this."

The time for debate was over. The *PC* was 30° off the starboard bow at about 700 yards and closing at 12 knots, time for a change in plans. I dropped painfully into the conning tower with a thud, and raced to the attack scope. It took forever for it to raise back into position. On the back side of the scope are indices to read the bearing from a target. I set it on 20° to starboard, then moved back to make the shooting observation. This would happen fast. And faster than I would have liked, the bow of the *PC* came into view. This was it. One of those moments in life. I slapped the periscope paddles up out of habit, making the two steps to the firing button in a flash and hit the plunger. The boat shuddered. The torpedo had fired! My confirmation came from the hatch overhead, hoots of excitement and one serious "oh shit" as in *you've done it now.*

Back at the scope, I caught sight of the stream of exhaust and air bubbles left by the torpedo. By the speed of the torpedo and the speed of the approaching *PC,* I knew I had a hit. I raced up the ladder as fast as I could hobble to the bridge to watch. It was like every submarine movie I had ever seen, the torpedo wake off the bow, the target steaming into its path.

The MK XIV had a horrible history in the war due to faulty firing pins. It took them over two years to figure out the problem while Japanese merchantmen and man o' war marveled at the torpedoes that routinely bounced harmlessly off their hulls. Were these firing pins modified? My answer was a huge explosion such as this aviator has never seen. Instinctively, we all ducked down behind the fairwater seeking refuge from flying debris. It was a wise move. Tons of water, fiberglass, and wreckage rained down upon the *Dogfish.* The night was lit like day for a second or two. I risked a glance over the bridge, aghast at the sight, because as the airborne water met the sea, there was nothing left of the yacht *PC.* She was gone.

"It never rains 'til the flight's on the ground."
—*Ramp rats*

CHAPTER 23

Johnston

Tug *Edgar* met us 65 miles southwest of Morro Bay where we reluctantly dropped off some of our crew. Fran refused to leave and, of course, Manny stays with the boat. Mike and Brian had two very different handshakes, and we were sad to see them go. Like TJ, they wanted to stay aboard, but they all had trips to fly. Under the circumstances, we all agreed it would be best for them to be there. Manny's pals, too, thought it best to be elsewhere, and most of the marina crew had to fly back to Tacoma and work. Bob and Margaret agreed to make the trip with us. As we watched the tug steam eastward over the horizon, the mood aboard the boat turned almost somber and very quiet.

Angie had ridden out on the tug for the ride and brought us up to date on the latest news. If she fell over the side, she'd go straight to the bottom. Her purse was bulging from tips that grew in proportion to the length of her necklines and the hem of her miniskirt. The news she brought us wasn't good.

We'd caused a fair amount of trouble for Morro Bay that we hadn't counted on. Feds, wearing their different ball caps and matching windbreakers that advertised their branch of service were all over the little village. They investigated everyone and every business in town for anything they could think of. In particular they were searching for a certain airline captain rumored to be living aboard a phantom submarine that none of them believed existed in the first place.

Intertwined yellow crime scene tapes from multiple agencies desecrated Morro Bay's quaint waterfront, not so far from *The Dog's* makeshift berth under Rose's Cantina. According to Angie, round after round after round of taxpayer funded fluids were served to the guardians of the Republic For Which We Stood in spite of their declined federal visa cards. Several of the executive types were incredulous to learn after several days in Morro Bay that Rose's actually served food. Heavily engaged in non-pertinent discussion, they were oblivious of the make-shift submarine pen over which they were seated.

The Morro Bay police, frustrated by a lack of crime and a Winchell's, threw themselves into their work. They did a thriving business in DWIs that would never see a court date, nor would they draw a fine or fill a cell for even one night. During one routine search, an ATF agent found and duly confiscated a revolver composed mostly of rust under a pallet of rabbit feed. This necessitated the immediate closure of the feed store and the street for a half block in either direction in the interest of public safety. Morro Bay is a small town. It wasn't long before the word was out. The feed store never did have a good cash flow. Not just another bankruptcy, but liquidation.

Well . . . technically, at least, weapons had been stockpiled in the feed store with the Morro Bay middle school less than a mile away. Observing the ATF agents shop-to-shop search for weapons, George Sandstrom, owner of Guns N' Gold paid a quick visit to Annie's Attic, a few doors away. After placing several souvenirs from the Wermacht under the counter, he displayed a 1950's era quarantine sign "Closed for Mumps" in his display case. He told Angie that he made sure any prying eyes would notice the flag first. George hastily erased the Hitler style mustache he'd drawn on Janet Reno, then returned her portrait to the usual spot flanking the display case, right next to the presidents. George told Angie over a bowl of chowder that it seemed like a good time to see if they were biting on Lake Shasta.

Angie went on to say that the antique shops like Annie's Attic, where George got his sign, were run by little old ladies who were under intense scrutiny. Were the quaint fifty-year old, hand-painted window signs applied with a federally approved paint? What of the glass the sign was painted on? Could there be—horrors—*lead* in the glass? *What if someone ate it?* Was the sign painter an approved and properly licensed, bonded, and insured sign painter? Had federal, state, county, and local taxes—not to mention social security *contributions*—been properly confiscated from his pay? Had the very necessary permits been in place and properly displayed and had the appropriate fees for those permits been lawfully extorted? All excellent questions, but it was the Border Patrol executive who had stopped by for a nooner, that brought up *the* most important of all questions:

Where . . . was this painter of signs, this person who was causing all the trouble . . . *from?* What if the sign painter had been an illegal alien! With Mexico a scant 343 miles to the south, the obvious conclusion was reached without delay. Surely the combined resources of the federal government and the State of California could locate him. Or her. Or his/her descendants. After all, this person had to be experiencing some type of health care crisis by now that would require the finest of care regardless of any actual need. He or she might be pregnant. Rumor had it that Oregon had recently established a precedent requiring each live male in the state to be insured against his own pregnancy. It was agreed that this precedent should be maintained in California. Additional meetings were held well into the night at Rose's to formulate plans to submit the Oregon plan to the State of California. Real thinkers were envisioning this as a national policy.

Dove tailing nicely into budget discussions, the health, welfare, and programming of the alien sign painter's existing children and possibly their children simply had to be considered. Angie didn't get it all right since she was hearing their conversation only when she delivered more drinks. But they had a lot of drinks.

She overheard enough to make sense . . . at least, enough for me to understand what she was trying to say. Allocated welfare funds had to be completely disbursed to those who qualified in order to prepare for the submission of the next federal budget. As "qualified" and "in need" are not necessarily the same thing, what better way to increase the next budget? The Task Force had discovered an entirely new minority group!

The elusive sign painter, well not the actual person who had ornately lettered the antique shop windows, but a theoretical one established for planning purposes, had become a serious problem and was the subject of multiple inter-agency meetings, again held conveniently at Rose's Cantina overlooking the water.

One of the environmental agency heads, having taken the afternoon off from the tremendous strain of the investigations, took in a flick at the family oriented Bay Theater. During the film, *Patch Adams*, the environmental implications of the fifty-year old screen came to him as if in a vision. He actually made an attempt to be quiet on his cell phone while he bounced the issue off his colleagues in Washington D.C. Thinking more of Angie than the movie, he soon lost interest and decided to take the bull by the horns. Following a very minor traffic accident, he returned to Rose's Cantina to report in with Angie in person and consider the matter in greater detail.

She said he had an annoying habit of tinking on his glass with his wedding ring, of all things. "Tink-tink-slurp." Then he bragged to Angie that the DWI he was issued at the accident scene would be dismissed. Professional courtesy. Somehow, she said, this was supposed to entice her into the sack. She said she didn't see it quite that way. "I really let him have it," she said. "Here's this fat SOB pouring down $7 doubles like they were water with me running his federal visa card! I may only be a cocktail waitress, but I'm not stupid. It is I—me, Angie, who is paying for his damned drinks! The bastards take ten percent of my ring out, besides what they take from my check. Max, I get minimum wage *and* they tax my tips whether I get any or not!"

As the Jack Daniel's flowed, he explained to her that thanks to *him*, the tiny glass beads on the theater's screen might be seen in an entirely different light. It was possible they might impact the health of the imaginary sign painter who, they had agreed, might also have been called upon to maintain the theaters in San Luis Obispo, and for that matter, even Paso Robles. That the worker might have worn some type of mask or other protective gear completely negating the entire subject was rejected out of hand.

DEA came on board, openly wondering about his addictions. The two parties came to quick agreement that since this person was not only Spanish, but *Mexican* Spanish, he must therefore be addicted to something. Counseling would be crucial and as the sign painter had been officially designated an illegal alien, the counselors would have to be bi or perhaps even tri—lingual. She overhead them discussing temporary housing concerns and a seemingly endless list of other related items. Angie said they were nothing if not thorough.

Enjoying a fine buzz from the Jack and soda, he shared his vision of a Federal Task Force with Angie, suggesting they get together after hours to explore the possibilities thereof. There would be a new title, a new office, possibly with a window and even a photograph with the vice president. His budget would certainly fund a well cared for private secretary, and that secretary could be Angie if she played her cards right. That Angie would rather sling hash in Morro Bay rather than do anything for any price in Washington D.C. never entered his bureaucratic mind.

Switching to gin, he gazed out on the harbor at the boats swinging with the tide, musing over one of the perks of his new Division Chief title he envisioned by being at the right place at the right time. Rather than merely having a photo with the VP, he could become the Vice President, leaving only one rung of the federal ladder left to climb, and climb it he could. He was sure. Other buffoons had. Recently.

Of course, Angie's news wasn't all bad since the feds have to eat and sleep like the rest of us, albeit a little more of each. The sleepy little town experienced a federally funded miniboom. There were those who considered it a partial tax refund. Angie's boss was happy to learn that they all seemed to enjoy the food and atmosphere as well as the cute high school girl waitresses, although he was distressed to learn that two of them had been reported missing by their parents.

Angie said that the local motels were doing a thriving business, their parking lots full of generic automobiles sporting a variety of tax-exempt license plates, several years newer than most residents of the town could afford.

She said that Happy Jack's, Manny's favorite saloon on Morro Bay Boulevard and Main, was voted to have gained the most from the invasion of Federal Rambo wannabes. Sponsoring inter-agency pool tournaments and dart games, kegs and kegs of draft beer flowed like a Pacific tide under a harvest moon.

Angie said that on a higher level, the pastel-shirt-and-neck-tie/white-patent-leather-belt wearing Keystone bureaucrats held marathon planning sessions, and their inter-agency meetings in Rose's Cantina from lunch, when the doors opened, through happy hour and on into the night. The Embarcadero was closed in order to accommodate their vehicles that ferried each man to and from the distant motels located a block or two away. Instinctively each fed knew that in order to create a need for more federal revenue, he had to do something about it. Somehow he must personally contribute to the combined waste of federal tax dollars in order to get more and more of them. So while other, more efficient methods were being sought, many of them did so in the best way they knew how. While carrying on hour-long, international, cell phone conference calls with their counterparts in other countries, generating reports, memos, directives, e-mails, and faxes, they simply consumed the tax dollars themselves.

Meanwhile, as the Submarine *Dogfish* and her crew of all five of us moved north along the fog shrouded California coast, Angie's stories convinced me that the *Dogfish* could never go home to Morro Bay again. That left only one place, and our present course would take us there.

On the bridge, my favorite spot on the boat, I was enjoying

the monotony of the voyage. I could go on like this forever, listening to the powerful diesels, the hiss of the bow wake, the sloshing of the seas while the boat rose and fell slowly on the long ocean swells. I was mildly annoyed at the distraction when the battle phone rang. "Bridge."

"Hungry?" It was Frannie.

"Uh, yeah I am. You gonna bring me a sandwich?" She said she and Margaret had made a little snack and that I should slither on down and see for myself. She sounded like she was in a good mood, something one does not often see, nor take for granted in Ms. Olson. So I took a good sweep of the horizon with the 7 x 50s. Observing no traffic, I dropped down into the conning tower and, yes, it still hurt. Immediately I was enveloped in the heavenly aroma of a Thanksgiving turkey dinner, not from hydraulically smashed leavings in a box but carved from the dead carcass of a real live turkey. When I tried to hug her for the feast she'd made— mashed potatoes, gravy, dressing, real cranberries, home-made rolls, and three pumpkin pies—she hit me over the head with a wooden spoon and told me get out of *her* galley. "Go tell Manny it's time to eat, and both of you wash your hands!" I think it's instinctive with them. Wash your hands, brush your teeth, do your homework, that kind of crap.

As I rarely did what my own mother told me to do, I decided to carry on the tradition by making a quick check of the SD radar in the control room. I hollered at Manny on the 1MC, which is in effect a PA system throughout the boat. He called back immediately, "What, jew crazy, Pendejo? Ju gonna wake everyone up!" I figured I'd better let that one slide cause there wasn't anyone to wake up. Except possibly for his shipmates from 1945.

In a few minutes, the five of us gave thanks for our deliverance, so far, and feasted on the best meal I could recall in a long, long time.

*   *   *

Commencement Bay
N 33° W 144' 0310 PST

The engine room telegraph answered up ALL STOP as the
tug *Marlin IV* gently edged the boat in between the *Tatiltiga* and
the *Gray Ghost*, two half-salvaged ships serving as a part of the
marina's breakwater where more than one bureaucrat has
mysteriously disappeared. In spite of the hour, there were a half-
dozen now familiar and sleepy faces peering out from foul weather
gear to greet us because as it does on a daily basis, it was raining.
And, of course, it was cold.

The dock committee went about their business of securing
The Dog with heavy, otter-shit-encrusted hawser. Fifty-amp electrical
power was snaked through to the modified connection near the
cigarette deck, and her fresh water tank was topped off using a fire
hose from the marina's fresh water fire fighting system. The
submarine *Dogfish* was home, leaving only one remaining item
prior to stringing camouflage over her periscope shears.

"We're damn near on the bottom now . . . no real reading on
the depth sounder. What do you estimate the depth at?" I half
shouted over to the skipper on the *Marlin IV*.

"It's seventy-three feet by lead line!" He shouted back.

"Das jus' about right," said Manny who, after an arthritic climb,
had joined me on the bridge. "Anyway, what choice do wee have?"
That one. And if it weren't for the thirty years I'd known Margaret,
the marina manager, we wouldn't have had that choice either. After
the boat was completely secured, we took the members of the
committee who hadn't seen the boat in Morro Bay below for a
look-see. No stranger to ships of the same era, they were
nevertheless blown away by the like new condition of the sub, at
least below decks. Fran went to work in the galley again, and soon
the committee, Manny, Fran, and myself—were full, content, and
very sleepy. It was time for all going ashore to haul ass.

"Nap time for us, Margaret. You're all welcome to stay, grab a bunk for yourselves. But, if you do, it'll be . . ." I moved to consult the tide guide in the *Coastal Pilot*, but Bob Stipp was way ahead of me. These guys live by the tide.

"Hell, it'll be late afternoon before we could leave again." Poor bastards. Everyone had to get back to work at the marina. Everyone except Bob and Margaret who were just as worn out as us.

It took us three tries and a lot of compressed air, but we finally got the boat to lie on the bottom on an even keel. And then, after nine days of very little sleep, we did.

* * *

Fran and I grabbed jump seats on Alaska Airlines to Los Angeles. I had no idea what was in store for me when I reported for my scheduled trip after my "vacation," half expecting to be arrested when we walked in the door as the IRS had done several times with some of our more militant tax-protesting captains.

The flags lining Mariah's circular drive were flown at half mast, apparently out of respect for the victims of the yachting "accident" from which Franco, Adoni, the honorable senators and their colleagues, their cocaine, and our money were missing and presumed drowned. They might have been little bites for them, but the Great Whites finally did get the meal Francisco Franco had promised.

The first thing I noticed inside the G.O. was that people I didn't know were saying "hi" to me, shaking my hand, and welcoming me back. Another group, flight attendants mostly, surrounded Fran until we had to excuse ourselves to check in for our Tokyo trip. As we walked through the corridors of the airline, doors began to open, and people stepped out into the halls. One man on the second floor, leaning over the rail, began to applaud and soon the entire mass of gathered employees were applauding, cheering, and whistling, giving us the equivalent of a ticker tape parade. At first I was embarrassed, and not at all pleased that the gig was out in the open, but before long I succumbed to the once in a life-time party. *What the hell.*

We rode the tram to the employee bus stop at gate 66, wrestled our bags to the ground to begin the short walk to 69 and our 747 flight to Tokyo. The first thing that caught my eye was a new 727 at gate 67 with a new, *complete* Mariah paint job. "I didn't think they were building those anymore," said Fran.

"They aren't. FedEx got the last one a few years ago. Let's have a peek, shall we?" I set my flight bag and carry-on down by the aft stairs while Fran arranged her multiple suitcases and garment bags on her wheeled cart against the stairs. As usual, they promptly fell over into a heap.

Dwarfed under the T-Tail, mindful of falling drops of kerosene or oil, we started up the stairs. "This is spooky," she said reflectively. "The last time I was in a stairwell like this, it was on fire." I thought back to that night and shuddered, thankful and more than a little amazed we had survived. I threw the heavy latch hard over to open the massive door that makes up the aft pressure bulkhead and stepped inside. She had the smell of new. My naturally curious nature lead me past the coach section, through a now small first class section and galley to the cockpit while Fran lagged behind to inspect the cabin. I wasn't prepared for, nor did I like what I saw. I leaned against the doorframe to take in the view of a brand new two-man glass cockpit.

The second officer's position had been removed. The 727's comparatively spacious cockpit with three crew positions and two jump seats had been redesigned into a tiny, two-man version, half the size of a Volkswagen beetle. The bulkhead, separating cockpit from cabin, had been moved forward, allowing the forward galley and biffy to be replaced by five extra knee-crunching rows of coach seating aft. But the part that caught my eye the most was the glass cockpit.

Flight instruments, save for one toy altimeter, had been removed and replaced by two 12" CRT screens. Two keypads denoted the method this grand lady would be flown by in the future which would involve very little manipulation of the controls by the pilots who are slowly being designed out of the cockpits. I would not win the debate of "steam" where pilots fly the airplane using flight instruments, the autopilot, and other computers to aid them over "glass" where the airplane is flown solely by computer as the "flight managers" watch, for the battle had already been lost. I settled into the left seat to take it all in.

The familiar feel of the 727, one of the grandest achievements in all of mankind's history, was compromised, but still there. The original yoke with the word *BOEING* staring at me as it had for so many thousands of hours appeared to be all that remained of the original cockpit. Instinctively, as Fran rushed in the doorway, something made me grab hold of the yoke. Something was familiar.

"Max!" She cried, "I think this—"

"Yeah. I know." Staring at the burned windshield wiper, I turned to a bewildered Frannie. "It's the same airplane."

"But how—?"

In a flash, I ran the whole caper through my mind from beginning to end. The fire when I thought I'd lost Frannie, Blake, our ordeal on the *PC*. The Keystone bureaucrats and their goons, and finally Buck Don Breeding whom we learned had been "elected" to the Board of Directors of Mariah. There may yet come an envelope with a FAA return address that could take my license or a pair of handcuffs with my name on them. Worst of all, this brand new "airplane." They'd transformed one of the finest airliners ever built into a computerized flying rabbit warren. An expendable rabbit warren. I reached the only possible conclusion. "Frannie," I said, "the bad guys are winning."

The End

GLOSSARY

4-1	Shift Early morning shift 0400-1300
A system	1 of B727's 3 Hydraulic systems
Accumulator	Hydraulic device to store small amount of pressure and protect system from shock.
AGL	Above Ground Level
Approach plate	Diagram of headings, altitudes and other data used in instrument approach to an airport.
APU	Small jet engine that provides electrical and pneumatic power for ground use only on 727
Avo	Avocado dip, with salsa
Baro	Slang for Barometer or Barometric Pressure
Benjo	Very primitive Japanese toilet
Biffies	Airplane lavatory. Also Blue Room, Loo, etc.
Big cues	Giant Cumulous clouds
Brodie	Slang for a 6 wheel drifting turn
C band radar	Old non-color technology radar
Catering Cover	A plastic plug preventing objects from entering a jet engine intake
CH	Call Home feature on Max's GPS
Coast Out Last	nav check point before oceanic air space
Detent	A notch to insure positive flap selection
Dutch Roll	Violent rolling motion
EGT as in No. 2's EGT	Exhaust Gas Temperature
EPR	Engine Pressure Ratio, measurement of

	power
Flaps-two	Initial flap setting on B727
G.O.	Airline General Offices
GPS	Global Positioning System for navigation by earth orbiting satellites
GRD	Ground start position of start switch
HEMLO	Navigational fix determined by Lat/Long's
HSI	Horizontal Situation Indicator; provides visual relation of aircraft position to desired course
IFR	Instrument Flight Rules
IVSI	Instant read out of climb or descent in feet
Lat/longs	Latitude and Longitude
Mach number	Airspeed expressed as a percentage of the speed of sound.
Malletize it	Beat on it with a hammer
MSL as in 7, 342 MSL	Mean Sea Level, as in altitude above.
N1	Compressor section of a jet engine
N2	Turbine section of a jet engine
Nav Lights	Red green white wing tip & tail navigation lights
On the deck	Flying at a *very low* altitude
PC	Yacht *Politically Correct*
Pitot tubes	Probe providing input to airspeed indicator
Radome	Nose of airplane under which radar antenna is located.
Ramp rat	Loader of baggage. AKA Baggage Smasher
Revenue Trip	Normal flight carrying passengers and/or cargo
Safety-gate	Method of insuring positive flap position.
Spin the dogs free	To turn a wheel that will open a hatch

Spooled/Spooling	Acceleration/deceleration of a jet engine
Squawk	Discrete transponder code for radar identification.
STBY	Stand by
Sterile cockpit	Environment below 10,000 feet where non-pertinent conversation is prohibited.
Stockholm Syndrome	Condition where victims of hijackings tend to identify or side with their captors.
TORPEX	Explosive used in torpedoes
Trim (nose up/down)	Method of relieving pressure from controls
T-Tail	Top mounted elevator as on DC-9 B-727
Tumblehome	Rounded sides of submarine hull
U Check	A systematic check of all systems on S/O panel.
VFR	Visual Flight Rules
Wet	Airplane rented with fuel included in the rate.
WOXOF	Ceiling and visibility zero in fog